SPECIAL MESSAGE TO READERS

In one form or another, Andy Jones has always been a writer. At school he passed notes in class and scribbled rude words on lamp posts. At university he wrote a PhD in biochemistry and forged tickets to various balls, and as an advertising copywriter he has written adverts for everything from baby food to booze. But it wasn't until he was well into his thirties that Andy started writing fiction. If he could write a letter to his younger self, it would urge him to stop messing around and get on with it. *Four* is his fourth novel, but it should probably be his tenth.

FOUR

In the time they've known each other, Sally, Al and Mike have shared — well, almost everything. Sally and Al have been married for seven years, but now their relationship is hanging by a thread. Sally and Mike have been best friends since university. Mike and Al have been friends for many years. Yet with Al poised to become Mike's boss, their relationship is coming under threat. And now there's Mike and Faye. They haven't been together long, but Mike's pretty sure that this time it's the real deal. As the three old friends sit on a train heading towards Brighton to meet Faye, little do they know that after this weekend, the four of them will have shared . . . everything. They all know they have made a mistake. But they could never have imagined the consequences.

ANDY JONES

FOUR

Complete and Unabridged

CHARNWOOD
Leicester

First published in Great Britain in 2018 by
Hodder & Stoughton
London

First Charnwood Edition
published 2019
by arrangement with
Hodder & Stoughton
An Hachette UK company
London

A catalogue record for this book is available
from the British Library.

ISBN 978–1–4448–4281–4

Published by
F. A. Thorpe (Publishing)
Anstey, Leicestershire

Set by Words & Graphics Ltd.
Anstey, Leicestershire
Printed and bound in Great Britain by
T. J. International Ltd., Padstow, Cornwall

This book is printed on acid-free paper

Stan, this one's for you.

1

The train hit a clockwise bend in the tracks, and Sally watched her plastic glass of champagne glide across the table . . . drifting in relentless centimetres towards the window, where it would either topple or come to a gentle halt.

The journey from London to Brighton was scheduled to take a little under one hour, but as the train barrelled through the spectacular countryside of High Weald, Sally found herself wishing the journey were perhaps half as long again. Autumn was waiting in the wings, and it would be dusk by the time they arrived, but now, with sun still visible above the treetops, the landscape was etched with layered greens and deepening shadow.

Sally's glass reached its own destination now, bumping up against the glass, tottering on its stem and coming to rest with not a drop spilled. She picked it up and took a sip, savouring the still-cold bubbles as the scenery receded away from her.

They had just departed Three Bridges station, marking an approximate midpoint in their trip south, but Sally would have welcomed an extra hour to fully decompress from the week at her back. She'd been in the surgery since nine this morning — a conveyor belt of imagined patholo-gies, repeat prescriptions, intimate examinations and hopeless cases; the anxious, the ill, the lonely, the depressed. In a pair of three-hour sessions bracketing two and a half hours for paperwork and a rushed sandwich, she had seen upwards of two dozen patients today; well over a hundred throughout the course of the week.

It was her imagination, she knew, but as Sally raised the champagne to her lips, she fancied she could smell the succession of latex gloves she had pulled on and off throughout the day. She recalled her penultimate appointment — a smiling and quietly charming Indian gentleman in his mid-forties.

Mr Johara had been suffering with intermittent stomach pains for several weeks and had only made the appointment at his wife's insistence. 'Probably nothing,' he'd said, but after palpating his stomach Sally didn't share the man's optimism. He was borderline obese and almost certainly pre-diabetic, but what had concerned Sally was the possible lump she had felt in the region of his pancreas — although his weight made it hard to be either sure or precise. She'd sent him to the nurse with paperwork for a thorough set of blood tests, including those for jaundice, liver function and various tumour markers.

Mr Johara had two children, both girls under the age of ten, and if Sally's suspicions were correct, it was unlikely he'd see them into their teens. It was tragic, cruel and indiscriminate but, in the way a labourer's hands thicken with callouses, Sally had long since acquired the tough layer of professional indifference that is no less important to a general practitioner than her

2

knowledge, training and the standard trick-bag of diagnostic equipment. In truth, she had stopped worrying about Mr Johara before she had arrived at Victoria to meet Mike and Alistair, and it was only the phantom whiff of latex that dragged her mind back to him now.

Her need for decompression was based on more personal concerns, but it was going to take more than an extra hour's train ride to work through those. She and Alistair had attended their third session at couples' counselling last night. They'd both gone through a lot of tissues — although certainly not £100 an hour's worth — and Joyce, their counsellor, had said things were likely to get worse before they got better. But Sally couldn't help wondering if, rather like for Mr Johara, things would instead continue to decline as the sustaining systems, restorative mechanisms and vital processes broke down, and the thing they were trying to save faded and died. Maybe that was the real reason her thoughts had returned to the smiling man who insisted his cancer was nothing more serious than indigestion.

She turned her gaze from the window to Mike and Alistair, who had been picking over some titbit of office scandal — infidelity; stupidity, humiliation; the usual. Alistair was animated with laughter and you'd never guess he'd been sobbing into a Kleenex at marriage guidance just twenty-four hours earlier.

We find our own ways to cope, Sally thought.

The advertising agency where Mike and Alistair worked opened the beer fridges at four-thirty, and the boys were at least two bottles in by the time Sally met them at the station. Alistair had opened the champagne as soon as they took their seats, and was now debating with Mike whether to open a second. Probably Sally should have travelled down on her own, meeting the boys at the house they had rented for the weekend. But it would have offended Alistair and disappointed Mike. She smiled inwardly at the expression — the boys. Both approaching forty, but still and forever the boys. She had known Mike for over half her life now, since meeting him — God, twenty-one years ago — during their first week at university. Twelve years on, Mike had introduced her to Alistair, the man she would marry three quick years later.

'It was the Queen Mum's favourite,' Alistair said, tapping the cork of the unopened champagne.

Heidsieck Monopole Blue Top, the same brand they'd served at their wedding, and Sally wondered if it was a deliberate romantic gesture for her benefit.

'You'd think they'd make more of the fact,' Mike said. 'Imagine the poster: the Queen Mum's dentures floating in a glass of Heidsieck while the old girl sleeps in her four-poster. She's wearing a blue nightcap and the headline reads: 'One's favourite Blue Top'.'

Alistair clapped his hands together. 'I knew there was a reason we paid you so much.'

A man standing in the aisle — a plasterer or decorator, judging by his clothes — looked down on Alistair, taking in the champagne, the haircut,

4

the attaché case, then looked away, rolling his eyes.

Sally saw her embarrassment echoed in Mike's face, and again found herself wishing she'd travelled down on her own.

'Anyway,' she said. 'I thought the Queen Mother was dead.'

Alistair sighed. 'Fair enough. So' — he tapped the cork again — 'what does the doctor suggest?'

Sally checked her watch; the train would arrive at Brighton in around twenty-five minutes. Not long enough to properly enjoy a bottle of champagne, plus they had a long night ahead of them so it didn't make sense to peak too early. They were meeting Mike's new squeeze, the glamorous actress, and Sally didn't want to do it smashed. They were going to watch her in a play — *This Life*, she seemed to recall — and Sally knew that if she drank too much she'd end up sleeping through most of it. She quite liked dozing in the cinema, thought there was something innocuously decadent about it, but snoozing through your best friend's girlfriend's play, well that was just rude.

But Alistair had laid the decision at her feet. If she suggested they wait, then she'd be cast as the killjoy. Who knows, maybe she was. Ten years ago she wouldn't have hesitated to open the second bottle — so what had changed? Was it growing up or growing old?

At counselling, Alistair had chosen his words carefully: he wanted them to 'get back to the way they were'. But the way they were was thirty years old and no matter how hard you tried you couldn't talk the clock backwards. The counsellor had smiled indulgently at Alistair's declaration. As if she'd been expecting it, waiting for it so she could deliver her well-worn response:

'You can't go back to the way you were,' she'd said. 'You have to build something new.'

Counselling had been Al's suggestion, but Sally, whose job it was to send people along this path, had modest expectations. This idea, though, of building something new, had resonated with her. She wasn't happy, hadn't been for years, and to some extent — great or small — she had to accept that she was responsible for her own dissatisfaction. Maybe she had lost her way; her spontaneity, her compassion. Perhaps she needed to open herself up again, to let go.

On the train now, Al smiled at her warmly. He sat back in his seat, half winked at her and gently placed the bottle on the table — deferring graciously to Sally's common sense.

Sally slid her plastic glass towards him. 'Well we'll have to drink fast,' she said.

Alistair's smile broadened, not from getting his own way, she thought, but out of gratitude, or maybe even love.

She smiled back, the expression feeling like an old item of once-loved clothing that may or may not fit any more. 'And if I pass out in the theatre, I'm blaming you.'

Al dropped his voice and leaned in conspiratorially. 'Not much chance of that.'

'What do you mean?'

They were sitting at a table for four, Mike and Al facing forward, Sally in the window seat on

6

the opposite side. A boy of about eleven sat to her right, buried in his headphones while the rest of his family sat at the table across the aisle. Alistair glanced at the kid to make sure he wasn't earwigging, then tapped the side of his nose. 'Little cheeky-beaky to keep us going?'

Mike glanced at Sally and half grinned, half smiled — a gesture of complicity and apology. She wondered if he knew they were in counselling. Al had asked her to keep the information private, but the boys went back a long way and she wouldn't be surprised if Al decided to confide in Mike. Staking the first claim on their mutual friend.

Sally mouthed the word across the table: *Coke?*

She could see Alistair wondering if he'd made a mistake. She knew he occasionally dabbled with recreationals, but they had come to a tacit agreement that he would pretend he didn't and she would pretend not to know any better. Perhaps he'd been emboldened by Sally's agreement to an additional bottle of champagne.

'Molly,' he whispered.

'Who?'

'MDMA,' Mike said. 'It's cleaner.'

'Really?'

She turned to look out of the window. The day was fading into grey, turning the glass into a weak mirror and showing Sally her expression of weary exasperation. She adjusted it to one of nonchalance and took a sip of her champagne. 'Fuck it,' she said. 'In for a penny and all that.'

Mike tapped his glass against hers. 'Well put.'

Sally laughed, and now all three touched glasses across the table.

She glanced at the man standing in the aisle, not really caring what he thought any more, but curious nevertheless. The man caught her eye, winked, then went back to talking on his phone.

'So, tell me about this actress.'

'Faye,' Mike said, his face opening in a broad smile. 'You'll like her.'

'We'll be the judge of that,' Al said.

Sally turned to her husband. 'You haven't met her?'

Al shook his head. 'I thought he was making her up to compensate for his shallow lonely existence.'

For the second time in ten minutes, Sally cringed at her husband's lack of tact. Mike had been divorced for more than four years, but it seemed to Sally it had aged him by eight. As if every year after the break-up, his ex-wife Kim had found a new way to keep the wounds open — remarriage, a new baby, and approximately one year ago, moving back to the States and taking Jojo, Mike's then five-year-old daughter with her. And as much as Sally wanted to hate Kim for doing this to her closest and most enduring friend, she couldn't. She had always liked Kim and found her funny, generous and engaging. Not that she thought Kim and Mike were particularly compatible — they were too similar for that; both a little needy, driven by their insecurities and need to be liked. Wanting support and reassurance to a greater extent than they were wired to give it, perhaps. She was playing amateur psychologist, but you learn a lot about a person in twenty-one years.

In the months following Jojo's departure, Mike retreated into himself, and when Sally did see him, it felt to her that he was fading, losing colour and definition, his optimism and spark. He started smoking again, drank too much, talked about pointlessness — the latter point worrying Sally more than the rest. She took him to his own GP, not revealing her professional credentials but gently steering the conversation towards a low dose of Seroxat.

On the pavement outside, Mike had hugged her for a long time, wetting her neck with his snot and tears, before disengaging and giving the prescription to Sally for safe-keeping. 'You can't trust doctors,' he'd told her, and it had been the first time she'd seen him laugh in months. He joined a gym, bought a cookbook, stopped drinking from Sunday to Thursday. And, of course, had started dating. Maybe that was the trick. He looked healthier and happier than he had done for years. He looked good.

Sally leaned across the table now and kissed him.

'What's that for?'

'I'm happy for you. That's all. So, how long's it been? You and this actress.'

Mike held up six fingers.

'Weeks?'

Mike shook his head and smiled. 'Months.'

Sally punched him on the shoulder. 'Mike!'

'Ow! Make your mind up.'

'Well why haven't we met her yet?'

He shrugged. 'She's been busy. We've been . . . ' A smirk. ' . . . busy.'

Al elbowed him a little harder than necessary. 'I bet you have.'

'How old?'

Mike screwed up his face in a faux-wince. 'Have you heard about the half plus seven rule?'

'No. Wait. Half what? Your age?'

Mike took a sip of champagne, nodded.

'Plus seven,' Sally went on. 'So in your case — '

'In all of our cases.'

'Twenty-seven!' Alistair's eyes went wide — like a kid coveting his best friend's new toy, Sally thought. 'Are you telling me you're f — ' and then, lowering his voice to a whisper, 'you're fucking a twenty-seven-year-old?'

'Actually, I'm living with one.'

'Shut up, Michael Doyle. Shut. Up.'

Mike shrugged. 'What can I tell you, I'm a catch.'

'When?'

'Two weeks ago. We even bought cushions.'

Sally tilted her head to one side. 'You look happy.'

'I am,' he said. 'I am.'

Alistair downed his champagne and then tilted the empty tumbler first at Sally and then at Mike, inviting them to follow suit.

'So,' he said, as he went about refilling their glasses, 'any pictures?'

'You'll see her for yourself in an hour.'

'How will I know which one she is?'

'She'll be the one with no clothes on.'

10

2

Faye twisted the spoon into the ice-cream, raising her elbow to shoulder height to generate the necessary downward force. She was wearing a fawn-coloured vest top, no bra, and the muscles in her arm — fine, downy hairs from wrist to elbow — flexed as she attempted to dig into the goods. 'Mother . . . fucker.'

'Still frozen?'

Using the spoon as a handle now, Faye banged the tub against the table — the resulting thud rattling the glassware. 'Like concrete.'

'Rocky road?' Sally said.

'Funny.'

'Mint choc brick,' Mike offered. 'Don't let me forget to replace it tomorrow.'

'You already said.'

'Did I?'

'Three times.'

'At least.'

They were renting the house for two nights through a website that connected home-owners with temporary renters. Part of the new 'shareconomy', although the terms of the contract hadn't extended to sharing the contents of the permanent residents' fridge.

After depositing their bags, Sally had run downstairs to take a shower before the play, while Mike and Alistair went to the local supermarket for bacon, eggs, bread, milk, coffee, pastries. But — big oversight — nothing they wanted to eat at one in the morning, drunk on champagne and wired on MDMA. Faye undertook a search of the house, finding three large tubs of ice-cream in a chest freezer hidden away in the utility room.

Faye pushed the spoon down the side of the tub and began working it around the perimeter. 'Right,' she said. 'Never have I ever r — '

Someone groaned. 'No more!' This said in a half-joking, half-pleading tone.

The rules of the game stated that if you ever had, you drank.

'Never have I ever . . . ' Looking across the table, taking in their faces one at a time, holding their eyes for a second before moving on to the next ' . . . regretted sleeping with someone.'

Sally gave Faye an incredulous stare. '*Never?*'

Faye shook her head slowly. 'Nuh-huh.'

'Well you will,' Sally said. 'Trust me, you will.'

Mike made a big deal of clearing his throat. 'Ahem?'

Sally laughed at her gaffe, then gesticulated at Mike. 'Sorry. Present company excepted and whatnot.'

Mike bowed his head graciously. 'Apology accepted.'

'Anyway,' said Faye. 'You only regret the things you didn't do, don't they say?'

'Well *they*,' said Mike, 'have clearly never invaded Poland.'

'Or twatted their thumb with a hammer.'

'Or shagged Craig Plimpton.'

Alistair looked inquisitively at his wife.

12

'Upper sixth,' Sally said, shuddering. 'Spotty back, spotty bum.'

Faye leaned across the table and hugged Sally. 'You crack me up. Honestly. I think we're going to be good friends, me and you.'

Sally blushed, and was surprised at the sudden pulse of embarrassment.

'Yes,' she said, 'I hope so.'

'I know so.' Faye released the hug then, and inclined her head to the boys in a parody of impatience. 'Well?'

They answered in unison. 'Well what?'

'Never have I ever regretted sleeping with someone?'

Mike took a drink. 'God yes.'

Al did likewise. 'Everyone who wasn't my beautiful wife.'

Everyone groaned, and Al made a show of offence. 'You saying she's not beautiful?'

'Fuck no,' Faye said. 'She's gorge.' Going up on tiptoes, she attempted again to force the spoon into the ice-cream. Her hand slid down the shaft and her knuckles banged hard against the table. 'Bastard!'

'Here,' Alistair extended his hand towards Faye. 'Give it to me.'

As Faye reached across the table, her vest fell loose, briefly exposing her breasts. Small and neatly upturned.

Earlier that evening — last night by the pedantic kitchen clock — she had spent ninety naked minutes on stage, every curve and crease of her flesh exposed to the polite audience. From the front row of the theatre (the top floor of a

Victorian pub, converted for the purpose, Al could see more than most in the modest audience. The crop of freckles at the small of her back; the geometric asymmetry of her dark areolae; the colour and extent of her pubic hair, grown out at the director's insistence; the ghost of a tan line across her buttocks.

In spite of which, this fleeting demi-crescent of flesh was somehow more provocative than the full-lit feature-length exposure from three hours ago. Maybe it was the drugs, maybe it was the champagne. Maybe it was something about Faye.

Sally observed Alistair; the furtive glance, the inner struggle as he tried to resist staring too hard, or too obviously. More than anything else, Sally found it endearing. She took another spoonful of ice-cream from the tub she was currently hogging, then slid it across to Faye. 'Take mine.'

Faye took the tub, licked the spoon clean then dragged it through the ice-cream. 'Flavour is it?'

Sally shook her head. 'Everything tastes like MDMA.'

Faye threw back her head and laughed. 'Ben and whatshisname, Jerry, should get right on that. I'd buy it.'

Sally glanced at Mike and smiled. She cocked her head in Faye's direction, a small sideways tick seeming to say *Get this one.* A gesture of approval.

Faye caught the exchange. 'Don't blame me, blame the MDwhatsaname. What's all that stand for anyway?'

14

Mike turned to Sally. 'Doc?'

'Methysomething, methyphety . . . amphet-ymeth . . . '

'Any more?'

'Ice-cream or whatsaname?'

'Either or.'

Alistair skimmed a small envelope of drugs across the table.

'You only regret the things you didn't do.'

★ ★ ★

The play had, in fact, been called *A Still Life*. A two-act piece centred on an affair between an A-level art teacher and his pupil, Rose — her name being an allusion, perhaps, to blossoming. The play opens with the couple in an expansive double bed — revealed in dialogue to belong to Rose's parents. With the benefit of post-coital clarity, it becomes apparent to the teacher that he's made a colossal mistake, a realisation intuited by the wise-beyond-her-years Rose.

Mr Martin pulls on his jeans and begins stripping the bed, while Rose, parading, posing and cavorting in front of him, asks, 'Why the rush? My parents won't be home for at least two hours.' Adding a clever element of real-time jeopardy. Suddenly in a panic, Mr Martin can't decide whether to continue stripping the bed, pull on the rest of his clothes, or simply jump out of the window.

Act one ends with the laundry safely deposited inside the washing machine, and act two begins with it being transferred into the dryer. The

drying cycle will take fifty minutes, we are told
— with Faye breaking the fourth wall as she
turns to the audience and muses: 'Hmm, roughly
the length of a short play's second act.'

There is some back and forth then, as Rose
— still naked — convinces her art teacher to
sketch her while they wait for the sheets to dry.
Here the play loses a little momentum as teacher
and student discuss the nature of art and youth
and life and love. And then, in the final ten
minutes, there is some well choreographed
physical comedy as the lovers remade the bed
against the expiring time left to them. As
foreshadowed at the start of the play, Mr Martin
leaves via the bedroom window as Rose's parents
clatter in through the front door. The teenager
hurriedly pulls on her clothes and exits the set,
shouting a girlish greeting to her folks. But in her
haste, she leaves behind the charcoal sketch
(initialled, of course, by Mr Martin) of her naked
self, posing on the armchair in her parents'
bedroom.

⋆   ⋆   ⋆

'I don't know how you do it,' Sally said.

The unfinished remnants of the ice-cream sat
melting in their respective tubs. Alistair still held
a spoon, rotating it around his fingers as they all
talked at once, revealing small secrets and
theories and recollections and regrets. Interrupting themselves and each other, dropping threads
and picking up new ones. Occasionally they
would fall silent as an anecdote ended or petered

out, or they simultaneously lost focus and direction. And then they would start again, one at a time or all at once.

'All those people looking at you in the . . . ' Sally shuddered. 'I could never do it.'

'Course you could, you've got a gorgeous body.'

'Thank you. But — '

'You do, though! Doesn't she?' — Faye addressing Mike and Alistair — 'She's bloody gorgeous.'

Alistair raised his glass. 'I'll drink to that.' The champagne was gone now and they were drinking a bottle of peach schnapps someone had unearthed. Mike had worried about replacing such an arcane item, but they'd decided they could simply top up the bottle with a substitute. 'To Sally's gorgeousnessness,' Alistair said. 'Is that a word?'

'It is now.'

Four hands reached across the table to seal the toast and touch glasses. A confusion of contacts, each clinking against one then another, struggling to keep track yet determined no one would be missed. They clattered and crossed and came close to breaking their glasses.

'You have to make eye contact,' Faye said.

'Who?'

'Everyone. When you toast. If you don't make eye contact it's seven years' bad sex.'

'No one told me.'

'Now you know.'

Someone raised a toast to good sex, and again they chimed their glasses together, making

17

sincere and determined eye contact as they did.

'Anyway,' said Sally, 'I just don't know how you do it.'

'What?'

'You know what, I really can't remember.'

* * *

Seven years, Alistair thought, would take them back to their engagement, roughly six months away from the big day. The venue booked probably, but Sal had taken care of all the arrangements so he couldn't be sure. They had enjoyed a good sex life, making love often and with none of the tensions and disappointments that would lie ahead. It wasn't so much that they had bad sex these days, but that they rarely made love at all. But Sally seemed more relaxed tonight than she had for a long time, and Alistair wondered if this version of his wife would make it as far as their bedroom. And the thought that she might made him faintly apprehensive — *had it really been that long?*

He felt eyes on him and looked up to see Faye watching him with amusement. Almost as if she could read his thoughts.

* * *

Faye guessed they were the same age, but Alistair looked younger than Mike. Then again, he hadn't been through a divorce, didn't have a child halfway around the world, didn't smoke as far as she could tell. And he had a doctor at

18

home to take care of him. He had the beginnings of a paunch, and she wondered if Sally nagged him about this. But he was tall and broad, the combination going well with the good haircut and expensive shoes. Handsome too, but his awareness of the fact subtracted something from the overall effect.

He looked at her, as if sensing her eyes on him, and Faye smiled before looking away.

★   ★   ★

Mike watched with amusement as Sally further interrogated Faye about the awkwardness and excitement of performing nude. He watched her eyes go wide as Faye described a small piece of flesh-coloured Lycra she called a 'pussy patch'. Faye was right, he thought; Sally was gorgeous. She always had been, but looking at her now it seemed to him that she had grown into herself. She was a yoga junkie, he knew, cultivating a figure that would have made the younger — softer — Sally envious. She wore some life on her face now, her skin faintly lined around the eyes and mouth. Mike thought it suited her.

★   ★   ★

They had sat three abreast during the play, Sally in the middle with Alistair to her left and Mike on her right. At the point in the second act when Faye's character had urged her teacher to draw her, Sally had dug her elbow — as Mike had imagined she might — into his side. He had

19

glanced at her and muttered the word *Cliché*. To which Sally had nodded slowly, pressing a thumb to her lips as she struggled to contain a headful of nostalgia and laughter.

Cliché.

Despite receiving an A from the Joint Matriculation Board, Mike had never held any illusions about making a living as an artist. His A-level portraits and abstracts were fine, but he realised early on that the only people ever likely to hang them on a wall were the same people who had tacked his crayon rainbows to the fridge door. And he also realised that he didn't much care.

Even so, he enjoyed filling a page, and after settling into the rhythms of university, he joined a life-drawing group that met on Wednesday afternoons in a basement room of the Student Union.

He and Sally had recognised each other immediately, each experiencing a flutter of excitement and a slight quickening of the pulse.

They had met once before, over a month earlier during freshers' week. Waiting to get served at the bar, they had shared a look of wry disdain for a huddle of excited students throwing themselves to the ground during the chorus of Chumbawamba's student anthem 'Tubthumping', and then, of course, getting right back up again.

Mike was served first, but he remained at the bar while Sally waited for her own drink. Perhaps he considered paying for this stranger's vodka and tonic, but embarrassment would have prevented him from putting the thought into action. He managed 'Hello', and that turned out to be enough. Names were exchanged, and they had moved easily enough through the checklist of *Where are you from? What are you studying? Where are you staying?* before stumbling over that shifting awkwardness that comes from mutual attraction. As they progressed through music and film and books, they felt their discomfort grow as they approached the point where the small talk would run out — not because they had nothing to say, but because they had so much they wanted to reveal and learn and do. They could never agree on who, but someone's friend or course-mate lurched up to the bar, positioning themselves between the two and — in retrospect — saving them from the embarrassment of themselves.

They said they would see each other around, glanced once more over their shoulders and disappeared into the crowd of anonymous bodies.

After her GCSEs, Sally had dropped art so she could concentrate on the four A-levels that would get her into medical school. Her decision, and one she never doubted or regretted. She had wanted to be a doctor for as long as she could remember, and she was single-minded in her focus.

At the same time, she had always been enthralled and delighted by scientific illustrations, captivated not only by the miracles they elucidated, but by the unambiguity of their clean lines, cross-hatchings and annotations. Not yet seventeen, she had constructed a retirement fantasy, warming to the image of herself hunched over a draughtsman's board, her bunned hair a grey nest of pencils as she sketched the chambers of an exposed heart. Holding on to the image throughout her A-level studies and carrying it with her to university, Sally joined the Wednesday afternoon life-drawing class as a means both of relaxing from her academic studies and of keeping her pencils sharp.

And they recognised each other immediately.

They sat next to each other whenever they could, talking more easily now they had discovered something mutual, sharing jokes and gossip and offering encouragement as they drew. Sally remembers a particularly well-endowed model, a big man in all respects — solidly fat, large-featured, heavy-limbed, wide-shouldered and heftily appendaged. She had lost herself in a daydream, speculating at his comorbidities — diabetes, arthritis, hypertension, hyperlipidaemia — when she became aware of Mike watching her. He glanced at his work, inviting her attention to the charcoal man on his easel. Mike was talented, for sure, more so than herself, but his work was undisciplined and uneven — accurate to a point and then growing diffuse and loose as he lost interest. Drawn from a three-quarter angle, he appeared to have sketched this man with more focus than normal, the centrepiece being the man's faithfully rendered but drastically reduced genitals. It was all there — the uncircumcised penis lying lazily to the left of his testicles — only imagined at

22

approximately a third of their actual size. Like a grotesque joke of nature; an ogre cursed with a cherub's cock.

He had watched Sally's face contort under a widening smile, feeling something profound for her as she pressed her thumb to her lips to contain the escaping laughter. That was the first night they slept together.

The first of perhaps one hundred scattered nights, although they never managed to string more than a handful together at any one time. Believing themselves — in their naïve sincerity — to be beyond the trite conventions of boyfriend-girlfriend.

Alistair knew that Mike and Sally had — in the way of old university friends — enjoyed the occasional, low-intensity drunken fumble. He knew they had kissed, he guessed they had laid their hands on each other. He was ignorant, however, of the fact that his wife and very close friend had been habitual lovers during three overlapping student years and — with decreasing frequency, passion and expectation — for almost a decade after.

There is a window of time for sharing old and intimate secrets, and whilst Mike and Sally had intended to share theirs with their best friend and new man, the moment had proved elusive, and that window on the past was a long time closed.

Months after that first night two decades ago, comfortable now with their naked bodies, Mike had asked Sally if he could draw her. They were in her room and Mike had picked up her pad and flipped to a blank page. 'Let me draw you,' he'd said, giving voice to a notion he had been playing with for some time — since the first time, in fact, that they had pulled their stools together on a Wednesday afternoon.

Sally had looked at him, expressionless, for maybe three seconds or maybe a hundred years before laughing and then saying, 'One word, Mike Doyle. Cliché.'

Cliché.

When he had mouthed the word to her in the theatre, there was something else behind the suppressed laughter and a shared joke. Something they knew each other well enough to experience mutually.

Mike had leaned into her, pressing his shoulder against hers in something like a hug. And Sally had pushed back.

★   ★   ★

'Never have I ever been unfaithful.'

No one was drinking now, not seriously, not to get drunk. That mission had been well and truly accomplished and surpassed. Occasionally someone would raise a glass to their lips, but only for something to do with their hands. They had taken down the kitchen clock because no one liked what it had to say. They should go to bed, but as tired as they were was as wired as they were.

'We're in this together,' they had agreed, making a pact that no one would retire until they all retired.

'Never?'

Faye shook her head. 'Ever ever.'

'I thought actors were all in and out of bed with each other.'

'They are,' Faye laughed. 'And I'm not saying I've never slept with someone who was cheating on someone else.' She looked at Mike and winced apologetically. Mike batted it away nonchalantly. 'But that's their problem,' Faye said, a hint of coldness in her tone maybe. 'Not mine.'

'What about kissing someone on stage?'

'What about it?'

'What's it like? Being passionate or intimate with someone who isn't your boyfriend.'

'It's called acting.'

'Sorry, I didn't mean to . . . '

Faye laughed. 'It's fine. It's just . . . it's just make-believe, isn't it? Just pretend. So, never have I ever . . . ?'

Mike, Alistair and Sally all picked up their drinks and took a sip.

★ ★ ★

Like actors in a play.

Isn't that what they were now? All of them pretending to be something they weren't; this rented house the stage, the set.

Faye, it seemed, was flirting with Al. Maybe teasing Mike, maybe trying to ingratiate herself with his best friend. Or was it an attempt to flatter Sal, by showing approval for her choice of husband?

25

Were they really flirting or were they pretending? These hands across the table, the touched shoulders and blown kisses, the clumsy allusions.

★ ★ ★

After the initial rush and buzz of each inhaled and hacked-back line, they had come to anticipate the slow slide to a point below baseline. The confidence and thrust gradually displaced by a mithering sensation of absence and edge. It was bad stuff and good stuff; potion and poison and antidote to itself. While it's there it's wanted, but when it's done it's gone. So they snorted one more rail of white powder, felt the circuits firing and began again to blurt their lines and hurry their jokes before the inexorable slide.

★ ★ ★

The boys were doing impressions, attempting to one-up each other. Rattling off second-rate De Niros, Pescis, Walkens, Brandos.

Sally watched Mike do the famous speech from *On the Waterfront*, and while the other two laughed at his 'I coulda been a contender', Sally found it profoundly sad. The swelling emotions caught her off balance, and as the tears rose to her eyes, she excused herself to the toilet before they began rolling down her cheeks.

★ ★ ★

'How much did you bring?'

Al grimaced like a little boy found out. 'Two.'

'Jesus, one would have been enough.'

'More than.'

'Nice though, it's . . . it's nice, isn't it?'

'I feel like I'm grinding my teeth. Am I grinding my teeth?'

'I really need to go to the dentist.'

'Good God it's moreish.'

'I'd be struck off.'

'One would have been enough.'

'You only regret the things you don't do.'

'In that case . . . '

★ ★ ★

'Never have I ever kissed a member of the same sex.'

They watched each other, waiting, eyes moving from one to the other but tending to linger on Faye. Faye, however, refused to be drawn by such presumptive scrutiny.

'Not me,' said Alistair. 'Not that I have anything against, you know . . . it's just' — he placed a hand on Mike's shoulder — 'sorry mate, I just don't see you that way.'

'I'll get over it. And no, me neither.'

Sally shook her head. 'Nuh-huh.'

Faye leaned across the table and kissed her full on the lips. For maybe one second longer than was comfortable. 'You have now,' she said. 'Drink.'

★ ★ ★

Al watched Faye kiss his wife. Tilting her head to create a more intimate angle, maintaining eye contact as she leaned in, holding her mouth against Sally's for . . . one, two, maybe three seconds. She was standing, bent at the waist with locked legs and a flat back as if performing one of the yoga poses his wife practised. Again her vest fell loose, but as she braced herself against the table, her arm obscured a second glimpse of her breast. His eyes scanned along the line of her back to the cut-off denim shorts, the curve of her buttocks and sweep of her thighs. He brought back the image of her from earlier that evening, the fading tan line, the crescent of her navel, the dark hair at her crotch. Faye met his eye and smiled.

★ ★ ★

MDMA increased the levels of three neurotrans-mitters: dopamine, serotonin and something else, Sally couldn't remember. She went on to list the drug's effects, an altogether easier task with the full catalogue now in evidence around the drug-dusted kitchen table: euphoria, a sense of empathy, loquaciousness. Distorted perception, decreased inhibitions.

★ ★ ★

'Define *infidelity*.'
    'Well it's cheating, isn't it?'
    'What if you separate the physical from the emotional? What then?'

'It's still cheating,'
'What if it's consensual?'
'Consensually physical or emotional?'
'Hold on, you've lost me.'

★ ★ ★

'I'm going to look like the Bride of Frankula tomorrow.'

'Frankula?'

'I'm off my whatsit. Druckula, fuckula, you know what I mean. Thank the Lord for hair and make-up. Thank fuckula. Your friends are a bad influence, Mikey pie.'

'You only regret the things you don't do.'

The platitude had become their chorus, a punchline they leaned on when the conversation — or what passed for it — veered off track or lost momentum.

But they were circling around something too.

The talk returned — in a tightening spiral, it seemed — to sexuality, fidelity and trust.

★ ★ ★

Sally tuned out of the conversation, troubled by some revelation she could only vaguely recall making. They were talking about the nature of infidelity, and she thought maybe this was related to the anxious thought she couldn't quite snare.

★ ★ ★

'Everyone's kissed my wife.' Al banged the table as if at a sudden insight. 'Everyone at this table has kissed my wife.'

Faye raised her eyebrows at Mike.

'University,' Mike said, by way of explanation. 'Anything . . . else?'

Alistair laughed: 'He wishes!'

Sally and Mike glanced at each other, their eyes connecting briefly before both looked away.

Faye shrugged. 'You only regret the things you don't do.'

★   ★   ★

Distorted perception, high body temperature, increased heart rate, teeth clenching, depression.

★   ★   ★

Sally remembered now. She had told them about the old couple coming in together, holding hands nervously as they got to the point and asked for a prescription of 'the Viagra'. Sally had justified the anecdote as a sweet example of enduring romance, but maybe she was kidding herself. Maybe it was nothing nobler than a crass indiscretion designed to make her look smart and funny and irreverent. To narrow the gap between her and Faye.

★   ★   ★

Someone had suggested that when all the glasses on the table were empty, that's when they would head upstairs and down, to toss and turn and deal with their insomnia. So they nursed their glasses, watching each other, waiting for each other.

★　★　★

'This is the last of it.'
  'Thank God for that.'
  'One for the road?'
  'Only don't you do what you regret.'

★　★　★

Something bothered Faye but she couldn't put her finger on what. She couldn't remember if it was a significant or a trivial thing, but it was there. Something about Mike and Sally, she thought. About them kissing at university, perhaps — but why would that be agitating her? She wondered at the dynamic between the three friends. Sally, her husband and their mutual friend — she had been told the sequence of events and introductions, but it eluded her now.

★　★　★

The glasses were almost empty.
  'Never have I ever had a foursome,' someone said.
  There was a little laughter at this, but no one raised a glass to his or her lips.
  Something on the stereo. Silence seeming to fill the spaces between the notes.

31

'Never,' someone ventured, 'have I ever . . . swapped.'

All four glasses remained on the table; rolled between finger and thumb, maybe. Tilted in contemplation, perhaps. But no one drank.

'Never have I ever been tempted?'

They all held their glasses in their hands. One and maybe another were lifted from the table.

Sally looked at Mike.

Alistair looked at Faye.

One of the four raised their glass, rolled the viscous liquid around the base and then drank. And when one drank the others followed. No one was sure who had initiated this sequence; locked on to a single pair of eyes, everything else was peripheral, slow motion and low resolution. Someone pushed their chair back from the table and stood.

3

Anxious, depressed, paranoid, hungover and hurting, fuzzed out, dehydrated and sick. Angry, confused, rejected, betrayed and wracked with guilt. Each in the same bed as the person they might — at a dinner party, say — introduce as their other half, their better half, my girlfriend, my man, my husband, my wife. The person they relinquished last night, the person who gave them away to another. The person who smells of someone else, their skin tacky with dried spit and sweat and cum.

What have I done?
What did we do?
How could we?
Why did we?

Four bodies feigning sleep, four minds trying to untangle threads and motives and initiatives. Blame the drugs, blame the drink. Blame Mike, blame Faye, blame Sally, blame Al. Blame yourself.

★ ★ ★

Faye's stomach felt liquid, her guts contracting around the stale booze and congealing ice-cream. She slid out of bed, not believing Mike was asleep, but taking care to move silently just in case. She walked into the en-suite bathroom, head throbbing with her pulse, hand shaking a little as she closed the door behind herself. She ran the shower and under cover of the noise, vomited into the toilet bowl.

There was urine on the toilet seat; it could have been anyone's.

Hers, Mike's, Alistair's, the people who owned this flat even.

Not Sally's, though — she had slept in her own room and was innocent, at least, of this transgression. She had liked Sally. Instantly and with a growing warmth throughout the night. She was familiar with the synthetic affections inspired by drink and drugs; knew they seldom persisted beyond the inevitable comedown of the next day. But this hadn't felt like that, it had seemed from the minute they met that she and Sally connected. And now she had slept with this funny, intelligent, attentive woman's husband. She had fucked her boyfriend's best friend. And Mike had endorsed it, whilst simultaneously returning the favour.

What did we do?

She asked herself the question again, not out of abstract self-pity but out of genuine bafflement. *What did we do?*

*   *   *

Mike rolled onto his back and opened his eyes. Running his tongue over his teeth, his mind flashed to the feel of Sally's tongue pushing against his own. Today they were going to walk on the beach, find an arcade and drop two-pence pieces into the rigged cascade, play mini-golf. A movie montage of friends on a carefree weekend away. Maybe go for cocktails while Faye performed for the Saturday night crowd. Maybe watch the show again. But the script had been changed now.

While they were in their own rooms, behind a closed door, they were insulated from whatever would happen next. The narrow house had an esoteric floor plan ranging over three levels. One bedroom, one bathroom and a utility room in an excavated basement; kitchen and living room and small study on the ground floor; second bedroom with en-suite bathroom on the floor above. Had the layout been more conventional — adjoining bedrooms — maybe they would have nothing more than their physical symptoms to contend with this morning.

Proceeding to their bedrooms as a four might feasibly have broken whatever spell held them. But as they moved upstairs and down, the four were separated from their partners and any sobering effects of self-conciousness.

Last night, earlier this morning, after Mike left Sally in bed, he had waited in the kitchen, distracting himself with the domestic banalities. Throwing the tubs of melted ice-cream into the bin, the empty bottles into the recycling, washing the glasses and spoons. He leaned out of the kitchen window and smoked a cigarette. He made a cup of tea.

How did it happen? was the question he returned to, but the answer wasn't readily apparent. Faye had certainly seemed . . . what? Restless, provocative? Maybe she had done this before. Maybe it was de rigueur in thespian circles. But wasn't it perhaps a little disingenuous to single out Faye as the instigator? It had felt like there was something in the air — something beyond the invisible miasma of powdered ecstasy. He had sensed something between Sally and Alistair, a tension maybe. And what of him and Sal? The events and their sequence were incomplete and disordered in his mind. Gaps and overlaps and scenes that seemed to play from multiple perspectives — as if observed on a screen rather than from within.

He may have dozed in his chair at the kitchen table; it was hard to tell.

Al was buttoning his shirt as he came into the room. They hugged, holding each other in an embrace that didn't know what it wanted to articulate. Not a coy wrapping around of arms, but a tight and intimate clinch of acceptance or forgiveness or understanding. Something.

When Mike went up to his room last night, Faye had been in the shower. Lying in bed eight hours later, listening again to the sound of drumming water coming from the bathroom, he imagined twisting the architecture of the house. Rotating the three floors as if they were pieces in a puzzle, separating them, breaking them apart and sending them in different directions — transporting himself back to south London, sending Sally and Alistair to the north. With miles between them, and months and years too, maybe this ungraspable feeling would fade. They would come to view it as a moment of shared madness and trust and friendship — something

36

they could only have done with each other. He pictured the four of them at a dinner party, kissing cheeks in the hallway on arrival, telling each other how well they looked, a squeeze of the shoulder or upper arm acknowledging that they had a special bond now — something the other guests could never know or guess. As the night progressed, they would find themselves isolated as a four, and one would say, 'So, how have you been?' But what he or she would really be saying was: *Remember that time?* They would exchange knowing smiles, laugh and shake their heads: *What were we thinking?* And then they would move on, talk about work, holidays, the state of the nation. But as Mike's mind lingered over the imagined scene, he saw himself catch Sally's eye — saw a further, deeper, understanding pass between the two of them.

★　★　★

Down two flights of stairs, on the other side of a second bedroom door, Sally lay curled on her side. Her right hand under the pillow, her left between her knees. Her lips, tongue and gums were dry from a night of breathing through her mouth. The membranes in her nose swollen and blocked from a million fine grains of MDMA.

Methylenedioxymethamphetamine, the unlovely chemical name she couldn't conjure last night. Knowledge and wisdom after the fact. Her mind was a kaleidoscope of images and thoughts, remembered sensations and murmured words. Had she been alone, she may have allowed herself to examine these, to attempt to assemble them into some kind of sequence. But Al was breathing at her back — awake or asleep, she didn't know — and she was afraid of what the images might reveal. Last night would need decoding, analysing, understanding — but not now. Her levels were off, her biochemistry was wrong, her emotions were stretched thin. Stretched to snapping point.

'You awake?' Al's hand on her shoulder.

3,4-Methylenedioxymethamphetamine. She spelled out the twenty-nine letters inside her head. Carbon, hydrogen, oxygen, nitrogen. The stuff of stuff, it just depends on how you arrange the pieces — water, medicine, poison, food.

'Babes. You okay?'

It was too easy, though, to blame the drugs. To blame the booze, to blame someone else. Was blame even the right word? It was too soon to tell. Of all the emotions she should be or could be struggling with — guilt, regret, anger, embarrassment — perhaps the dominant feeling was one of loss. But for what or who exactly, she didn't have the clarity of mind to answer. She had no answers.

She wasn't sure she had the right questions.

Alistair's hand squeezing the muscles at her shoulder. His lips on her neck.

After Mike left she had pulled on a pair of clean knickers and a T-shirt. It had been another fifteen minutes before Alistair came back to their room, climbing quietly into their bed, kissing the back of her neck like he had just done now. She had listened to his slowing breath, to the catch of air at the back of his throat as he slid into sleep, to the low rattling rumble of his familiar and comforting snore.

Sally rolled over now, and rested her head on her husband's chest.

★   ★   ★

Alistair remembered closing the door behind him as he left Faye. He had debated with himself — for how long? A second? Two? — whether or not this was the right thing to do. If there was a protocol for these kinds of situations, he was ignorant of it. Should he close the door for Faye, or leave it open for Mike? Closing it seemed more appropriate, somehow — as if resetting some mechanism, perhaps. He had descended two or three steps, then stopped, listening to the stillness of the house. Listening for movement from Faye, maybe. Imagining she might come to the door, beckon him back for one more kiss. She didn't.

Three, four, five more steps and his attention shifted to the room in the basement. What if he heard them? No time limit had been set, so it was possible they were still in bed. It was the first time — the first of many — that he would wonder about their comparative performances. He didn't know how long he had been in bed with Faye; time felt bent out of shape. It could have been an hour. Less, possibly, but unlikely to be much more. He had worried that the Molly and the Blue Top would undo him at the moment of truth, but those concerns had vanished at the first touch of Faye's naked body. Watching her in the play earlier he had wondered what it must be like to be Mike, to share a bed with this young, confident actress. And now he knew.

Like his anxieties, Alistair's control had been short-lived that first time. *A compliment*, Faye had said. Or were they his words? Faye had been hesitant about going again, but he had made a game of it — tickling her sides and kissing her breasts and, soon, she was kissing him back, pushing her mouth hard against his. He did better the second time; pacing himself, distracting his attention with little feats of memory: song lyrics, old jokes, stations on the underground.

As Alistair came into the kitchen, Mike was dozing in a chair, a cup of tea on the table in front of him. Alistair had smiled at the small victory — outperforming his friend — then cleared his throat before walking into the room.

As Sally placed her head on his chest now, Alistair kissed her hair, smoothing it flat with his hand.

They had lost their way, to borrow the idiom of their counsellor — her of the reassuring smile and shifting metaphor. There was no going back to the way they were, Joyce had explained; the task now was to build something new. Build what, though?

You heard about open marriages, but Al thought the concept was a contrivance, espoused by unhappy people in unhappy marriages. Was he being narrow-minded, missing a trick? The cosy familiarity of another half at home, with

40

occasional distractions on the side. Someone to love and some other one to fuck. Was that the new thing? Or an older thing built around the dual necessities of protection and procreation.

Perhaps. But not like last night.

He could handle, he thought, the idea of consensual and anonymous affairs. But as much as he had enjoyed — very much enjoyed — an hour with Faye, the idea of Sally with Mike was less frivolous. Ego, maybe, but there it was.

She shifted slightly on his chest.

'Do we need to talk about this?' he asked.

Sally took a deep breath. 'I don't know. I don't think so. Do you?'

'I don't think I'd know where to start.'

Sally made a small noise of acknowledgement, the first breath of a laugh. 'No.'

'Are you upset?'

'With who?'

'Me.'

'How can I be? We all . . . you know.'

'Yeah.'

'Have you ever fantasised,' she said, 'when we make love? Have you ever fantasised about someone else? Be honest.'

'Once or twice perhaps. Have you?'

Sally nodded.

Al laughed, a short *hah* that sounded a little like bravado. 'Who?'

Sally shrugged against him. 'Doesn't matter. Anyone. No one.'

'So what are you saying?'

'I'm saying it's . . . just a fantasy. It's . . . it's fine.'

Al kissed her hair again. 'I love you. You know that, don't you?'

'I love you too.'

What else could she say?

4

Faye checked her watch, again. She had been waiting twenty minutes now for an 11.35 call, which meant she was going to be late back to the office. 11.35, the call sheet said, printed in bold ink and highlighted in yellow. Why be so fucking precise if they couldn't even keep to their own schedule? She took a compact mirror from her handbag and checked her make-up. Nope, it hadn't somehow vanished or smudged in the five minutes since she had last checked.

The door to the casting suite opened and Faye overheard a male voice telling the outgoing actress it had been great meeting her; they'd be in touch. The actress made some joke, some remark Faye couldn't quite discern and the invisible others inside the room laughed. We'll be in touch, the man said again, and if you believed the sincerity in his voice then the rest of them were wasting their time.

It had been two weeks since the Brighton play (an inward cringe at the associated memories, before pushing them back and turning away) had run its natural course. It had received good reviews in the local press and on a few popular websites, but so far, Hollywood hadn't come calling. Pinewood either, for that matter. 'You're not an actor if you don't act,' someone had once said. 'You're just someone who attends auditions.'

'Aspiring' was the tag invented to deflect such snidery, or 'resting' or 'struggling' — or 'starving', if you wanted to be cute about it. But 'aspiring' had an expiry date, after which your prefix simply became 'deluded'.

Funny Girl was smiling as she left the room, stepping into the corridor where the rest of the hopefuls sat with perfect posture on their plastic chairs. She was trying not to appear smug, but she wasn't that good an actress. Perhaps she didn't need to be. Funny Girl looked younger than Faye, taller, skinny with big tits. Perhaps not as pretty as Faye, but there were some things you couldn't measure in increments. Even so, Faye should probably start running again. One of the girls at work was on a fad diet — surviving on an apple and a boiled egg for two days a week, then eating whatever the fuck she wanted for the other five. Maybe Faye should give it a try; she had skipped breakfast this morning, after all. Although not out of any dietary considerations, rather that her period was due and she was suffering from the mother of all cramps. But this was to be expected.

She'd been back-to-backing her pill during the play's run — a dangling tampon string not being part of the director's vision — and now her cycle was all screwed up. She'd done it before, skipping the seven-day hiatus that came after every twenty-one pills, to hold back a period so it wouldn't compromise a summer holiday in Ibiza. But after she'd returned and stopped taking her pill, it had taken around a fortnight for her body to get back to normal. *The things we do to ourselves.*

The casting director called out another name that wasn't Faye's and escorted the owner into the room. Faye didn't even bother checking her watch; she was late and there was nothing she could do about it. Except, she supposed, walk out and sprint across Soho in her heels. But these — her late twenties — were the make-or-break years, so she stayed put and looked again at the script. Nine words in a thirty-second commercial for a price-comparison website. Her character was identified as 'Attractive Woman #2'.

At least it wasn't 'Fit Bird #2'. *How very progressive.*

It had been easier when she was in drama college. You were encouraged to attend as many auditions as possible and no one tutted if you had to skip out of a workshop or a lecture to run across town and wait your turn to read your lines. Beyond graduation, however, the real world gave precious few fucks for your talent and ambition. These phones need answering, these groceries need scanning, these tyres need changing. It's why so many thesps work in restaurants and bars — flexible hours, empty daytimes, colleagues who will cover you for the time it takes to run from here to there, give your name and agent to the camera, profile left and profile right, say your lines then hightail it back to serve table thirty their tiramisu. But the mid-shift waitress was neither a good look nor an attractive perfume, and besides, the job had a way of sucking you in. You're unlikely to get the part, anyway, so you skip the audition and perform instead for the family of fat Americans on table twenty-two; they should be good for a twenty-quid tip.

She'd done it for a while, they all had, but Faye had hung up her stripy braces years ago. Now she temped as a receptionist; reasonable cash, convenient location and it didn't make your clothes stink. Plus, most of the companies were reasonably amenable to the occasional, brief, cross-town flit. Although this one was no longer brief, and there was only so far that reasonable amiability could stretch. And then where would she be?

Mike hadn't used the words explicitly, but when she moved in, he'd let it be known he would support Faye. Be supportive of, at any rate. He wouldn't accept rent and had needed his arm twisting to take a token payment towards bills and groceries. Even so, without the money she earned from temping, she would go from being a live-in girlfriend to a financial dependant. And she wasn't ready for that, even if Mike was — which was by no means a foregone conclusion.

After Brighton, very little was.

The first two weeks after moving in with Mike had felt something like a honeymoon. They — he — had bought new bedding, new drawers, new mugs. Leading towards what, she hadn't known, but the exuberant frivolity that had characterised the early part of their relationship was giving way to something more settled. Exchanging the trendy restaurants, private views and members' clubs for a pair of matching Habitat towels and a set of Rob Ryan egg cups. And, yes, all that cosy domesticity *was* nice, but she hadn't realised it was an either/or deal. She liked Mike, cared for him. He was a catch, if you liked the older man kind of thing. And Faye liked that kind of thing. Since the age of sixteen, in fact, she had been attracted to the calm confidence of men one and two decades older than herself. There was more to Mike, though, than the number of candles on his cake. Besides being financially secure and comfortable in his skin, he was funny, sharply intelligent, considerate and generally laid back.

But this felt like seven years married, without the first six and a half years.

Was that why Faye had behaved the way she had in Brighton? A reaction to the his 'n' hers towels, the designer egg cups and half a bottle of wine in front of a TV box set? Talk about using a mallet to crack a soft-boiled egg.

Faye's eyes dropped to the script in her lap, to the three lines she was still waiting to perform:

Attractive Woman #2 throws her arms around the neck of the lifeguard.

'*And I saved one hundred pounds on my holiday!*'

They look into each other's eyes and kiss.

Her attention closed in on the last word. Something was gnawing — an apt description, bringing to mind a tattered item riddled with holes — at her memory. She recalled kissing Sally at the table, making a big show of it for the boys, and she sighed aloud. What had provoked her to do that; who was she trying to impress; what was she trying to prove? Was it simply the

47

drugs and drink or something more? If it really was a reaction to the safe routine of life with Mike, it was surely an overreaction.

And what of the rest of it?

The words she used when considering this question coloured her view. The shift from 'screwed' to 'slept with' adjusting the context from base to metropolitan; and likewise, the difference between 'fucking' and 'making love' changing the event from something brutal to something urbane — or from playful to insidious, depending on your point of view. Perhaps it should be no more shocking than a penchant for bondage or role-play. Other people, after all, did these things. And not just your movie stars and rock stars, billionaires and moguls. More, in all likelihood, than we knew — the couple down the road, the man opposite you on the tube, the guy driving your bus, the lady scanning your groceries. Who knew, perhaps the occasional bout of consensual infidelity was the secret to a successful and happy relationship. Look at the old marrieds who barely noticed the other's existence. You could bet your boots — knee-high or otherwise — that these indifferent partners didn't fuck their neighbours. They didn't fuck anyone. As a waitress, Faye had seen them every week, staring through their partners as if time had worn them invisible — as if their once true loves had become as familiar and as interesting as the hairs on the back of their own knuckles.

If she and Mike ever became an old couple, would they discuss the events of Brighton over their anniversary supper? Fondly recalling

— Remember that time? — their youthful audacity. Maybe. Then again, maybe not — they'd done a pretty good job of avoiding the subject so far.

They had asked each other — with a look that made it clear to what the question pertained — *Are you okay? Are we okay?* And they had both answered *Yes. Yes, everything is fine.* Maybe they hadn't asked each other about the specifics of their encounter because they hadn't wanted to discuss the details of their own. Ask no questions and all that. Besides which, it hadn't seemed like the thing to do. Funny, to be considering matters of form, but reliving and retelling the intimate aspects had felt — to Faye, anyway — both tawdry and futile. Or maybe it was simply too awkward, too humiliating, too much. Instead, the default position had been to dismiss it as an innocuous and amusing faux pas. Crossed eyes at some associated prompt or mutually felt recollection. Raised eyebrows at the ice-cream fridge in Waitrose; the words *Blimey, Bonkers* or *Fucking mental* muttered at some TV infidelity or magazine gossip. Although lately, the crossed eyes had given way to wrinkled smiles and sideways glances.

She wondered if the same went for Alistair and Sally. Were the married couple talking it through or laughing it off? And what about Mike and Al? Avoiding each other in the office, or bumping fists perhaps in the lift? With regards to the latter, Faye didn't think Mike was the type, but the jury was out on Al. The flesh on the back of her neck prickled.

The morning after, the first thing Mike had said was 'Are you okay?' And he'd said it like he cared about the answer. He had kissed her, very gently and sincerely. A white crust dried at the corner of his mouth — maybe it was toothpaste, but she couldn't recall him brushing his teeth. Faye had smiled and told him yes, she was fine, but Jesus Christ this was some hangover.

There had been a sound from the kitchen — Al, Sally, both of them? — and the events of just a few hours prior coalesced around her symptoms, intensifying her headache and nausea and tooth-grinding comedown. Mike had made some attempt at diffusive humour. Something about bed and breakfast, but Faye couldn't have forced a laugh if Steven Spielberg himself had asked her to. Mike took his turn in the shower and Faye must have fallen asleep, because the next thing she knew he was sitting on her side of the bed, dressed and smelling of soap and toothpaste. He was going to face the music, he said. And would Faye care to join him? 'Later,' she told him, but later — she surfaced mid-afternoon — Sally and Alistair were gone.

A relief for the most part, but it had also denied them the chance to move past it as a group. To broach the uncomfortable subject in the diluting space of Brighton beach, throwing stones into the oncoming waves. Maybe going for a small glass of wine, clinking glasses and saying *You only regret the things you don't do.* It would have drawn a line under the previous night, and they would have all moved on.

Sal and Al had sent a card and flowers. A short

50

note saying it had been fun, 'Crazy but fun', the glaring absence of any reference to the explicit details seeming to say: *We'd rather not hold a post mortem, if it's all the same to you.* And then the suggestion of dinner sometime: 'Let's pick a nice restaurant' — a subtle but clear message that there would be no encore. Which was fine with Faye.

After Sally and Alistair left — some excuse about Sally having work to catch up on — Faye and Mike had gone for a long walk. Holding hands but saying little. They went for lunch, Faye thinking it might settle her stomach. With hindsight, a bowl of fried calamari probably wasn't such a good idea, and the few pieces Faye managed to eat didn't stay in her stomach for long. In fact, she kept little down all weekend, and by Sunday evening her stomach muscles ached from exertion. On the upside, her waistline had looked as tight as a ballerina's for closing night.

From somewhere in the depths of her bag, her phone rang. Probably the office calling to find out where the hell she was or to tell her not to bother coming back. But the name that came up was Sandra, her agent. Calling to see how the casting had gone, no doubt.

'Sandra, hi.'

'Hey, sweetie. How'd it go?'

Faye lowered her voice and cupped her hand around the mouthpiece. 'It hasn't. Still bloody waiting.'

'Ah well, par for the whatnot. Anyway, that's not why I called.'

'Tell me something good, for God's sake.'

'Well, I've good news and bad. Shall we start with the bad? Convention dictates, after all.'

'So long as you're not dumping me.'

'God no. I've high hopes for you.'

'I bet you say that to all your girls.'

'And boys. But I happen to mean it where you're concerned.'

'So, you were saying something about bad news?'

'That's right, sweetie. You'll have to let the lady garden grow for a while, I'm afraid.'

'Sandra, you've lost me.'

'Your whatsit, sweetie; your pussy.'

Faye doubted anyone could hear her agent on the other end of the phone, but she glanced around nevertheless. 'My . . . whatsit?'

'*A Still Life*, darling. It's been picked up by the Brixton Playhouse.'

'You're kidding?'

'Never. It's not the Old Vic, but it's a great little fringe place — not that little actually; you could have close to three hundred pairs of eyes on you. Two weeks to start with, maybe more. Little bump in the bank account too, but I'm pushing for a little bump more.'

'This is . . . amazing. When?'

'I *know*. Within a month, I should think, maybe sooner. So, let the lady garden grow, darling. Let it grow.'

'Will do. Am doing right now, in fact. Thank you.'

'*De nada*, darling. Right, I must dash. Good luck with the other thing — you'll be fab.'

'If I ever get in there. Take care, Sandra. And thanks again.'

'We'll speak soon. Bye sweetie.'

Faye dropped her phone into her bag.

'Faye White?' The tone suggesting this was at least the second time of asking.

Faye glanced again at the script: *Attractive Woman #2.*

'Yes,' she said, rising from her seat and fixing a smile on her face. 'That's me.'

The casting director motioned Faye into the room. 'Okay with kissing?'

'Sure,' Faye said, and again, something worried at her subconscious.

5

Sally glanced at the clock. This was their fourth session, and she had become accustomed to the structure. They were forty minutes in now, meaning their counsellor would soon wrap up the session with a discussion of last week's 'homework' before setting a new assignment for the following week. She experienced the conflicting emotions of relief and anxiety. Relief that they would soon be out of this neutral room and this polite inquisition. The anxiety stemming from the same source. Each passing session brought them one week closer to the end of this exercise — they had set no limit, but one must exist nevertheless. Sooner or later they would deliver their final homework and write their final cheque. And then — to quote her father — it would be time to do something or stop pretending.

This was their fourth session, but it should have been their fifth. Sally had postponed the session immediately after Brighton — almost three weeks ago now — not able to face Joyce, her knowing smile and sincere empathy, so soon after everything that had happened.

Tell me about your weekend?

Let's talk about mutual friends?

Have you been intimate this week?

They were there to share, but surely you can share too much? And more than the embarrassment, or shame, or call it what you will of the revelation — *I fucked my friend; Al fucked his girlfriend* — she feared the inevitable follow-up question: *And how does that make you feel?* Because, really, Sally didn't know.

She had, in fact, wanted to cancel all their sessions — it felt too much like a farce now — but doing that meant making a decision and she wasn't ready for that. Not yet.

The thought of being alone frightened her, and the idea of starting again was worse — new people, new baggage, new secrets and hang-ups and bad habits.

Mike had started again. He had Faye — talented, magnetic, beautiful. Unpredictable. But Sally wasn't sure it was making him happy. Did happy people do what they had done in Brighton? Some people did, she supposed, but she had known Mike for more than twenty years and that scene didn't fit the man she thought she knew. But people change — wasn't that why she was in this room, watching this slow clock?

She knew it was possible to separate sex from love, but to separate love from fidelity was a harder concept to grasp. Possessiveness was part of it too. The saying asserts that if you love someone, you set them free. But it doesn't say you should give them away. Surely to love means to own, and to be loved means to be owned. Not in the way of control and obedience and presumption, but in terms of mutual proprietorial trust. We give ourselves to the one we love, don't we? And they give themselves to us.

She hadn't seen Mike since, but they had sent short, non-committal text messages to each other, asking and confirming that one and the other was 'okay'. She wanted to talk to him, to ask what had happened and how, but at the same time, she was fearful of a dismissive reply — *It was nothing. Just a bit of fun. Don't overthink it.*

Maybe he was happy, and maybe she should concentrate on fixing her own marriage instead of wrecking her best friend's new relationship.

Don't overthink it.

Easier thought than not done; the thing they had done had a gravity that dragged at the mind. Regret mixed with a muted, guilty exhilaration. She cringed at her sketchy memories of the build-up, the showing off and flirting and suggesting and everything else that passed, under the circumstances, for a kind of fore-play. When her mind went back to these short scenes, she turned instead to the too-short hour she had spent feeling Mike's skin against hers. Scandalous, perhaps, but it was one of the few pockets of time from that night that didn't feel contrived.

She had felt happy and loved in a way that had been missing from her life for a long time. But then it was over, and what it revealed was hard to look at. Hardest of all, perhaps, was how little she cared about Al screwing someone else.

'Sally?'

'Sorry?'

Joyce leaned forward in her chair. 'Did you find time to look at your homework?'

What attracted you to each other when you first met?

'Right, yes.'

Alistair opened his attaché case, rummaging

56

about inside for his notebook. 'I made a list.'

He'd bought one for each of them — matching black Moleskines — so they could take notes, record thoughts and do their homework. It was sweet, in a way; a demonstration of how seriously he was taking this. But Sally also found it a little . . . ridiculous? Embarrassing? Controlling? As with so much lately, she struggled to land on the right word, or find the appropriate emotion. To hold a clear line of thought.

Take Joyce's homework:

What attracted you to each other when you first met?

To answer the *what* meant thinking about the *when*.

It had been Mike's thirtieth birthday party. Friday night in a fashionable Soho bar, all Mike's guests adhering to an ironic dress code stipulating 'anything black' to mark the demise of the young man's youth. Almost ten years later, Sally still had the jacket she wore that night. There was a good chance it still fitted, but the odds of it being in fashion were more remote.

After a period of several months, during which they had scarcely talked let alone laid eyes on each other, both Sally and Mike had become suddenly and not unhappily single. Sally had been the first to exit her relationship of eight months with a charming but over-sincere child psychologist. And less than two weeks later (what else but serendipity?) Mike had parted ways with a vegetarian banker who, despite the Mulberry handbag, wore her dietary preferences like a badge of honour. Mike and Sally had talked on the phone, met for coffee, then lunch, then cocktails, taking turns to air the details and the absolutely no-regrets of their recent and respective break-ups. Conversations concluded, more often than not, in the bedroom.

But something had changed. The physical charge that had been the hallmark of their relationship appeared to have faded. Or perhaps it had simply burnt out through overuse.

Despite what they may have believed at the time, they had been kids when they met in that university bar. Eighteen years old and with school uniforms — autographed by the friends they had yet to forget — still neatly folded in a cupboard at their childhood homes.

But they had felt so grown up and wise and so very fucking cool — sneaking around campus, indulging their urges, but resisting the simple thing they both felt but were too young and too stupid to acknowledge or grasp.

They met other people, slept with each other in fits of jealousy and candour behind those other people's backs. There was what passes for guilt in a pair of naked teens, but it was a small thing compared to the excitement and easy compatibility of their furtive hours and occasional nights together. What had started out as something like a game — playing grown-ups, perhaps — became something shared and secure.

Their friendship was not worth jeopardising, they agreed with forced sincerity. Nineteen now, and experienced in the ways of the world and heart, they had seen friends become couples become enemies and were determined not to make the same mistakes, each simultaneously believing and doubting this idea — although to differing extents and at different times. They took turns at taking offence, alternating between being the wrong and the wronged. Each making their declarations and demands and promises and excuses and apologies.

And there they were again, on the cusp of their thirties, their school uniforms long ago thrown out, and this game outgrown.

A new phrase had entered the vernacular. Two short words that fitted them well, exposing all their prevarication and self-justification for the silly bullshit it was. But Sally didn't want to *fuck*, and she didn't need another *buddy*. The thing they had sought to preserve was unravelling after all, and, to quote her father again, it was time to do something or stop pretending.

And then Mike's invitation dropped onto Sally's doormat: 'Anything black.'

Her first thought was to buy a new LBD and a pair of strappy heels. But most of Mike's crowd were advertising types and Sally didn't want to look like the token try-hard geek. Something more relaxed then; skirt and top, shorts and shirt, jeans and vest, long sleeves or bare arms, romantic or metal or skate, lace or cotton or denim, or how about leather? The single colour was maddening in its variety, and Sally must have tried on every black item in a size 10 up and down the King's Road and Oxford Street. In the final analysis, though, it scarcely mattered. The bar was as dark as a hole in the ground, and if Mike noticed or appreciated the skinny, three-quarter-length Versace jeans, the vintage adidas, the Vivienne Westwood shirt with black mother-of-pearl buttons, the French Connection leather biker jacket, he certainly didn't comment. Worse than this, though, the vegetarian banker was there — dressed as some kind of gothic ballerina and accessorising herself with Mike.

Sally and Mike talked and laughed and drank tequila, but the banker — Monica — was always lurking on the periphery, aloof and proprietorial, her thin bulimic lips fixed in a rictus of nonchalant superiority. Mike hadn't explicitly said that he and Monica had got back together, but it had been obvious enough to Sally.

And then, to return to the question posed by Joyce, there was Alistair. Mike's colleague and one-time flatmate. Tall, burly and confident. He liked the sound of his own opinion, but he was informed and funny and he held Sally's eye throughout, never looking over her shoulder for someone else to whom he could hold forth. He listened, too, sincerely and with a flattering degree of admiration for Sally's chosen career. When she told this charming man that she had recently become fully qualified as a GP, Alistair had insisted on buying a bottle of bubbly. They found a nook where they could drink it together, touching hands, now, as they talked. They left sometime after midnight, arm in arm, buzzed on champagne and anticipation.

They made love again in the morning, and Sally had been relieved to find Alistair still handsome and still entertaining. He wasn't Mike, but Sally had grown accustomed to that reality, and had learned the trick of looking away.

'I wonder what Mike will make of this?' Al had said, their heartbeats still elevated from their exertions. 'I think he has a thing for you.'

'He's like a brother to me.'

'Nothing else?'

'We kissed at uni. Once, maybe twice.'

'Well he's more of an idiot than I thought.'

Yes, Sally had thought. *Yes he is.*

'I guess one of us should tell him,' Alistair had said, Sally sensing Al rather fancied the task for himself.

'Knock yourself out,' she had replied, sliding out of bed and pulling on last night's clothes: the black adidas, the black shirt, the black leather jacket. 'I'm popping out to get bread.'

Not because she was hungry, but because the mention of Mike's name had amplified his absence in her small room and Sally didn't want to hear it again. Not today, not for a long time.

It was a scene she had returned to several times last week as she contemplated Joyce's assignment:

What attracted you to each other when you first met?

Alistair had finished reading the list in his notebook: Sally's eyes, her hair, her legs — the list went on, as if Alistair feared that by complimenting one aspect of her appearance he might be insulting another. Her smile, her skin, the freckles on the bridge of her nose. He had liked her laugh, he said — that it was sincere and

61

infectious. He liked her energy and lack of inhibitions. He admired her intelligence and career. She was the only woman he'd met who liked Bob Dylan and Woody Allen. Sally couldn't hold a tune with both hands and a handle, he said, but it didn't stop her singing along to 'It's Alright, Ma' whilst strumming an invisible guitar, and this too he found endearing. It was sweet and sincere, but diluted to translucence by its own rigour.

Sally opened her own notebook, her eyes going to the ragged scraps of torn paper between the pages. She had used her nails to pick away the remnants — the evidence — of a removed page, but a few stubborn pieces remained in the fold. She had spent a long time thinking about it, but her efforts looked mean compared to Alistair's thorough inventory. A bullet-pointed list of prompts rather than a crafted declaration.

'There was an immediate physical attraction,' Sally said. 'He was handsome, masculine. And he had this palpable confidence, like it occupied the space in front of him — you could be intimidated by it, I think. But I found him charming. Charismatic. There was this whole party thing going on around us, but he was totally intent on me and it didn't feel like an act. Telling me about himself, making jokes, asking questions. And listening like he really cared what I had to say. It was flattering . . . '

Sally looked at the list in her notebook: *handsome, strong, confident, intelligent, charming*. Beneath this she could make out the faint impression of an additional line, where the pen had pushed through the torn-out sheet above. Or maybe she was imagining it in the carefully muted light of the counsellor's office.

Writing the list on her lunch break yesterday, Sally had again replayed the night she met Alistair, but instead of recalling her husband's broad shoulders, wide smile or potent swagger, her mind had focused on her own sense of disappointment, excavating it from beneath the protective layers of resignation, self-deception and defiance. Because when all was said and done and written in ink, the best thing about Alistair that night was that he was the next best thing to Mike. She wrote it in her pad, pressing hard on her biro, forcing the blue ink into the fabric of the paper: *next best thing.*

That's your answer, Joyce. He was the next best thing to Mike.

Joyce inclined her head slightly towards Sally — *Are you finished?* — and Sally nodded.

'It's good to remind ourselves,' Joyce said, insinuating herself into their relationship, 'of what first attracted us to each other. To remind ourselves of the foundation our marriage is built upon. Now' — she glanced at the clock — 'I want you to say what still attracts you to each other today. Alistair?'

Alistair looked at the closed notebook in his hands — as if trying to see through the cover to the list printed inside. To remind himself, perhaps, of the catalogue he must now reiterate. 'Some things have changed,' he said. 'I mean, we're ten years older. We've changed.'

Joyce nodded, raising her eyebrows as she did

so, as if saying *Well done, you figured it out.*
Joyce had said she was 'on the side of the
relationship', and maybe that was true, but at the
same time, Sally couldn't help feeling that their
counsellor had a favourite pupil. And it wasn't
Sally.

Alistair shifted in his chair so that he was
facing Sally. 'I still find you beautiful; I'm still in
awe of what you do. You can still make me laugh;
maybe not in the overt, deliberate way you used
to — you're more thoughtful now, more
measured. It's a good change, though. And . . . I
know you more now, we've been through some
hard times, we have a history. And I love that
too, if that makes sense.'

Sally nodded: *Thank you.* Al's eyes were
sheened with tears, and Sally thought she might
cry if she opened her mouth.

Joyce filled the silence for her. 'Thank you,
Alistair. Sally?'

Of course their marriage wasn't built entirely
around the fact that Alistair was the next best
thing to Mike. In the weeks and months and
years that followed they immersed themselves in
each other, moved through attraction to
understanding and commonality, trust, affection
and love. They did the things couples do, the
things she and Mike never had. They went on
holidays, met each other's friends and family,
they made plans and grew and — to use
Alistair's phrase — they created a history.

They had undergone a decade of change, but
change can happen in three hundred and sixty
degrees — some traits are diminished, some lost

64

and some entrenched. The context shifts, too, throwing new shadows of unexpected shapes. What passed for confidence in a twenty-one-year-old can become brash arrogance in a man approaching forty. Charisma can mutate into boorishness. Humour can grate, anecdotes grow old and opinion can harden into belligerence.

Sally's notebook remained open in her lap and she ran her thumb along the deckled edge of the torn-out page. She traced her finger over the faint impression of the words — *next best thing*.

She said to Alistair, 'I see you now the same way I saw you then.'

Alistair smiled and reached across the small table to take hold of his wife's hand.

6

The midday sunlight was forgiving, lending flattering but dishonest highlights of blue and orange to the Thames, high today and animated by a moderate breeze. No two ways about it, the view from the new offices was spectacular. A collage of history and progress and clashing architecture that made Mike ashamed of his ignorance. He felt he should know the names of these buildings, their styles and periods and stories, but aside from several obvious land-marks, he knew no more and probably less than the average American tourist.

He checked the time on his laptop. Jojo should have called five minutes ago, and Mike was getting antsy. It would be just after 8 a.m. in New York, and his daughter would be getting ready to leave for school. Evening calls were less hurried affairs, made from the comfort of his own armchair, but if Faye was home Jojo invariably showed more interest in Daddy's girlfriend than anything Daddy himself might have to say.

After a tentative start on both sides of the Atlantic, Faye and Jojo had grown close after a fashion, coining nicknames and developing a limited rapport. But Mike was wary of letting Jojo get too close to Faye, particularly at the moment. He didn't want his daughter — grow-ing more inquisitive and perceptive by the week

— forming the idea that women were objects of transience in her father's life.

From behind his desk, Mike's eye-line faced east, taking in the steep dome of St Paul's Cathedral and the cluster of inelegant tower blocks lurking behind. If he were to press his forehead to the plate-glass window of his seventh-floor office and twist his head to the left, he could make out Waterloo Bridge, and the wide façade of Somerset House, largely obscured by a wall of autumn oaks. Further still to the northwest was the familiar structure of the old BT Tower, stabbed into the heart of Fitzrovia like a dirty syringe.

When Mike and Alistair had joined the agency — both with crisp degree certificates and full heads of hair — the offices had been located within a hundred yards of that same iconic column. Occasionally, if the sun was high and bright enough, the tower's long shadow would darken the window beside Mike's desk. A phenomenon the old creative director took as a cue to open the beer fridges, even if it happened before lunchtime. The 'good old days' people called them, their hazy memories editing out the wrecked marriages, ruined careers and shot livers.

Eighteen years he and Al had worked there now, remarkable in a fickle industry character-ised by sackings, redundancies and restlessness. They had outlasted hundreds of colleagues and weathered multiple business and economic crises. And now they had survived the old building in Fitzrovia, condemned to be razed before the end of the year.

Beyond his office window, a tugboat hauled an improbably large cargo of junk, dragging it slowly but inexorably upriver. Relocation had been briefly exhilarating: the grand vista, the smart 'elevators', the rooftop bar. But only three months in, the thrill of the new had dulled. He was still sitting behind the same desk, still doing the same job he'd been doing since he left university. All he had done was swap one view for another.

The word — *swap* — dragged his memory back, pulling it against the tide of six heavy weeks to the thing they had done in Brighton.

It sounded juvenile and frivolous; the word bringing to mind childhood exchanges of marbles and comics. But how else to describe it? On the playground, you would only exchange an item of which you had grown tired, or had perhaps damaged in some way known only to you. No one swapped the thing they prized.

And what of Brighton? No one had objected and no one had been coerced. Each of the four had been culpable to the same extent. More or less. Al had slept with Mike's girlfriend; but Mike had slept with Al's wife of almost seven years — considered in these terms, the scales of blame appeared less evenly balanced.

In an office of close to three hundred busy people, ranged over five floors and a warren of corridors, Mike had hoped for a few days' grace — maybe even a week — before, inevitably, bumping into Alistair in some lift, stairwell or meeting room. But when he had arrived at work on the Monday morning after they had swapped a wife for a stranger and a girlfriend for an old flame, Mike had walked into his office to find Alistair waiting, two cups of Starbucks coffee on the desk.

Al, sitting at Mike's desk, had slid one of the coffees forward. 'Just how you like it,' he said. 'White and sweet.'

Mike acknowledged the joke with a tight smile. 'Thanks.'

'Sorry,' Al said, 'it sounded funnier in my head. Less . . . dickish.'

Mike nodded. 'It's fine, it's . . . '

'Awkward.'

'That's one word for it.' Mike walked up to the window, leaving the coffee where it was.

Al spoke to his back. 'How was your weekend? After . . . after we left.'

A deep breath. 'A little . . . weird.'

'Only a little?'

Mike allowed himself a small laugh. 'Okay, a lot weird.'

Al came around the table, positioning himself behind Mike as they both stared out across the Thames, and Mike imagined he could feel Al's eyes on the back of his neck. 'Have you . . . have you ever done that before?'

Mike shook his head. 'First time. Last time.'

Al made a noise that sounded like agreement.

'I blame you,' Mike said, turning from the window.

'Me?'

'You're the one who brought a bag full of class-A drugs.'

Al understood that no personal blame was being apportioned. He nodded. 'You only regret the things you don't do, right?'

Mike raised his eyebrows at this. *Debatable.* 'How was your weekend? Is . . . is Sal okay?'

Al looked away briefly, before again finding Mike's eyes. 'She's a bit . . . you know. She's fine. We're fine.'

Mike nodded, but said nothing.

'Do you think we should . . . ' Al cringed, not knowing where this might be headed.

'I don't think there's any need to . . . '

'No.'

'No.'

'Right.'

. . .

Mike laughed. 'It'll get easier.'

'Good God I hope so.'

The two men hugged and it felt like the right thing to do. Neither one diminishing the gesture with the self-conscious banter that suggested itself. But as Al turned to leave the office, he hesitated in the doorway and said, 'You're a lucky guy.'

Mike hadn't been sure whether it was intended as a simple compliment, or a sly reference to the hour Al had spent in bed with Faye.

You're a lucky guy.

You too was the reply that had come to Mike's mind, but the words caught in his throat. Their truth making them too large, too painful to speak.

Sally, after all, was the one that got away. No

70

sense pretending she wasn't.

There had been a turning point — at the end of their second year he thinks, or maybe halfway through their third. They had gone home between terms, he is confident of that detail because he remembers missing Sally. He remembers, too, sitting on the stairs in his parents' house, the phone pressed to his ear for an hour or more, the calls — rather like those to Jojo — heightening his sense of apartness rather than assuaging it. He had grown tired of the charade, jealous of her 'others', uninterested in anyone else. As soon as he returned to university, as soon as he saw her again, he would tell her: *We should be together.*

And she would look at him and smile, as if she had been waiting for Mike to arrive at this inevitable conclusion. She would shake her head ruefully and say, *What took you so long, Michael Doyle?* She would wrap her arms around him, they would kiss, make love, walk about campus like all the other couples, become inseparable and nauseate their friends with their unabashed, unapologetic love. It was so obvious, so clear. He had his hair cut the day before catching the train to Birmingham.

Favouring the element of surprise, Mike made no arrangements to meet Sally, instead turning up unannounced at the flat she shared with two other medics and a dentist. He had wine in a carrier bag, holding it behind his back as he waited for her to come to the door. One of her flatmates — again, the detail is lost — answered the door, telling him Sally was studying at the library. A gap in his memory then — of walking to the library, locating her in the stacks or sitting at a table, of what she was wearing or how she greeted him — and the next scene he has is of them sitting on the lawn outside the library. A sequence of felt attitudes rather than remembered particulars — a coldness when she told him that she had to study, her annoyance at his attempts to cajole, her refusal to meet him that night. Her lack of excitement at seeing him. Maybe she was with someone else, or maybe he'd simply waited too long, but pride forbade him from asking. He didn't share the thoughts that had galvanised him over the term break, he told her it was no big deal and walked away. Where to he can't recall.

He wondered now if he should have tried harder, but he already knew the answer.

Even so, it was hard to fully embrace the regret when his daughter had been a direct consequence of his failure to be with Sally. Had he been with Sally, he wouldn't have been with Kim, and regardless of how that relationship had worked out, he would not turn back the clock if it meant unmaking Jojo. If anything, he should have been a better husband to Kim; they weren't perfect — would never have been — but they could have made it work, and then he'd be going home to his daughter rather than waiting for her to call from across several thousand miles of water.

But miracles of creation aside, yes, Sally was the one who got away.

That brief hour making love in Brighton had

been a glimpse both of the past and of the future they might have enjoyed. They hadn't talked about what they were doing; they didn't squander their time by asking questions or debating or even thinking. They kissed — gently — the second the door closed behind them, taking their time, reacquainting themselves with the shape and feel of each other's face.

A blurred detail that had been troubling him since that day came back to Mike as he stared out across the Thames.

That slow, lingering kiss hadn't been the first time they had tasted each other's mouths that night. Al had gone down to his and Sally's bedroom for some reason — or had he gone searching the house for drink? And Faye had gone outside for a cigarette, leaving Mike and Sally alone in the kitchen. By that time they were already jangling with drugs and champagne and . . . They had embraced, telling each other again how good it was to catch up, that it had been too long, that they missed one another. And then they were kissing.

A peck on the cheek, a brushing of lips, a tentative kiss and then another, the contact extending across the number of seconds that would take it from something innocent to something more. How long? He didn't know; the entire night felt like it was made up of badly edited scenes jump cut out of sequence, shot from nonsensical angles, drifting in and out of focus. Replaying that kiss, he saw it from different, unreliable perspectives, as if watching from a point removed. But as he watched the

73

kiss, over and over again, it was as if Mike and Sally were co-conspirators; the only two in on the secret of how the night would develop from that point forward. As if they had set the whole thing in motion.

A trilling noise snapped Mike's attention to his laptop, Jojo's grinning face filling the screen.

He clicked an icon to accept the call.

'Baby girl!'

'Daddoo!' Her head was moving erratically, as if being pulled by strings connected to the back of her head.

'Everything okay?'

Kim's face moved into the frame from behind their daughter's. She waved with a hairbrush. 'Hey, Mike. Sorry we're late.'

Mike thought about saying something sarcastic, but the calls were short enough without getting into it with his ex-wife. 'It happens.'

'Tell your dad why we're late, Jojobee.'

In response, Jojo hooked her index and middle fingers into the corners of her mouth, pulling them wide to expose her teeth as she gooned at the camera.

'I loss anovver tooff, Daddy.'

'No! How many's that now?'

'Five, but this one's wobbly, too. Stephanie Fielding's lost six, and the tooth fairy gives her two dollars a tooth and six times two is twelve, so Stephanie's had twelve dollars now.'

'That's a lot of money! How much do you get?'

From behind Jojo, Kim bunnied two fingers over her daughter's head.

'Two too,' said Jojo.

'Like the dress?'

Jojo scowled in incomprehension. 'What?'

'Never mind, baby. It was a bad joke.'

'A dad joke,' said Kim, and this time Jojo laughed.

'But I didn't get any money yet today, because my tooth just came out in my breakfast.'

'No way!'

Jojo nodded. 'Cheerios.'

A quip suggested itself — about bidding farewell to teeth, and milk teeth at that: *Cheerio!* But it was doomed to fall flat — another bad joke, another dad joke. Mike's own father used the same semi-archaic expression at the end of phone calls — *Cheerio, son.* The quaint word contrasting with his hard Geordie accent. His hard life. It's not until we become parents, Mike thought, that we appreciate what a poor job we make of being children. We learn the neediness that our parents hid from us (or not), because we feel it first-hand. These fleeting thoughts more like a series of intuited facts rather than an articulated line of reasoning; he resolved to call his parents this evening, to visit soon after.

Kim twisted and tied Jojo's hair into perfectly symmetrical bunches. 'Couple of minutes, Jojobee. Sorry, Mike. We can try again tonight? Six o'clock our time?'

Mike hesitated; Faye would be home tonight. 'Can you do tomorrow instead?'

'T-ball,' Kim said. 'Sorry.'

'What's T-ball?'

'Like baseball,' Jojo told him. 'But the ball's on

75

a tee. Can I see Paul's Cathedral again?'

'Sure, baby. Tonight's fine,' he said to Kim.

Mike stood from his chair, walking around his desk and taking his laptop to the window so Jojo could see the view.

'Was Paul the best at cathedrals, Daddoo?'

Mike laughed. 'No, they just made it to remember him.'

'Why?'

'He was a nice man, I suppose.'

Kim smiled. 'Some would say a saint.'

He missed her easy humour, and wondered, again, if they couldn't have made their marriage work for the sake of their daughter. Or did he mean for the sake of himself?

'How big is Paul's Cathedral?'

'We can go and see it when you visit,' he said, positioning himself in front of the computer and imposing himself on the view.

'Visit?' Jojo turned to her mother.

Kim kissed Jojo on the top of the head. 'Your daddy will tell you.'

Daddy. Did she call Brendan 'Daddy'? Good for her if she did, but he hoped that she didn't.

'Your mummy and me thought you'd like to come and see me in London?'

'Really?' Again, looking to Kim for approval, and only on receiving it, turning back to her father.

'Really really.'

'Are we all going, Mummy?'

Kim shook her head, widening her eyes to tell Jojo this was something exciting rather than frightening. 'On your own. Someone on the plane will look after you, you can watch films, play on your iPad. Although it'll be bedtime, really, so you'll be able to sleep in the sky! And when you wake up . . . '

'I'll be waiting for you at the airport,' Mike said.

Jojo looked from one to the other, struggling to take the idea in; the corners of her mouth turned down, her chin dimpled and, despite Jojo's best efforts, the tears came.

'Hey,' Mike said. 'Hey, it'll be fine. It'll be fine, baby.' Desperate to reach through the monitor and take hold of his daughter's hands.

Kim put her arms around Jojo's shoulders and pressed her face against her cheek, so they were both facing the computer. She grimaced quickly at Mike — *Yikes* — then said, 'You don't have to, angel, but it'll be *such* an adventure. Imagine how jealous your friends will be.'

'And there's something else,' Mike said, the thought just that moment occurring to him. 'You get to travel business class.'

Kim looked at him: *Have you lost your mind?*

Jojo asked, 'What's a buisner's class?'

'Business class, sweetheart. It's the best bit of the plane, where all the pop stars travel.'

Kim exchanged a look with Mike, making it plain that any pop star worthy of the moniker wouldn't be seen dead or otherwise in business class.

'Like Little Mix?' asked Jojo.

'Sure,' Kim said.

'Will they be on the aeroplane? In buisner's class?'

'Maybe not on your flight, honey. But you never know.'

Kim turned from Jojo to Mike: *Are you sure?*

'Air miles,' Mike said, reasonably sure he didn't have enough for an in-flight coffee let alone a buisner's class upgrade.

But fuck it; if Bono could send his hat first class, Mike could bring his daughter in the section next door. The corners of Jojo's mouth had levelled out and the look of panic had begun to fade. 'We'll go and see St Paul's,' Mike said, gently. 'The aquarium, the Natural History Museum. We can go to Buckingham Palace, where the Queen lives. We'll go and see Gran and Granddad too.'

'Will the Queen be home?'

'I don't know, but if not we'll go and blow raspberries at her waxwork.'

'What's a waxwork?'

'A statue. Made of wax.'

'Why's it ma — '

'That's it, Jojobee.' Kim, having vanished for a moment, reappeared holding a coat. 'Say goodbye to Daddy and we can call him after supper tonight. Maybe he'll read you a story before bed?'

'Nothing I'd like more. Bye bye, Jojo. You have a great day at school, okay?'

'Okay, Daddoo. Love you.' She blew him a kiss, which he caught before sending his own through the laptop monitor.

'Love you, baby girl.' He blew another kiss, but Jojo was already leaning in to end the call.

Her face — so real and animated and proximal

just a moment ago — was replaced by the desktop image of her on his computer. She had changed so much in the eighteen months since the picture was taken, and more fundamentally than by the simple subtraction of five baby teeth. The baby fat was leaving her face, revealing the soft angles of a child in transition — the promise of her mother's cheekbones and a hint of the girl his daughter was becoming.

'Daddoo' she had called him, as she always had, but any day now she would outgrow the cutesy epithet just as she would outgrow milk at bedtime and bunches in her hair.

'Baby girl,' he said to himself as he looked out across the city towards the old BT Tower — a totem, if one were needed, that instead of progressing, his life had merely drifted.

She would be with him soon. And whilst Jojo might be excited at an itinerary of tourist attractions and gift shops, the thing Mike anticipated so much he could feel it was the presence and warmth of his daughter's small soft body. Her chops, before they vanished forever, against his cheek; her hand in his, the soft curves of her tummy and bottom as she nestled against him.

A trio of firm raps on the door snapped his attention back to the present. He knew the signature well — one knock, a pause, and then two more in quick succession — and was already holding up a hand to acknowledge Al as he turned his back on the river.

On the other side of the glass door, Al jerked his thumb down the corridor. Mike checked his watch and saw their meeting was due to start in a few minutes — the final pre-production check for a big-budget car shoot. The sort of thing that would have excited him eighteen, fifteen or even ten years ago, but now, it was just another two-hour exercise in going through the motions and laughing at the client's jokes. He gave Al a thumbs-up, and made a gesture toward his desk, suggesting he needed to gather a few things before following on. Al nodded curtly and tapped his wrist-watch before setting off down the corridor.

Mike turned for one final look out across the Thames, the tugboat continuing its slow progress past his window. He watched for several minutes until the boat disappeared from view, then took a deep breath and went to join the meeting.

7

Al, the most senior agency member in the room, was pouring coffees and teas. The junior account exec, to whom this task traditionally fell, would spend the meeting worrying he hadn't offered the clients coffee quickly enough, but he needn't have concerned himself. This was Al's shtick. In an industry still dominated by kids from private schools and affluent middle-class families, Al played up to the image of working-class lad done well, judiciously dropping 'g's and 'h's, and making damn sure everyone had a hot drink and a biscuit.

He'd just completed his circuit of the table when Mike walked into the room, five minutes late and too cool to acknowledge or apologise for the fact.

'Nice of you to join us,' Al said. 'I saved you a seat next to me. Have to keep an eye on these creative types,' he said to Karl, and the client nodded at the quip.

All three were on familiar terms, and Mike nodded to Karl as he took his seat.

This meeting was more than a formality, but most of the decisions had been made and this was an exercise in ratification more than anything else. A final chance to go through the details of the production and address any outstanding concerns. It would be led by the production company and the middle-level team who had written the script. Mike and Al were there primarily to keep the troops on song and the client happy.

Al poured Mike's coffee, added milk and a single lump of sugar.

Jody, the agency producer, cooed. 'Ah, they're like an old married couple.'

It occurred to Al to make some remark — *More than you know, Jody!* — but he resisted, patting Mike on the shoulder before taking his seat and handing over the meeting to the production company.

On several occasions recently, he hadn't been so restrained, making glib asides that he later regretted. Last week, he had held a door open for Mike, muttering, 'After you' as his old friend walked past. A juvenile remark made without premeditation, but — he had to admit — not without some small degree of satisfaction.

In his typical blase fashion, Mike had said it would 'get easier', but for Alistair, it had become anything but. He and Sally were in the worst kind of limbo; they had attended eight sessions now, five of those since Brighton, but if they were closing in on a conclusion, it didn't feel like a happy one.

At their first session, Joyce had said things would get worse before they got better. But instead of building something new, it felt to Al like they were picking something apart. They had discussed in polite measured tones the day they met and the points at which they had begun to drift; they remembered their affections but aired their grievances and deconstructed past arguments.

They opened old wounds.

Their situation had indeed worsened — but in spite of the counselling, Alistair felt, not because of it. Their situation, their love and trust and optimism, had deteriorated because of Brighton. Because of Faye, because of Mike.

He regretted his own part in the whole exchange, and wished he'd had the presence of mind to ask, incredulously, 'Are we fucking serious?' But he had been as caught up in the thrill and tease as everyone else. He knew it was self-serving, but Alistair considered his own motivations the most understandable, the most . . . honest of the four. Faye was gorgeous, a twenty-seven-year-old actress, sexual, provocative, seductive. What man wouldn't have his head turned? Yes, he had strayed, but there had been consent and mutuality. It made his breath catch to think of what Sally had done, but, to an extent, he could understand that too. Their marriage was on the rocks and she had a history of sorts with Mike. Perhaps taking him to bed was a way of taking herself back to her youth, to a less troubled, less complicated time. He didn't like it, but it had a ring of plausibility.

What Faye had been thinking that night, Al couldn't guess. Perhaps random acts of blithe promiscuity weren't so unusual in her world of on-stage nudity and rehearsed intimacy. And besides, Alistair and Sally were strangers to her; there was no history and as such no betrayal. But Mike? Alistair couldn't begin to unravel his old friend's motivations. If anyone had had a moral responsibility to cut that whole game short, surely it had been Mike.

Alistair had suggested discussing the issue with Joyce, but Sally had refused under threat of ending the whole exercise. And if that happened, how long would it be before everything else fell apart?

Mike had just made some joke that Alistair had missed, but everyone around the table was laughing. Genuine laughter, rather than the polite kind they reserved for him. Like so much else, this humour, this light touch, came easy to Mike. No self-deprecating office-boy shtick needed there. Alistair realised he was gritting his teeth and had to make a deliberate effort to relax his jaw.

Mike handed over to Jean, the copywriter who had penned the script. Jean cleared her throat and began reading from a sheet of A4 paper:

A woman — young and beautiful, of course — sits behind the wheel of a £90,000 German estate car. She pushes the ignition, programmes the sat-nav and checks her expensive earrings in the rear-view mirror.

The dash console lights up with an incoming message: 'Don't forget the package. Don't be late.'

The woman adjusts the rear-view mirror, showing us a brown paper-wrapped parcel on the back seat. She hits play on the stereo and pulls away to the strains of Lalo Schifrin (although the rights to the track are proving prohibitively expensive, so alternatives will need to be discussed).

As she exits the car park, however, a second

car — this one a £110,000 coupé — pulls away from the kerb, tailing the mysterious brunette through the night-time streets of (probably) Prague. The driver of the second car — a handsome male, naturally — is careful to follow at a discreet distance, but his quarry is no amateur. She has seen him and she smiles. What follows is a vehicular game of cat and mouse, following many of the familiar conventions involving traffic lights, stray footballs and narrow alleys — although nobody exceeds the speed limit and at no point are any pedestrians' lives imperilled.

But all is not as it seems (giving the viewer, who had suspected as much, a nice warm feeling for being so dam smart). The final destination is revealed to be a primary school, the two cars arriving together and taking adjacent spaces. The drivers smile at each other.

A quick interior shot shows a cast of six-year-old kids taking their places on a small stage. One of the children — an adorable, gap-toothed girl — is visibly more nervous than the others.

Back in the car park, husband and wife kiss. 'What kept you?' asks the woman.

'Traffic was a nightmare,' he tells her, and they kiss again.

They set off, arm in arm, before she remembers the package on the back seat. Which is revealed to contain a pair of fairy wings for — yes — their adorable daughter, the star of this particular show.

The client had loved the script since first

hearing it, but there had been much debate about why exactly this husband and wife would travel in separate cars from the same departure point to the same destination. That was the point, Mike had argued — they did it because they wanted to, not because they needed to. It was a testament to the joy of driving these gleaming pieces of precision German engineering. This couple were beautiful, spontaneous, successful, happy — who wouldn't want to be like them?

Bullshit really, but whilst the premise may have been flimsy, Alistair understood that the principle was sound. It wasn't the sat-nav, the parking assist or the badge on the bonnet they were flogging, it was the family. *Buy this and be like them*, the commercial said. The car was simply the packaging.

Yeah, who wouldn't want to be like them?

Alistair would; he would *love* to be like them. He even had the car, bought off the production line with a thirty per cent corporate discount. He had the wife, too (for now, at least), but the child had never happened. Instead of the school plays and angel wings and missing teeth, his and Sally's story had been one of trial, failure and false hope. Years of disappointment and bitterness that had damaged their marriage and eroded the margins of their happiness.

A child, of course, was no guarantee of happiness — Alistair need only turn his head to the left to see the evidence; it was drawn across Mike's face. Children and family brought their own pressures, demands and complications, he knew that, but he would have embraced them and faced them and made them work. He wouldn't have thrown it away the way Mike had. Mike's problem — one of them — was that he didn't appreciate what he had. Even now, when he was finally rebuilding the shambles of his life, he had treated Faye like something cheap and disposable. He didn't deserve what he had.

Alistair closed his eyes — as if considering the current discussion about what colour cars to use in the shoot — and in his mind's eye he saw Faye naked. Not the clear unobstructed vision from the play, but the way she had looked as he moved on top of her: the shallow crater of a chickenpox scar at her temple, her stark clavicles, her small breasts flattened under his hand. Her dark hair sweat-stuck against her face. He saw her on top of him and astride his hips — her pliant body pulled tight against its internal structures, her throat and ribs, the ligaments at her inner thighs.

Al opened his eyes and took in the room, nodding as if in agreement or thought.

He and Sally had not made love since Brighton, but Alistair had returned to that loft bedroom many times in his mind, refining the memory and its sensory details, layering sounds over the image, the staccato gasp of her breath, the taste of alcohol and ice-cream — imagined or otherwise — on her lips and tongue, the texture of fine hairs at the nape of her neck.

Masturbation, however, was not what it used to be. The furtive but guiltless pleasure of his teens and twenties now came with associations of failure and disappointment. He managed, of course — while Sally was at work, the gym or sleeping. He had even jerked off in the toilets at work a couple of times — but these brief interludes of self-pleasure recalled the scheduled ejaculations of three failed cycles of IVF. He remembered the creased 'literature' in the clinic lavatories, the embarrassment he felt on handing over the vials of warm semen to the nurse, the anticipation, the wait, the frustration. But he thought of Faye, and he managed.

In the room, everyone turned their folders to the page headed 'casting'. Mother, father and simply adorable daughter.

'Made for each other,' said Karl. 'They're perfect.'

Jody, the agency producer, tapped something into her laptop. 'I'll get contracts sent out today.'

'Er ... ' Everyone turned to the young executive, clearly doubting the wisdom of this sudden interjection.

Alistair turned his smile on the lad. 'Yes?'

'The mum,' he said, tapping the actor's image on the sheet.

Bruce, the director, took the bait first. 'What about her?'

'Did anyone see *Grand Designs* last night?'

All eyes narrowed at the boy, as if whatever followed was now his responsibility.

'Was she on it?' Alistair asked.

The lad shook his head. 'A commercial. During the break.'

At least five people said 'What?'

'What was it for?' Mike asked.

'Diarrhoea. I mean not *for* diarrhoea, for a

drink thing to stop it.'

Karl spoke next. 'Was she just . . . an extra, or was she . . . you know?'

The exec shook his head. 'She was pretty much on the toilet for the whole commercial.'

Bruce banged his fist on the table. 'Fuck. Fucking . . . fucking actors. Sorry Karl.'

Karl held up a palm — *It's fine.* 'Did we ask?'

Jody nodded. 'At casting and call-backs. She didn't declare anything.'

'Embarrassed, probably.'

'So,' said Mike, all smiles and no worries. 'We need a new mum.'

Easy come, easy go? Alistair thought, but he bit his tongue. He turned to Jody. 'How long do we have?'

'Four weeks. But it's jammed — location recce, rehearsals, wardrobe, foreign unit, visas if we need them.'

'Where are we shooting?'

Bruce said, 'Prague would be ideal, but we're looking at Ontario, South Africa, Edinburgh.'

'Edinburgh? Really?'

'Don't worry; it wouldn't look like Edinburgh. There are some nice brownstones, though. Good cobbles.'

'Realistically,' Jody said, 'we need to sort the casting this week.'

'It's Wednesday.'

Karl shook his head. 'Diarrhoea.'

'Tell me about it.' Alistair said.

He wanted to blame Mike, but knew he couldn't — the simple truth was, these things happened. They said you should never work with

89

children or animals, but in Alistair's experience the maxim could be broadened to include the entire thespian community.

Normal rules didn't apply where actors were concerned.

Take Faye, for example. Alistair had tried on several occasions to backtrack through his memories of that night, to arrive at the nucleus of the thing. The closest he could come was that stupid parlour game she had initiated — *Never have I ever.*

Never have I ever regretted sleeping with someone.

Never have I ever kissed a member of the same sex.

Never have I ever been unfaithful.

The way she dressed and behaved, the way she had kissed Sally, the way she had looked at him.

'Never have I ever had a foursome,' someone had ventured — it wasn't him, and it wouldn't have been Sally or Mike. Would it? Surely it could only have been the actress, playing a part she'd written for herself. And then . . . 'Never have I ever swapped.' Who had said that? Could it have been him? He wasn't sure. But by that point a force of inevitability had gathered around them.

Cut to the following morning in the kitchen where it had all begun the night before. Faye hadn't been there, just Alistair, Mike and Sally. Him the cuckold, drinking tea with his wife and the man who'd just fucked her. If Faye had shown her face there might have been some balance — some relief from the suffocating humiliation and resentment. But no, Faye — so bold the night before — had hidden away upstairs while the rest of them sipped their tea in the small kitchen, not knowing where to look or what to say.

In the meeting room now, Mike, Jody and Bruce were going through the logistics of a second casting at short notice. They had selected actors not only on the basis of their talent and demographic appeal, but on their authenticity as a family unit — the girl's straight chestnut hair matching her mother's, for example. You could dye hair, of course, but it was better to find a more natural match.

He pictured again Faye's brown hair, wet with sweat and stuck to her shoulders and face and breasts. The same chestnut brown as the actress they were now going to jettison on account of her publicly liquefied bowels.

'Actually,' said Al, enjoying his authority as the chatter died down, 'I think I know the perfect person.'

He turned to Mike and smiled at the look of dawning comprehension. Mike's eyes narrowed, he took a short inhalation and pursed his lips as if he were about to speak, forming the shape for a 'W', perhaps — Who? — but Mike already knew who.

Karl asked the question for him.

'A mutual friend of mine and Mike's,' Alistair said. 'Well, she's a little more than that, hey Mike?'

Mike forced a smile. 'Right.'

'Faye is Mike's girlfriend.'

Mike shook his head. 'You know, I don't think — '

Al dismissed Mike's attempted objection with a wave of his hand. 'We're like that' — he crossed his middle finger over his index, showing it first to Karl, then to Mike — 'aren't we, Mike?'

For the second time in under a minute, Mike's words caught on his lips, and whatever he wanted to say now, it began with a hard 'F'.

Alistair smiled. '*And* . . . she's a *very* talented actress. Trust me, I've seen her perform. Haven't I, Mike?'

* * *

Alistair turned to the client. 'Gorgeous and talented, Karl. Certainly wasted on this sad old reprobate, right, Mike?'

Mike laughed along with everyone else. He didn't want to encourage Al any further, but neither did he want to antagonise him. Al was in a pugnacious mood and he didn't want to exacerbate the situation. 'I'm a lucky guy,' Mike said.

'Hang on.' Al picked up his phone from the table. 'I might have a picture.' Glancing at Mike. 'You know, from Brighton.'

'Mate,' Mike reached for Al's phone, but Al twisted away from him. 'I'll get her agent to send over her head shots.'

'So professional,' Al teased. He continued scrolling through the thumbnail pictures on his phone. 'I'm afraid these are all rather . . . Ah! Here's a good one — backstage after the play.'

92

He held the phone towards Karl, who regarded the picture over the top of his spectacles. He turned the corners of his mouth down in deliberation, nodding to himself. 'She looks good,' he said, turning to Mike. 'Good for the part.'

Bruce walked around the table to look over Karl's shoulder.

'We should get her along to a casting,' he said. 'If you don't mind, Mike?'

As if Mike owned or controlled her.

But he did mind. Their relationship was drifting, coasting, tilting — and until it became clear where they might end up and in which direction they were heading, he didn't need this additional complication. A month and a half had passed since Brighton, and whilst they had yet to put that night fully behind them, it was beginning — by degrees — to recede into the background.

During the week, they ate supper together in front of the TV, talking about work, the weather, whatever programme they happened to be watching. Some weekends they would go to a restaurant or bar, finding themselves somehow more relaxed in the company of strangers and with a waiter to pour their wine. They made love too, although less frequently than they ate out. There was an air of self-consciousness about their intimacy now; it was not as dense as it had been in the first weeks after they'd given each other away, but it was still tangible against their naked skin.

And now this — working together on set while

they were still unsure if they worked together at home. He doubted Faye would go for it, but on the other hand, it would be a good cheque for a few days' work. Upwards of ten grand, maybe as much as fifteen. Enough, it occurred to him, to clear some debts and — if she were inclined — to move out and rent a place of her own.

'Sure,' Mike said to Bruce. 'Why not?'

Al failed to disguise his surprise, and maybe his disappointment at Mike's easy acquiescence. He slapped Mike on the back. 'Why not, indeed.'

Jody said, 'Would you like me to call her, Mike? To arrange a time for the casting?'

'Why don't I talk to her first, check she's okay with it then give her your number?'

'Sure. I'll give you my mobile?'

Mike opened his notebook and got three letters into Jody's name before his pen ran out. 'Sorry about this,' he said, flashing Jody the smile that all the girls seemed to like. 'It's never happened to me before.'

Alistair winced as everyone laughed. 'Yeah right! Here' — he held out a sleek brushed-steel retractable — 'use mine.'

Al held eye contact with Mike as his old friend reached for the pen, tightening his grip around the barrel so that it took Mike two attempts to tug the pen from his fingers.

Mike nodded as he took the pen. 'Thanks.'

'Hey man, what's mine is yours, right?'

8

Mike rubbed his hands together, warming the lotion before applying it to Faye's back, first working it into her neck and then circling his hands across the thin muscles of her shoulders. 'Is this going to give me brown hands?'

Faye stood naked and hunched, hands crossed over her breasts, fingers curled into her armpits. She looked up and into the bathroom mirror, Mike standing behind her, smiling as he presented his stained palms. 'Not if you get a move on,' she said.

Mike held out his hand. 'Little more?'

Faye reached for the dispenser and delivered a golf ball of fake tan into his palm. 'Keep it moving. Otherwise it'll go all streaky.'

'Well, you are a streaker.'

'Very funny. Come on.' She wiggled her bottom. 'Get a move on.'

'Don't be distracting me,' he said, grinning at her reflection.

Mike halved the dollop of lotion between his hands, then applied it to Faye's shoulder blades, amusing himself by daubing two angel wings across her back, using his fingertips to effect the illusion of feathered tips at the base.

'Hit me,' he said, reaching around for more lotion and then using it to vanish the daub into an even coating of light brown. 'Tomorrow's just a rehearsal, right?'

'Yuh-huh.'

'You're not doing it naked?'

Faye laughed. 'Not this time.'

'But later?'

Faye nodded. 'There's a new guy,' she said, glancing at Mike's reflection to gauge his reaction. 'A new teacher. Did I say that already?'

'Don't think so.'

Faye made a noise of mild surprise: *Must have slipped my mind.*

She had been waiting for a moment to tell Mike, but had backed away from it more than once. When Faye had first landed the part of Rose the teenage temptress, she and Mike had been dating for maybe three months, and the idea of her appearing naked on stage had been an exciting one. Something bold and provocative to match the mood of their new relationship. But now, the revelation that she would be derobing in front of another man felt like an admission of some sort. Or maybe it was an echo. The play, after all, was intimately and forever associated with the nightmare that was Brighton.

'So,' Mike said, 'what did you do with the old one?'

'He's got a part in some dragon and magic nonsense. Five weeks in New Zealand.'

'Sure it wasn't just an elaborate excuse to get away from you?'

The joke, such as it was, fell flat — the premise, perhaps, a little too close to home.

Mike smiled, held out his hand for more foam. 'Nervous?'

Faye nodded. 'A little.'

'You'll be fine,' he said. 'You'll be brilliant.'

'I'd better be.'

The audience would be larger this time, the expectations too. A play like this in a theatre like that could lead to something, and God knows she needed something. Faye had attended maybe a dozen auditions in the last month and a half, split evenly between commercial parts and what she thought of as 'proper acting' — theatre, TV, film. She'd had a handful of call-backs, including one for the part of Attractive Woman #2, but so far no one had offered her a part. Thank God for the naked schoolgirl; the money wasn't much, but she would be able to think of herself as a legitimate actor for a few weeks. Although how many more was anything but certain.

Her back was aching now, and the bathroom was cold. 'Finished?'

'Almost.' Mike smoothed the fake tan onto the sides of Faye's waist and the small of her back. 'Bend over a little.'

He slid his hands down her buttocks, across her hips and onto the front of her thighs, his fingers dragging against the tackiness of the drying lotion. He leaned in, kissing the back of Faye's head and continuing the slow drift of his hands, up her thighs and onto the soft curve of her belly.

Faye's stomach tensed reflexively, and she took a half-step forward, turning at the same time so that she was facing Mike. 'You'll smudge me.'

'You're goddamn right, I will.' A hint of an American accent to make the line play.

Faye laughed, but squeezed past him, going

through to the bedroom. 'You goddamn won't. That stuff costs thirty quid a bottle. And besides' — she took her dressing gown from a hook on the back of the door — 'my period started.'

'Right. I see.' Mike stepped back into the hallway, pointing his thumb over his shoulder towards the kitchen. 'I'll go and knock something up.'

'So to speak?'

Mike laughed. 'God, can you imagine?'

'No.' Faye shook her head. 'No I can't.'

★ ★ ★

He was standing at the hob when Faye walked into the kitchen. Frying a pan of onions and what smelled like too much garlic. She stood quietly for a moment, watching him casually fuss about the stove; adjusting the flame, agitating the pan, a pinch of sea salt, a dash more oil, a grind of black pepper — as if this intricate and unimportant task was as complex as life could get. As if a month and a half ago, he hadn't screwed one old friend while Faye fucked the other.

Mike turned to her. 'All dry?'

'Excuse me?'

'The tan?'

'Right, yes. As a bone.'

'There's wine open.'

Faye waved the offer away. 'I was thinking of taking a few weeks off. Give my' — she patted her side — 'give my liver a rest.'

Mike sliced open a pack of chicken strips and

dropped them into the pan. 'And what about your stomach?'

'Big lunch.'

'Small portion then? Lunch was a long time ago.'

'Don't daddy me.'

Mike held up his hands, one still holding a sharp kitchen knife. 'Sorry, I just . . . '

She shook her head. 'No, I'm sorry. I . . . ' She nodded to the knife. 'You're not going to stab me, are you?'

Mike pretended to consider this. 'God, think of the mess.'

Faye sat at a stool next to the breakfast bar and picked a slice of chorizo from the chopping board. 'There, I'm eating.'

Mike took a slice for himself. 'Jojo lost a tooth.'

'You spoke to her?'

His shoulders dropped. 'Not for long. I'm going to try her again later.'

'How is she?'

'Good, great. Too many miles away.'

The sad smile made Mike look vulnerable, and if he'd been standing on this side of the counter, Faye would have hugged him. She considered going up to him and doing it anyway, but even as she formed the thought the moment drifted.

She pushed her hair behind her ears. 'I saw the tooth fairy once.'

'Saw it?'

Faye nodded. 'Her.'

Mike regarded her for a moment, waiting for a

99

punchline that didn't come. 'Okay.'

'I know it didn't happen, can't have happened, but . . . I swear to God I saw her. She was so real, I could draw her, even now: red and gold dress, elfin eyes, hair like Audrey Hepburn in *Roman Holiday*.'

'Dreaming?'

'Either that or fairies really do exist.'

'What happened?'

'Nothing. I was meant to be asleep, so I just lay very still, watching her through half-closed eyes. You know the way kids think you can't tell when they're peeping through their eyelashes. Probably it was the pattern on my pillowcase or something, my brain turning it into something else. Anyway, I watched her through my eyelashes, shimmering, hovering above my pillow, and then' — Faye snapped her fingers — 'she was gone. First thing was, I panicked. Thought I'd scared her off before she had a chance to take my tooth. So, I slid my hand under the pillow, feeling about for the little piece of paper that Mum had folded my tooth into. What I found instead was a fifty-pence piece, still warm like it'd just been put there. Magic.'

'You should tell Jojo,' Mike said. 'I'll call her after supper.'

Faye smiled. 'Yeah, that'd be nice.'

Mike turned back to the stove, added the chorizo and a good shake of chilli powder to the pan. 'So, I have some other news.'

Faye waited a beat. 'Go on?'

'We've got this car commercial.'

'The chase thing?'

'The chase thing. Well, it turns out that our 'mum' is in a commercial for some diarrhoea remedy.'

'That's unfortunate.'

'It's a bloody disaster. We've got to recast.'

'God, I hate castings.'

Mike cleared his throat, moved the pan off the heat and turned to face Faye. 'Actually . . . '

'What? No.'

'Why not?'

'Because you're my . . . I'm . . . just because, that's why.'

'You'd have to audition, but . . . the client likes you. I think you've g — '

'The *client* likes me?'

Mike smiled apologetically. 'Al — he had a picture of you, backstage in . . . you know . . . '

Faye adjusted her dressing gown, pulling it closer around her shoulders. 'He's working on it?'

'It's a big account.'

'Right. How are you guys?'

Mike blew out a long stream of air. 'Awkward. Obviously. But . . . it'll pass.'

'Have you talked to Sally?'

Mike shook his head; then, before the denial took hold, added, 'We've sent a few texts. *How are you?* That kind of thing. Nothing . . . nothing else.'

Faye held his eye. 'Why did you never tell me you'd kissed her?'

Mike hesitated. 'What do you mean?'

'When we were . . . you know, Alistair said you and Sally kissed. At uni.'

'I suppose it never occurred to me. It was twenty years ago.'

'God, you really are old, aren't you?'

Mike picked up the knife and levelled it at Faye: 'It's not too late to get stabbed.'

She held up her hands in surrender. 'I wonder what she'd make of it. Me working with you and Alistair.'

Mike shrugged. 'She's a grown-up.'

Faye recoiled on her stool. 'And I'm not?'

'That's not what I meant.' Faye stared hard at him. 'Faye, that's not what I meant. I don't know what she thinks about it. If Al's told her, she probably finds it as weird as we do.'

Faye made a small nod, eased her posture forward again.

'But that's between them. Maybe this' — he gestured at thin air — 'the commercial. Maybe it's the thing to move us all past it. Move on.'

'How do you figure that's going to happen?'

'Well, if we shoot this film, then Brighton won't be the only thing we all did together.'

Faye shrugged — *Maybe*. 'When is it?'

'Month. Good money, too. Might play in Europe. Asia. Could be a *very* nice payday. You could quit the receptionist gig. Concentrate on auditions. Write that play you keep threatening to write.'

'I'm waiting for inspiration.'

'All the more reason, then.'

'Besides,' Faye said, 'the play'll be in full swing by then.'

'Not every night of the week, it won't. We'll work around your schedule.'

'Got an answer for everything, haven't you?' Knowing she wanted to take this opportunity, but feeling she should go through the motions of prevaricating for a little longer.

'Look, I know it's awkward. But — '

Faye huffed out a short laugh.

'Okay — *excruciating*. But . . . like I said, it's a great payday. We might even get a trip to Prague on expenses.'

She counted silently to five before answering. 'I've never been to Prague.'

'Is that a yes?'

'It's not a no.'

The thought suggested itself: *You only regret the things you don't do*. But they'd already proved that to be an absurd and self-evident lie.

9

Sally recalled her anatomy classes. The hand contains twenty-seven bones. Carpus, metacarpus and phalanges. Tendons, ligaments, muscles and connective tissue. Thousands upon thousands of touch receptors. Force and control. The median nerve moving the thumb in opposition; the muscles of the forearm contracting, closing Alistair's fingers around her hand.

Holding hands; an exercise in intimacy prescribed by Joyce — a healer with night-class qualifications, setting exercises inspired by whim and intuition. Sally had spent five years at university, two more on the wards as a junior doctor, then three years' vocational training as a GP. Ten years of work, study and experience; anatomy, biochemistry, haematology, pharmacology, radiology; she diagnosed, counselled, referred; prescribed molecules to suppress, stimulate, eradicate. And yet, perhaps her success rate was no more impressive than Joyce's, with her sixty-minute sessions of empathy and silly assignments:

Sit quietly, close your eyes and hold hands for fifteen minutes.

Sally had resisted the impulse to ask: *Shouldn't we hold hands* before *we close our eyes?* But she knew no one would find it funny, probably because it wasn't. Probably because it was symptomatic of something else. The glib humour obscuring the deeper emotions — the way a patient might josh in the face of a bad diagnosis, hiding their fear behind a display of bravery, optimism or indifference. Hiding it from themselves as much as from the doctor — no longer a healer, but the bearer of very bad news.

Like Mr Johara, grinning like a winner as he backed out of her office — what? Two months ago? — clutching his paperwork and a plastic sample cup. She hadn't seen him since, but she had seen his results; Mr Johara was the oncologist's problem now.

Sally wondered if Joyce had gleaned what had become clear to Sally — that this relationship was terminal. And what about Al, did he know it was over?

How long? The second question every patient asks — right after 'Are you sure?' and before 'Will it hurt?'

The honest answers — 'Yes', 'Not Long', 'Yes' — almost as predictable as the questions.

Not long.

The days were getting shorter and colder now, helping separate the events of that warm night in Brighton from the early dusks and dark evenings of here and now. And with distance had come an almost dispassionate clarity. In the immediate days and weeks after their casual and brutal infidelity, they'd existed in a state of something like shock — the way they might after surviving a highspeed car crash. Processing and adjusting and reconciling themselves to the reality — yes, it really happened — of what they had done. But healing is never perfect; it always leaves a mark

— something you hide, something that aches in bad weather. And no amount of silent hand-holding would change that.

Mike had held her hand in Brighton.

In the still, charged minutes before they made love, he had held both of her hands in his. They didn't talk in that frame of time, sensing perhaps that the thing around them, the moment, was fragile. But the way Mike gently held her hands, the way he looked into her eyes, she understood him as clearly as if he'd said the words: *Are you sure?*

And Sally had nodded, returning the pressure of his hands against hers: *I'm sure.*

Beside her now, Alistair cleared his throat.

How long had they been sitting here? Two minutes, five, eight? Sally resisted the urge to open her eyes, not because she felt any obligation to the exercise, but because she didn't want to risk meeting her husband's glance. Treat it like a meditation, Joyce had said. Meditate on intimacy, on the reasons why you first loved each other, on the reasons you still do.

Alistair's hand felt alien inside hers. Too big, too hot, too much subtle animation. He pressed his thumb against her skin, Sally's radial nerve registering the gentle insistent pressure on the back of her hand.

She didn't want to meet her husband's eyes, because she was sure this exercise had become, to him, a form of extended foreplay. When the timer pinged, he would try and take this to the bedroom.

In the diluted silence, she concentrated on the

sound of the kitchen clock in the next room, focusing on the second hand and extending each muted tick across the long beat of time before the next. Bringing the sound forward where it might cover the slow deliberate rhythm of her husband's breath.

His thumb found Sally's wedding band and the engagement ring nestled up against it, rotating the precious metal a few degrees one way and then the other, caressing the backs of her fingers. Sally tightened her grip on Alistair's hand; a fast firm squeeze before relaxing the pressure — a request for stillness.

The memory of Alistair proposing came into her mind; flowers, champagne, this same ring presented from one knee. The memory was displaced by a sequence of others: Mike marrying Kim, watching them dance their first dance and feeling a hard knot of confused sadness in her stomach — the sensation so readily recalled it was repeated now as she sat beside her husband. Alistair had been with her at the wedding, she was wearing his ring as she vomited into the hotel toilet from drinking too much wine. Less than nine months later she met Mike's day-old daughter for the first time, her skin too big for her small bones, her wide eyes fanned with her father's long black lashes. She recalled the night Mike told her he was divorcing Kim, and Sally wondered — *or did she know?* — if that was when the seeds of her own dissatisfaction had begun to germinate. She remembered Kim taking Jojo to the States, remembered holding Mike as he cried against her chest. His antidepressants were still in Sally's bedside drawer, where they'd been for the last year since Mike had asked her to take them for 'safe-keeping'.

Maybe she should have been grateful that she and Al weren't able to have children. But she wasn't. Despite it all, she wished with her heart and useless womb that they had been able to bring a child into the world, into their lives. Sally wondered if this made her selfish, but feeling this way wasn't a choice, just another aspect of her biology over which she had no control.

Sally focused again on the ticking of the kitchen clock, willing the second hand forward. This exercise in intimacy would soon be over.

A quiet alarm would chime at the end of fifteen minutes; they would open their eyes, smile at each other and — as per Joyce's instructions — talk about their thoughts and feelings. But Sally didn't want to talk about her feelings. Not to Al. She would listen and she would tell him some muted version of what he wanted to hear. She would tell him, too, that she had a headache, that she needed fresh air. As she buttoned her coat, Al would volunteer to walk with her, but Sally — smiling, thanking him, kissing him lightly on the lips — would decline the offer. She would ask him to put the kettle on while she walked to the shops for milk or paracetamol or anything at all they happened to be out of.

And when she was out of sight of the house, she would write a short text to Mike. She would ask if they could meet, she would tell him they needed to talk.

Sally's phone trilled its gentle alarm, and Alistair squeezed her hand. She sat for a moment longer with her eyes closed, bracing herself for the thing that came next.

'Time,' Alistair said gently.

'Yes.' Sally opened her eyes and smiled at her husband. 'Time.'

10

She had attended more castings than she could recall, but this was the first time anyone had offered her a cup of coffee. Neither was this a chipped mug of cheap instant; this was a flat white from an artisan coffee house three streets away, where — according to the runner — they roasted their own beans every morning. Benefits of being the creative director's girlfriend, she supposed. From hipster barista to enthusiastic runner, a great deal of craft and legwork had gone into bringing her this short cup of milky coffee, but now that she held it in her hand, Faye felt too tight with butterflies to drink it.

Maybe it was worse because there was no one else waiting to audition. Normally the area outside the casting suite was close with waiting bodies, an atmosphere of mute camaraderie with each wannabe absorbing their share of the nervous energy. But today it was just Faye, and the weight of expectation was all hers.

Mike had thought it best if he didn't attend — as a professional courtesy to the client and the director, he'd said. But Faye understood what that meant: if they didn't like her, it would be easier all round if they didn't have to tell him to his face. And besides, Faye and Mike had agreed it might be a little weird; Faye 'auditioning' for the man she lived with, turning their relationship — such as it currently was — into a professional arrangement, even if only for fifteen minutes.

Faye admired him for it, but sitting outside the casting suite now, she wished he were here to distract her with small talk. And yes, to sway the jury should persuasion be needed.

A young woman came out of the casting suite, closing the door behind her.

'You must be Faye?'

'That's me.'

'Thanks so much for coming, we've been hearing *all* about you.'

I sincerely hope not. Faye forced a smile.

'Oops, manners.' The woman extended her hand. 'Jody,' she said. 'Producer.'

'Pleased to meet you.' Faye went to stand at exactly the same time Jody went to sit; both hesitated, reversed the manoeuvre and found themselves back where they'd started.

'Sorry to keep you,' Jody said. 'Client's on a . . . ' She held an invisible phone to her ear. 'He'll only be a few minutes.'

'No problem.' Faye held up her coffee cup. 'I've been looked after.'

'They hand-roast the beans, you know.'

Faye made an expression of profound appreciation. 'Is that right?'

'So I'm told.'

'Amazing.'

The women smiled, looked away, found nothing diverting and looked back. They smiled again.

'So . . . ' said Jody. 'You're . . . '

Here it comes . . .

' . . . you and Mike?'

Faye tightened her smile, crinkled her eyes. 'Yep. Me and Mike.'

'Lovely guy. *Lovely* guy.'

'Yes,' said Faye. 'Thank you.'

They nodded slowly at the truth of this.

Jody said, 'It's good to see him, you know, *happy*.'

'Yes. He's . . . '

'A lovely guy.'

'Exactly. Lovely.'

Faye felt her smile slipping and took a sip of lukewarm artisan coffee to hide the fact.

Jody inspected a non-existent watch, nodded across her shoulder to the casting suite. 'I'll just . . . see if they're ready?'

'Great. Sure.'

Jody opened the casting suite door, leaned into the room and muttered something to the people on the other side.

There was a whiff of nepotism about today's proceedings, and Faye had worried she might be received with resentment or blank-faced tolerance, but Jody — despite the asphyxiating awkwardness — had seemed sincere enough. Hopefully the rest of the crew would be as accommodating.

Jody turned back to Faye, gave her a thumbs-up: 'Shall we?'

★   ★   ★

The first person she saw was Alistair, smiling at her, arms crossed, waiting. Jody was introducing the other people in the room — director, client,

112

writer, production assistant, casting agent — but Faye didn't hear their names. It was all she could do to meet their eyes. To not turn and walk out of the room.

'And,' said Jody, her voice rotating in his direction, 'I believe you already know Al.'

He opened his arms wide. 'Faye,' drawing out the syllable to twice its length on a rising note of familiarity and affection. 'It's been *too* long.'

'Alistair.'

Al waggled his fingertips, inviting Faye into an embrace. They kissed on both cheeks and Faye thought she caught a trace of alcohol on Al's breath as he hugged her tightly for one, two, three, four full seconds.

'Seriously,' he said, releasing her from the hug but holding her at arm's length by the shoulders, 'it's been *way* too long. I haven't seen you since . . . what? Brighton?'

We've heard all about you.

She doubted he would have revealed the details of their mutual debauchery, but he had probably laughed about seeing Mike's girlfriend naked on stage. It would explain why Jody had been so awkward. *We've heard all about you.*

Faye found her smile. 'It feels like a long time ago.'

Al released his grip on her shoulders and transferred his hands to his pockets. 'Hope you don't mind me gate-crashing. But when I heard Mike had *abandoned* you to this lot' — a wink towards the room — 'well, I thought you might appreciate a familiar, you know . . . face.'

'Thank you, Alistair, that's very sweet.'

113

Alistair winked. 'Well, you know me.'

Faye forced a small laugh, concentrated on maintaining a polite smile. 'It's lovely to see you again. And thank you, thanks for' — gesturing about the room — 'thanks for this.'

Alistair pulled in his chin. 'Well, let's not get ahead of ourselves. This is only an audition. Mike did explain that?'

'Right, of course. I — '

Alistair smacked his hands together in an abrupt and exaggerated clap that rang off the walls in the small room. 'Okay then. Let's get this show on the road, shall we?'

Faye turned her attention to the director. He flashed her a small smile, an incomplete twitch of the lips that didn't conceal his contempt for Alistair's theatrics. She met his smile with one of her own. If he read it the way she intended, he would gather that Faye felt the same way. It was a smile that said: *I know*.

11

Mid-afternoon in the middle of the week; kids in school, mums preparing supper, old folks taking an afternoon nap and workers still watching the office clock. It was cold, too, and they had the small park to themselves. Even the trees had lost their leaves.

Sally asked him: 'Did you tell Faye you were meeting me?'

Mike shook his head. 'Did you tell Al?'

'No. Did you?'

Mike laughed. 'Must have slipped my mind.'

'So, I guess this is . . . what do you call it — a tryst?'

They had arranged to meet in a coffee shop just a few yards from Sally's surgery. In the few minutes it took them to queue and order their drinks, she had exchanged hellos with two patients, one of whom — a lady of around seventy — attempted to solicit an on-the-spot consultation while Doctor Stevens waited for her latte.

'Incurable and contagious,' Sally had whispered to Mike as the lady shuffled off.

'What is it?'

'Age. Life. Loneliness. You name it.'

'What do you do for that?'

Sally shrugged. 'Give her some innocuous ointment and send her on her way.'

''Innocuous ointment'? Sounds like good

stuff; can I have some?'

'Are you lonely?'

'Not always,' he said.

They had taken their coffees to go, walking away from the high street and up through a wide avenue of large residential houses. When they drew level with a primary school, Sally steered them across the road to a neat playing field, perhaps twice the size of a rugby pitch and sloping like a lifted rug from the northeast corner to the southwest. They chose a bench furthest away from the gate, sitting close against each other, making the unnecessary excuse that they were sharing warmth.

Tryst. A secret and — if Mike's vocabulary served him correctly — romantic rendezvous.

He nodded, although Sally, staring straight ahead, wouldn't register the gesture. 'Yes,' he said. 'A tryst.'

'Story of our lives,' Sally said — no answer required and none expected. 'How's Faye?'

'Good. Busy. Rehearsing and auditioning.'

'Rehearsing what?'

He hesitated a moment before saying, 'The play. That we saw . . . in, you know . . . Brighton.'

Sally turned to him now. 'With the life drawing?'

The associations tracing a line behind them, leading to Brighton two months ago and twenty years further back to a pair of head-turned teenagers in a university basement.

'It's moved to London,' Mike said. 'Brixton.'

Sally turned her focus back to the open field,

worn thin in patches that wouldn't recover until next spring. 'I liked her.'

'Yeah . . . ' The implications of tense were clear in Mike's mind. 'Me too.'

'You said she's auditioning?'

'Al didn't tell you?'

'No. Tell me what?'

'We're shooting a car commercial, and there was a problem with the actress.'

'So you suggested Faye?'

Mike shook his head. 'Not me.'

From the corner of his eye, Mike watched Sally watching her coffee — turning the cup around in her hand, revealing and then vanishing her name, written on the side in slanting script. She took a sip, swallowed and exhaled a cloud of white vapour.

Mike imagined reaching out and passing his hand through her exhaled breath. 'On cold-weather shoots,' he said, watching his words form their own cumulus, 'we get the actors to suck ice-cubes.'

'Sounds sadistic.'

'That too. But mainly it's to stop their breath fogging.'

'We've been in counselling. Did you know?'

'No. Because of . . . you know?'

'Since before that. We've been to, I'm not sure, half a dozen sessions now.'

'I'm sorry, I didn't know. Is it . . . is it helping?'

Sally let out a hollow laugh. 'Depends how you mean, I suppose. Do you regret breaking up with Kim?'

Mike shifted on the bench, sitting at an angle so he was facing Sally directly. Her face was different now, leaner and more angular than when he'd first known her. In profile, her nose, cheekbones and jaw held parallel angles, making her look noble and proud and fragile. He smiled at her, at her settling beauty, at her sadness, at everything that had passed between them.

'Sometimes,' he said. 'They say you shouldn't stay together for the kids. But I don't know if that's right. I don't even know if it was possible. But . . . sometimes.'

'For Jojo?'

Mike nodded, watched a single tear roll along the precise geometry of Sally's cheek. 'I so wanted children. More than anything, more than being with Al, more than being without him. We tried so hard. We tried everything.'

'I'm sorry.'

Sally shook her head. More tears came now, a quiet stream catching the slanting light. 'But it didn't happen for us. For me.'

'Come here.' Sally let herself list sideways, resting her head against Mike's chest. Mike placed one arm around her shoulder, using the thumb of the other hand to wipe at her tears. 'Hey, it's okay.'

Sally looked out over the barren playing field, the grass scuffed to mud by other people's children, by families kicking balls and playing chase. 'We talked about it in counselling. We told our counsellor that before all the miscarriages and the IVF and the false hope, that before all of that we were good. Everything was fine. And it was trying to have children that changed us . . . that let all the disappointment and resentment in. And the worst thing is, I think Al believes it.'

12

For fifty of the commercial's sixty seconds, the actors would be positioned behind the steering wheels of their respective German automobiles — although much of that screen time would be taken up with exterior shots, or close-ups of the cars' interiors. The actors wouldn't even need driving licences, as all on-road shots were to be handled by professional drivers. When the camera did focus on the protagonists, it would be in tight profile, or framed by a rear-view mirror.

The part for which Faye had just auditioned had only three words of dialogue: 'What kept you?', delivered deadpan and with maybe a cocking of one eyebrow, but there had been debate as to whether this was a touch too far.

It had become clear that this was a 'look' casting, rather than an audition to gauge her acting chops. And yet the session had dragged on for close to thirty minutes.

Faye sitting on a plastic chair, holding an imaginary wheel.

Faye checking an imaginary rear-view mirror.

An imaginary wing mirror.

Faye entering and exiting the car.

Faye checking her watch.

Checking her hair.

Her earrings.

Faye executing a variety of smiles: coy, wry,

and amused to a degree of extents.

'Try seductive,' suggested Al.

Al, in fact, suggesting most of the action and variations.

'Sorry for interfering, but . . . '

'Do you think we might . . . ?'

'Indulge me, would you?'

And on.

Faye could only guess at Alistair's motivation — spite, sabotage, pride, professional rigour. Possibly he was trying to help, but she doubted it.

Handshakes on the way in, kisses on the way out.

Faye thanked everyone for their time. Big smiles all round and polite enthusiasm from the client. The director — 'You were great' — squeezing Faye's arm in a demonstration of sincerity.

'We'll be in touch,' Jody told her. 'Soon. Give my love to, you know, Mike.'

And Alistair was escorting her from the room.

Guiding her by the elbow through the door and the waiting area beyond, silently steering her through a second set of double doors leading onto the stairwell.

They stood in the echoing silence for a few seconds, the stairs turning two floors above and two below, blisters of peeling paint on the walls, a fine grid of wire laced through the windows giving on to the street below. Faye experienced a sensation of something like confinement. To be cornered, she thought, might feel like this. The actress part of her, filing away the dread sensation for future reference — a heroine in peril, facing attack, facing . . . worse.

Alistair smiled. 'Nailed it. Honestly, you were perfect.'

As he continued talking, Faye registered noises from the street outside — chatter and shouting and traffic — the sound ushering in colour that had been absent ten heartbeats ago. Teal paint, the red-stitched buttonhole on Alistair's lapel, her plum nail varnish.

Alistair said, 'I hope there are no hard feelings?'

'About . . . about what?'

Alistair laughed, a short triple huff that gained insincerity as it echoed through the stairwell. 'Oh, the whole, 'This is only an audition' business — I hope you don't think I was being off.'

'No, not at all.'

'I mean, if it were down to me — and who knows, maybe it is' — a knowing smile — 'you'd have the part already. But I can't be seen to play favourites. You understand?'

'Sure. Of course.'

She should never have agreed to do this. Any of this. Mike had said the commercial would be a good payday. As it transpired, it would be good for close to eighteen grand — and whatever happened next, eighteen grand would make it a whole lot less difficult.

'Here.' Alistair was holding out a white envelope.

'What's this?'

'Services rendered.'

'Excuse me?'

'Call-back fee,' Al said with a sideways smile.

'This isn't a call-back.'

Al shrugged. 'I pulled a few strings.'

Faye opened the envelope and counted five twenty-pound notes.

'They told me fifty was standard, but . . . this is hardly *standard*, if you know what I mean.'

Faye dropped the envelope into her bag. 'Thank you. You needn't have.'

'No . . . ' holding her eyes' . . . but I wanted to. What are friends for, right?'

'Right.'

'I mean, we are friends, aren't we?' Alistair took a half-step forwards.

'Of course.'

'After all, we did . . . you know.' He grimaced, as if recalling some laughable lapse of judgement — playing their music too loud, or dancing on the tables perhaps — rather than a clusterfuck of cynical infidelity.

Faye resisted the impulse to look away. Perhaps she looked defiant.

'Uh-oh! Elephant in the room! Or should I say *in the stairwell*?'

His loud braying laughter felt like a presence in the small space.

'I should go.'

Al shook his head. 'I mean — what were we *thinking*, Faye?'

'God only knows.'

'You regret it?' Al's tone crystallising into something hard and cold.

She pushed the question back. 'Don't you?'

Alistair's gaze drifted into the middle distance, as if the answer might be found there. 'It's not that simple,' he said, almost to himself now.

Faye glanced down the stairwell, the concentric coils of step and banister rail tightening as they wound down towards the exit. 'I really should go.'

Alistair regarded her again, as if suddenly remembering she was there. 'I thought maybe we could have a drink?'

'I have to be somewhere, actually.'

'Another time?'

'Sure.'

'Going anywhere nice?'

None of your business. 'A rehearsal.'

Al crossed his arms, nodded. 'Right, the, er . . . schoolgirl thing.' A smile that spoke of mental recall. 'It's getting cold now, they'll have to' — he mimed turning a dial — 'turn up the heat.'

'Well, I don't want to be late.'

'Of course. Maybe we'll come and see you, again. We could all, you know, get together.'

'We'll see.' It was hot in the stairwell, but Faye buttoned her coat nevertheless.

Al smiled sincerely, almost with resignation. 'Do I get a hug?'

Faye stepped up to him. 'Of course.'

Al wrapped one arm around her waist and one around her shoulders, pulling her close. 'It's been nice seeing you again,' he said into her neck. 'Really nice.'

'Yes,' Faye said.

Alistair continued to hold her. Was it her

imagination, or was his grip tightening? His breath was hot against her neck, a low sound like a quiet sigh or a faint moan. She could feel the full length of his body against hers; chest, belly, groin and thigh. She put her palms against his body, exerting a firm pressure, creating a space between them until he slackened his grip and took a half-step back.

'Break a leg,' he said. 'We'll let you know asap about the commercial. But' — and again, the knowing smile — 'I think it's safe to say we'll be seeing a lot more of each other.'

13

They had been sitting that way — Mike's arm around her shoulder, Sally's head resting on his chest — long enough that their coffee had turned cold.

Sally said, 'Why did we never get together, do you think?'

Her head moved gently with the rise and fall of Mike's chest. He inhaled deeply and let his lips brush against her hair before answering. 'Because we were young and stupid.'

'Don't be glib.'

'It's the only answer I have.'

'Remember that house?'

'Parade Street.'

'What was it you called it — Paradise Street?'

Mike laughed. 'That's right. Paradise Street.'

Sally's degree had kept her in the Midlands for another two years after Mike's graduation, but gravity and opportunity had pulled her south to London, leaving a soon-to-be-former boyfriend behind.

While she looked for a room to rent, Sally slept on a sofa in the terraced house Mike shared with three others. Two weeks and three days in Paradise Street, sneaking into his bedroom and sneaking out again an hour before the rest of the house rose. Making love, talking, reminiscing.

But while the old habit of secrecy persisted in the house (two of the tenants were work colleagues of Mike's, and he'd been through a brief fling with a friend of the third), they abandoned themselves to the plain-sight ano-nymity of the capital. Eating at tables for two, holding hands in the cinema, kissing on the top deck of the number 38 bus.

Then back to Paradise Street, waiting impa-tiently for Mike's housemates to take themselves to bed. The anxious interval as the house settled, the noises subsided, and the last light was switched off. The slow ascent up the stairs, the silent creep along the landing, the oblong of dim light as she opened the door to his room.

It was the closest they ever got to being the couple they might have been. And then she found a place south of the river, close to the hospital and available immediately.

On Sally's last night in Paradise Street, after the noises stopped and the lights went out, Sally didn't climb the stairs to Mike's room and he didn't come down to take her by the hand. In the morning, they drank their coffee, ate their toast and behaved just like the friends they pretended to be.

Mike was right; they were stupid.

Sitting on the bench now, Sally turned to face him. 'I think I'm going to leave Al. After Christmas.'

Mike placed his hand against her cheek and kissed her. She kissed him back — their lips separating and fitting around the other's. The softness of her skin against his; his stubble against her cheek and chin. Their faces knowing and remembering.

127

'Why do we fit so well?'

'We just do.'

Across the street a school bell rang, clear and sharp.

Sally said. 'Five minutes and this place will be full of kids and mums.'

'Patients?'

'Some.'

She drank the last of her cold coffee then placed the cup on the ground beside the bench.

Mike said, 'I want to see you again. Somewhere . . . somewhere else.'

'To fuck?'

'Don't.'

'Well isn't that what you mean?'

'Not like that.'

'What about Faye?'

Mike shook his head. 'We don't . . . I don't even know why she's still with me.'

'Maybe she's waiting for Christmas.'

'Maybe.'

'Why did she do it, do you think? I understand us . . . I understand Al, I suppose. I mean, Faye's beautiful. She's young, she's — '

'You're beautiful.'

'I'm nearly forty, I'm — '

Mike kissed her. 'You're beautiful.'

Sally pulled away from the kiss. 'I love you, Mike. Whatever that means. But I can't be the . . . the last choice. I won't be that.'

'I want to be with you, Sally.'

Sally picked up her coffee cup, felt its empty weight and set it back down on the ground. 'So, what do we do now?'

'We'll figure it out. As soon as this commercial's out of the way, I'll talk to Faye. And when you're ready, you talk to Al.'

'Will you be able to work with him still?'

Mike smiled, shook his head. 'This is it, you know.'

Sally took both of Mike's hands in hers. 'Me and you?'

Mike kissed her hands, first one and then the other. 'Always was.'

14

Sally pushed the paperwork aside, clicked off her computer and glanced at the wall-mounted clock. The one that was supposed to mark no more than ten minutes per appointment but seldom did. She should have finished an hour ago, but 'should have' was the story of her life so far.

She picked up the Starbucks cup from her desk, empty since two this afternoon, and dropped it into the bin. Every workday morning and lunchtime for the last week, Sally had queued up for her flat white, not expecting, but idly hoping Mike might be sitting at one of the tables. Unable to stay away from her. Unable to wait.

Another week at her back. Another week with the wrong man, in the wrong house, in the wrong life. A week of quiet suppers, civil chat, wooden hugs and artificial kisses. And, last night, another hour of counselling with Joyce.

'Describe your perfect future,' Joyce had said. Alistair talked about holidays, about domestic harmony, about a year travelling together, about a retirement cottage near the coast. About long walks, crosswords, the theatre, slow games of cribbage with a bottle of wine. Maybe a dog.

Sally's perfect future no longer existed; that version of events had been eroded by bad choices, bad luck, bad biology. But new futures are written every day, every hour, every thin slice of every second. And starting from seven days ago, from that stolen hour with Mike, something new was forming ahead of her.

Sitting in Joyce's office last night, Sally had imagined a far-away Christmas with Mike and his daughter Jojo, grown up now, and mother to an unruly brood; three children who sat on her knees and called her Gran. She would knit sweaters and bake cakes and show the giggling children pictures of their grandfather, Mike, as a young man.

The mental image had made Sally cry gently. The tears sparing her from having to construct some fiction for the benefit of her counsellor and her husband.

Joyce had nodded. 'The important question,' she said, 'is are you together?'

'Of course,' Al had answered.

'Yes,' Sally said. 'We'll be together.'

The deceit in the specific identity of that future 'we', if not in the words themselves. Even so, the lie lay heavily, folding itself into the empty spaces of the room, absorbing light and deadening the sound of her voice. So palpable, in fact, that she had worried Alistair would feel it too.

His mood had become unpredictable, shifting between surliness and doting affection. Their home had become somehow muted; they spoke gently and trod softly as if the house itself had decided this would be the new default. They moved around each other — Sally going to the gym before work, Alistair going to a bar somewhere after. Some days, the only words they spoke were good morning or goodnight. They still slept in the same bed, although they seldom entered it at the same time. Sally feigning sleep as Alistair quietly shifted and sighed. Lying with her back towards him, melting into the dark, dreading the weight of his hand on her waist.

Sally had told Mike she would wait until after Christmas, but the idea seemed absurd now. Making plans, exchanging gifts, visiting relatives, pretending to be happy. The idea of waiting had felt like a kindness, but it was the exact opposite.

A week had passed since she and Mike had sat beside each other in the empty park. Kissing in cold daylight and caring little who saw them. But now, with nothing but time between them and their future, they were reverting again to secrecy.

Another week of furtive messages and plans and promises.

Anticipation pushed against her organs and coated her skin; it gave her courage and strengthened her resolve. One week ago, Mike had said he wanted to meet 'somewhere else' and Sally winced as she remembered her reply. It had been as hypocritical as it had been hostile. Next week they were going to meet again, but had yet to confirm when or where, both circling the idea of privacy and intimacy. Of making love.

Neither had suggested a hotel yet, but someone would.

'To fuck?' was what she had said to Mike.

The remembered words stirred her now and she felt their heat and promise between her legs.

Her desk phone rang, and Sally glanced again

at the clock before answering. She was in no hurry to be home, but reception shouldn't be taking any more appointments at this time. Unless it was an emergency.

'Is there a problem?'

'Got a friend of yours here, says her name's Ivy.'

'Ivy?' Sally hadn't seen her old friend for six or seven months, since an unsuccessful dinner party where Sally had allowed Ivy — always tending to belligerence, but pathologically objectionable after too much wine — to drag her into an animated and unresolved argument about junior doctors' pay. They had kissed cheeks at the end of the night, agreed they must 'do it again soon', but Sally had thought she'd be happy to never do it ever again.

'That's right, Ivy. D'you know her?'

'Yes. I'll be out in a couple of minutes, tell her.'

'Will do — Oh, hold on a mo . . . Actually, Doctor, she's saying can she pop through?'

Assuming Ivy must have her reasons for turning up unannounced at the surgery, and that they might be serious, Sally told the receptionist to send her in. She checked her reflection in the mirror above the small hand basin, tidied her hair with her hands and checked her teeth for food or lipstick.

She should probably have opened the door instead of waiting for a knock, but the thought occurred to her half a second too late.

'Hey.' Forcing a little brightness into her voice. 'Come in.' She stood as the door opened, her arms lifting away from her sides in preparation for the obligatory hug.

'Hey,' said Faye, stepping around the door.

Sally took a second to process the switch in the script. 'Faye? The receptionist said . . . '

Faye bit her bottom lip as she nodded. 'I didn't want you to send me away. Sorry.'

Sally's arms drifted back to her sides. 'Well, this is a . . . you know, surprise.'

Faye nodded, pointed to a chair beside Sally's desk. 'Can I . . . ?'

'Please. Faye, are you . . . is everything okay?'

'Yep. Well, I think so. I mean you never . . . you never really know, do you?'

'No, you never do.'

Possibilities clamoured to suggest themselves, but Sally ignored them. She understood that these preliminaries, this moment of gentle preparation, was important.

'How did you know about Ivy?' she asked. 'Did I mention her in . . . in Brighton?'

'Poison Ivy, you called her.'

Sally laughed. 'I don't remember saying that. Actually, there's rather a lot I don't remember.'

'No, it was all a bit . . . ' Faye spiralled her fingers in the air.

'Right.'

Sally watched as Faye's cheeks coloured. 'Can I get you some water?'

Faye nodded and Sally poured water into two plastic cups from a bottle on her desk. 'So, how have you been?'

'Okay. Busy.'

'You're shooting a commercial with — '

'With Mike and Alistair. Do you mind?'

'Honestly . . . I don't know. I mean, I don't think you shouldn't do it, but . . . I don't know how I feel about it. Everything's, you know . . . ' She mimicked Faye's gesture of the spiralling fingers.

Faye allowed herself a small smile. 'Did you know the play has moved to London now?'

Sally did know; Mike had told her last week, moments before he had kissed her. Moments before he'd said he wanted to be with her. Maybe that was why Faye was here now.

Sally nodded. 'Brixton, right?'

'Rehearsals this week and last. Opens in' — Faye counted on her fingers — 'six days. I think.'

'Excited?'

Again Faye bit her lower lip, looking to Sally more like a child than the brazen provocateur she had met two months ago. 'We did the *undress* rehearsal today.'

'Seriously? They do that?'

'Yup. Get it out of the way — the awkwardness and whatnot — before you let it all hang out in front of an audience.'

'But haven't you already done that?'

'New actor.'

'Right. You did the whole thing, the whole play?'

'Scenes. Couple of scenes, just me and Gareth — he's the actor — me and Gareth and the director. Cosy little threeso — you know.'

Faye sipped her water, placed the cup on the desk and took a slow breath. 'I meant it when I

135

said we could have been friends, you know. I remember that much.'

Sally nodded. 'I remember.'

'Do you think we could have been friends, Sally?'

'Yes. Yes I do.'

They were closing in on it now. Sally recognised the signs; the subtle shift in posture and voice and expression.

'This is so hard.'

'It's okay, Faye. Whatever it is you can — '

'I think I'm pregnant.'

Sally stared at Faye, stared at her face and her belly. 'You think?'

'Haven't had a period since ... before Brighton.'

'That's ... ' Sally reached for a cardboard desk calendar.

'Nine weeks,' Faye said. 'I haven't had a period in about ten.'

'Have you taken a test?'

'Got three in my handbag. I keep buying them, but, I haven't got round to ... I haven't been able to face it.'

'Ten weeks?'

'I was back-to-backing my pill — for the play — so it's all a bit ... fucked up.'

Sally nodded. 'Yes it is. Have you told Mike?'

Faye shook her head. 'I told him I had my period. Last week.'

'You ... ' *Lied.* Sally swallowed the word. 'Why?'

'Because it was easier than telling him I might be pregnant.'

'Well if . . . wait — you said you're on the pill.'

Faye closed her eyes, a slow blink, said: 'I was sick. Threw up all weekend, actually. All the drugs and drink and I must have eaten half a tub of ice-cream. Rocky road. Remember saying that?'

Sally began to smile at the memory, but another thought killed it on her lips. 'But you and Al . . . you used condoms?'

Faye shook her head. 'Didn't have any. And I'm on the . . . you know.'

'Jesus, Faye! How could you be so — ' Sally took a breath, reminded herself who she was, where she was. 'I'm sorry. I'm . . . ' A *hypocrite*. 'I'm sorry.'

'No, I'm sorry. This . . . it's still new to you.'

'So it could be . . . '

Faye wiped a tear from her eye. 'It's no one's idea of good news, is it?'

'What about . . . what if it's Mike's?'

Faye sipped her water. She shook her head. 'I don't think we're . . . I don't think me and Mike are . . . '

'I'm . . . ' — hating herself for the pretence of it — 'I'm sorry.'

Faye considered Sally for a second before continuing. 'At rehearsals today, I had to kiss the actor.'

'Okay?'

'We kiss then we share that cigarette, remember. A prop cigarette?'

'Sure.'

'So after the scene, Gareth says he's going outside for the real thing. A real smoke, and I go out with him.' Faye registered the professional alarm in Sally's face. 'I haven't smoked anything for weeks, not since I first suspected I might be . . . ' Her hand fluttered towards her stomach. 'But we were talking and if I'm honest I quite fancied a bit of passive. So Gareth's having his cigarette and . . . ' Faye touched the tips of her index fingers together ' . . . it was like the two things, the kiss and the cigarette, came together.'

Sally narrowed her eyes. 'What are we talking about, Faye?'

'I remembered something. From Brighton.'

Sally sat back slightly, an inkling of comprehension beginning to form in her subconscious.

'When we were in Brighton,' Faye said, 'I went outside for a smoke. I'd had a few hanging out the window, but it was awkward and I felt like a bit of a try-hard. I'm not sure exactly when it was, but Alistair had gone hunting for drink or food or something.'

'He found that bottle of whatever it was.'

'Right. And I went downstairs to smoke a cigarette outside. It was a warm night, remember?'

Sally nodded that she did.

'And it was late. Quiet, no one about. The stars were out and I was having a little moment, like I had all of Brighton to myself, or something. And then this huge fucking fox appeared, stared at me, then bolted up the alley at the side of the house. Nearly gave me a heart attack. Funny that I didn't remember it sooner, but . . . well, what with everything that happened after.'

Faye took a sip of water then squinted, as if bringing the scene back to mind. 'So, I cross the road to get a better angle on the side street. See if the fox was lurking or whatever. Except, what I saw from the other side of the street was you and Mike in the kitchen.'

Kissing.

Sally considered her options — denial or dismissal, but either would be futile and self-defeating. And anyway, Faye knew.

'You saw us?'

'You and Mike,' Faye said. 'You did more than kiss at university?'

'Yes.'

'Does Alistair know?'

Sally shook her head.

'Are you having an affair?'

Another shake of the head. 'No.' *Not yet.*

'I've wondered how something like that could happen. How we all did what we did, where it started. Who started it. You know what I mean?'

'Yes. I know.'

'I think I was thinking about what I saw between you and Mike. I think maybe I was reacting to that. When I kissed you, remember, and started acting like a . . . Maybe it was me, maybe I started it.' She was crying now, breathing deeply to contain herself and only barely managing.

Sally considered passing a box of tissues to Faye, but it felt too much like a cold professional response — the doctor and the patient. Instead, she knelt beside Faye's chair and hugged her while the tears — both of theirs — fell silently.

'It wasn't you,' Sally said eventually. 'It wasn't your fault.'

Faye rested her head on top of Sally's and returned the hug.

'What will you do?' asked Sally. 'If you're pregnant?'

Faye sat up straight and dried her eyes. 'I suppose we'd better find out?'

Sally stood, opened a drawer and removed a small plastic beaker with a screw-on cap. 'There's a toilet at the end of the corridor.'

15

How did this happen?

The Thames was black oil, still tonight and dotted with reflected lights. Standing in front of the window of his office, Mike watched the people below and the slow traffic on the north side of the river; going home, going out, going to work, going to meet husbands and wives, friends and children and secret lovers, going to start something new or end something old. All of them drifting like silt.

Through his superimposed reflection, Mike wondered at the unfathomable sequence of circumstances, chance and choice that had delivered him into this situation. One break in the chain, one turn left instead of right, one delayed train, one drink more or less, a change in the weather or a change of heart, one moment of hesitation, one of courage, and everything might be different. Maybe better, possibly worse, but better was easier to imagine.

Last night . . .

How did this happen?

How do you think!

. . . things were thrown.

Mike turned his attention to the palm of his right hand, the strip of sticking plaster around the base of his thumb, the fabric already fraying and curled at the edges. The injury sustained in the clear-up, rather than the assault — Mike

141

picking up shards of smashed china while Faye wiped tears of milky tea from the kitchen walls.

He pulled his phone from his pocket, but there were no messages.

After the shock and confusion last night, after the shouting and crying and drawn blood, his thoughts had turned to Sally. He'd called this morning — the minute he left the flat for work — but Sally hadn't answered. He called again from his office, and again this afternoon, but besides a single text — *Head's a mess, Mike. Look after Faye x* — they hadn't talked.

It was now twenty-four hours since Mike had learned Faye was pregnant, with what could be either his or his friend's child. *You said it, Sally: head's a mess.*

Blinking red and white lights moved across the sky from left to right. Two or three hundred humans turning off their devices and returning their seats to an upright position; preparing to land, excited, tired, nervous. Last night he was supposed to call Jojo; his head full of plans and imagined snapshots. He made coffee in the mug she'd sent for his last birthday, changed into the T-shirt she sent last Christmas.

He was about to call when Faye arrived home, eyes red and frantic and frightened.

He sat her down, took her coat, made tea.

How did this happen?

Later — the mess cleared, his finger taped — he messaged Kim with a lie about working late, and received a predictably curt reply.

He hadn't seen his daughter for eight months, and felt her absence like hands tugging at his

142

guts and ribs. She was due to land in seventeen days, and Mike had been counting off the time every night and every morning. He visualised himself collecting her from the airport, a funny sign, *Welcome Princess Jojobee*, decorated with stars and flowers. He wanted her visit to be perfect, but right now it couldn't possibly be.

Daddy? Why is Faye throwing up in the bathroom?

She's sick, baby.

Mommy was sick when she was pregnant with Stephie. Is Faye going to have a baby?

I don't know, sweetheart.

If Faye did have a baby, would it be my sister?

I don't know baby. I honestly . . . don't know.

Maybe in a month or so, the run-up to Christmas or the start of the new year, maybe then they could enjoy their precious scrap of time together. He would discuss it with Kim; feed her another lie about work. Or maybe a minor medical procedure or the death of a relative, a house-fire, a flood, an infestation of rats. Anything but the truth.

Another set of aircraft lights crossed the dirty sky, outbound to somewhere.

To anywhere.

'Knock knock.'

Mike turned as Al walked into the office carrying two glasses and a bottle of something amber. Al closed the door with his foot, and set the glassware down on Mike's desk.

'I'm pretty sure they're unbreakable,' Al said, nodding at the huge window.

'I guess it depends what you throw at them.'

Al filled both glasses. 'Client gave me this last Christmas,' he said, showing Mike the bottle of whiskey. 'I was saving it for a special occasion.' He shrugged, passed a glass to Mike.

Mike took the drink and sipped, made a face. 'And this client likes you?'

'Whoever knows, Mike?'

'You all right?'

'I've been in meetings since nine this morning and I'd struggle to tell you two things I talked about. Thanks for sticking around.'

'Didn't have anything better to do.'

'Faye not home?'

'Final rehearsal.'

Al nodded, appearing to lose himself briefly in thought. 'She all right?'

'Confused, frightened . . . ' Mike glanced at the plaster on his thumb. 'Angry.'

'And you didn't know?'

'She told me — maybe a week ago — told me she was on her period.'

'Jesus. What's that about?'

Mike shook his head. 'She must have been freaking out all this time. Just keeping it to herself. Can you imagine?'

'Shoot's in two weeks,' Al said. 'Will she be . . . ' He held his free hand in front of his stomach. 'Will it be obvious?'

Mike remembered Kim's pregnancy, the slowly growing belly that surprised him every day. Their anticipation and happiness increasing at the same rate as that determined bump. The opposite of this.

Mike shook his head.

144

'Is that a yes or a no?'

'I shouldn't think so,' Mike said. 'Not much, anyway.'

'Small mercies, right?'

Mike turned to look out of the large window. 'How's Sally?'

'She's far from fucking happy, Mike. Beyond that . . . I honestly don't know. I rarely do these days. Did you know we were in counselling?'

Did Al know the answer to his own question; was he testing Mike?

'I'm sorry to hear that.'

Al gave a short humourless laugh. 'Yeah. Seven or eight sessions. And now this bullshit.'

Al emptied his glass and topped it up to within spilling distance of the rim. He didn't offer the bottle to Mike.

'Sally and I use contraception,' he said, staring straight into Mike's eyes. 'Did you know that?'

Mike shook his head.

'After the baby didn't happen, after all the IVF . . . every time we did it after that, every time we slept together, Sal would still hope that it might happen. And when it didn't, she'd go through the pain all over again. It was rubbing her out, Mike. So we started using condoms — no hope, no disappointment. Ironic, isn't it.'

'This must be hard for her too.'

Al sipped his whiskey.

'I was thinking about it last night,' he said. 'If you didn't know, it's because you didn't ask and Sally didn't tell. Which means you didn't use anything when you and my wife — '

'Do we need to do this, Al?'

'Why not? I mean, everything's all fucked up to high heaven, so why the fuck not?'

'Okay then, I didn't use anything. Just like you didn't, when you slept with Faye.'

'*Slept with*. Right.'

'Don't be a prick, Al.'

'At least I checked, Mike. At least I *asked*. Faye told me she was on the pill, didn't she?'

'She was. She is.'

'Well, fat lot of fucking good it did.' Alistair worried a plaited cotton bracelet around his left wrist, removing it and replacing it on his other hand. A charity wristband perhaps, or a nod to self-expression. 'Want to know what I think?'

'No, but I guess you're going to tell me.'

'I think Sally saw an opportunity, a slim chance, a last chance — fuck knows — but I think she saw a chance to get pregnant.'

'But she can't . . . '

'Go on, say it.'

'She can't have children.'

'Not with me, Michael. Not with *me*. And you know what made it worse? They couldn't find anything the fuck wrong with either of us. But you know the story, don't you? Nothing wrong with me, nothing wrong with her — we just don't 'work' together.'

Mike refilled his glass, then crossed the room to the short sofa against the far wall. 'I'm sorry,' he said, 'I guess I just assumed . . . '

'Yes. You did. And good old Sally, she just lay down and let you get on with it.'

'It wasn't like that.'

'Really? What was it like, then? Because I

146

would *love* to know.'

'Ask Sally then. Ask your wife.'

Al went to say something then stopped. He pointed his finger at Mike and wagged it slowly. 'You sound bitter. Sad and bitter.'

'Yeah? Well, maybe I am.'

Al walked across to the window, turning his back on Mike as he addressed him: 'Will you stay with her? With Faye?'

'Let's find out what's going on first.'

'I mean, either way, you're fucked, right? Either you've knocked up Faye, or I have — no happy ending either way. Not for you, anyway.'

'No. I suppose not.'

Al turned to face Mike. 'I'm assuming she'll have an abortion.'

'I don't know.'

'But you've discussed it?'

'Not explicitly.'

'Well don't you think you should? I mean, Jesus, Mike. I don't know about you, but *I* don't want it. I mean . . . *Christ*.'

'She doesn't know what she's going to do. She's upset and she's scared.'

'I'm not surprised. So talk to her, Mike. Talk some fucking sense into her.'

'Sense?'

'Don't look at me like that. Like you're not thinking the exact same thing. Oh' — as if it were an afterthought — 'about the shoot . . . '

'Yes?'

'I think it's best if you don't go.'

'What?'

'I've been chatting to Bob.'

The last of the founding partners to remain on the payroll, Bob was close to retirement now, and Alistair was the man tipped to take his place in the big office on the 6th floor. From which vantage he could fuck with or fire Mike whenever the mood took him. Although in effect, Alistair was pretty much at liberty to do these things now.

'Of course you have,' Mike said.

'We both think you're . . . coasting a little. Perhaps not taking the job as seriously as you used to. As the head of a department should.'

'You and Bob thought this, did you?'

'I told him you had a lot on your mind and that we should cut you some slack. That you and Faye were going through a rocky patch, so it might be for the best if you stayed back from the shoot. Give you a chance to get your shit together. You should thank me, really.'

'Wow. Are you this petty at home?'

'Fuck you. We used to be best friends, Mike. Best friends. But who fucks their best friend's wife? What kind of cunt does that?'

'We all did the same thing. We're all culpable.'

'Culpable — piss off. You see the thing is, it wasn't all the same. Sally saw a last chance; she used you to try and get knocked up, and I understand that. Me, I hadn't slept with my wife for as long as I can remember, and then you stick me in front of this naked twenty-whatever-year-old, you lay it all out on a plate. It ain't pretty and I'm not proud, but I understand that, too. Faye? Fuck knows; maybe she's kinky, or mental, or maybe you just don't do it for her; I have no idea, and frankly I don't care. But you, you fucked my wife. It's as simple and cold as that, mate. You were my best man. My best fucking man. So forgive me if I'm feeling a little 'petty'.'

'Figure all that out in counselling, did you?' Mike winced at his own words. 'I . . . '

Alistair levelled a finger at him. 'You know what, Mike? If I really wanted to be petty, you'd be out on your arse.'

'You'd be doing me a favour.'

'You think so? It's a young man's game, Mike, and you're already paying child support for one kid. So, have a word with your girlfriend and let's get this sorry mess over and done with.'

Al drained his glass and banged it down on Mike's desk. 'Keep the bottle, mate. Drown your sorrows.'

16

The crowd was scattered evenly throughout the twenty-one rows, and if Faye squinted she could pretend the theatre was packed to capacity. Still, it would be nice not to have to squint. And not simply for the till receipts; during the play's short run in Brighton, Faye had discovered an interesting inversion, in that the larger the crowd, the less uncovered she felt. As if the audience had to divide her nudity between everyone present, each owning only a small portion of her exposure.

Joseph, the director, was optimistic that they would approach a full house over the weekend; advance sales looked promising and last night's reviews had been generally positive. One reviewer had called Faye 'broodingly incandescent, capturing the fragile swagger of a confused girl on the cusp of womanhood'. Another critic had called her 'watchable', which felt to Faye like faint praise, even more so considering she was naked but for a layer of fake tan and a few hundred goosebumps.

They were at the part of the play now where Rose posed for Mr Martin, and whilst she remained naked, Faye was at least sitting. For the most part, the audience were in shadow, but every so often she would see a tell-tale flare of light reflected back from a pair of spectacles or a camera phone.

Could they tell?

Before tonight's performance, Faye had opened her robe and regarded her stomach in the dressing-room mirror. She was an 'apple', according to her mother: slim, with a gentle swell about the navel. Staring at her cold flesh, Faye had tried to detect any change since the month, the week, the night before.

Faye's agent had said that *A Still Life* was booked for a four-week run, possibly longer if the reviews and sales justified it. And no two ways about it, four weeks from now Faye would be showing, under bright lights in front of three hundred paying guests — some of them with binoculars.

After all, apples grew; all life did.

Unless she did something about it first.

There was a producer from the BBC sitting somewhere in the first row tonight, and Joseph had been almost unbearable before the performance, giving unnecessary direction, fussing over their make-up and urging Faye and Gareth to 'give it your fucking all, yes?' Faye had felt these words were directed at her rather than at her co-star, worrying that Joseph had picked up on something in her demeanour — an agitation, a lack of focus. And he wouldn't be wrong.

The play would adapt well to the small screen, but Faye held little hope of going along for the ride. They would cast a 'name', someone to bring in ratings and do the chat shows. But a TV adaptation would be good for the stage play, would extend its run and help it transition from the suburbs to the West End. And that would be

151

a move Faye *could* expect to make, so long as Joseph felt she was giving her 'fucking all'.

As Mr Martin sketched his student, Faye tensed her stomach and gazed into the faces on the first row. Maybe the life inside her already showed in her eyes. 'Brooding' and 'confused', the critic had said. *Well you got that right, A. J. Johnson of* Brixton Seen.

Faye had plans, but a baby wasn't part of them. In her future, absolutely, but not now and not on her own — which was the only way this story could play out. Mike had handled the news better than she had anticipated. He'd been shocked, of course, and annoyed that she'd lied about her period. But, on the whole, he had reacted calmly; with compassion rather than accusation — although Faye would have preferred the latter. At least then she could have claimed the high ground.

'It's not your fault,' he'd said.

He meant well, she knew, but in the absence of anything better to push against, she pushed against this. 'I know it's not my fucking *fault*.'

'I'm just saying.'

'Well just don't.'

It wasn't her fault but she was the problem, nevertheless; the crisis, the nightmare, the ticking fucking time bomb. So despite, or maybe because of, Mike's disappointing equanimity, she had done what time bombs do — she exploded.

She laid blame, hurled accusations, threw a mug.

Perhaps that's what Gray Cadwallader of *Southwest Buzz* had seen when he described her as 'incandescent'.

She had drawn blood, and even then, he had promised to 'support' her, neither asking what Fay intended to do, nor suggesting what he thought she should. But language was Mike's trade, and his careful words had suggested that whilst he would 'support' her, he wouldn't necessarily be with her.

And yet, after they had mopped up the blood and tea and shards of mug, they went to sleep in the same bed, Faye taking much-needed comfort from the warmth and closeness of his body as he lay behind her, his arm across her waist, his hand on her belly.

As a father, would Mike want her to keep the baby; or as a man with one absent child, would he be reluctant to have another?

In the last seven days she had made more than seventy resolute decisions, some lasting a minute, others surviving through the night before crumbling in the face of the compelling alternative. She had searched online and lurked on forums, she had read stories of empowerment and others of regret. Brighton was eleven weeks behind them, which meant Faye was now carrying a foetus in place of the more innocuous, less human, embryo. At eleven weeks, the child inside her womb would have arms and legs, fingers and toes. She would have a nose and ears and eyes.

In her relentlessly shifting resolve, Faye's starting point was always to cast Mike as the father. Perhaps because this was the least unpalatable of the available possibilities. But palatability had no influence on outcome, and

Faye had to acknowledge the possibility that her foetus was forming Alistair's eyes.

And what if that were the case — would it impact her decision whether to keep the baby or terminate its progress before it opened those newly formed eyes? The answer didn't make Faye feel particularly good about herself. It wasn't the baby's fault who her father was.

Maybe she was being unkind. Alistair and Faye had swapped a handful of texts in the last few days — short exchanges in which Alistair had come across as concerned and supportive. It was cynical, she knew, but Faye wondered if his real concern was whether or not she might quit his commercial. The thought had certainly crossed her mind, but the cheque was a bloody good one and God only knew when her next paying gig might be.

She would be flying out early on Monday morning; two nights in Ljubljana, and that episode, at least, would be behind her. Mike wasn't going now, which was no bad thing in itself, but the thought of being alone with Alistair made her skin itch.

Faye could feel the gathering life inside her. And the weight of it was enough to drive a pregnant girl to drink. But therein lay the irony and the dilemma.

Last night the cast and crew had gone to a chi-chi cocktail bar for first-night drinks. Claiming to have been recently topped up anytime anyone came near her with a bottle, Faye had made a single glass of champagne last all night. Everyone else had been too drunk to notice. Gareth, in particular, had been garrulously, flirtatiously sozzled — telling Faye at close range how he admired her talent; lauding their chemistry over and again; his eyes, body language and tactility implying a layer of subtext that became less subtle the more he drank. Perhaps it was nothing more than sincere companionable banter; Gareth was 'happily married', and had talked at length about his two children, one on either side of their teens. Even so, when they'd kissed goodnight, Faye had sensed (the prolonged contact of their lips, the low murmur of affection, the firm pressure of his hand against her waist) that Gareth may be as replete with shit as every other middle-aged married man she had talked to in a dimly lit bar.

On stage now, in his role as Mr Martin the horny art teacher, Gareth looked up from his sketchbook and said:

'It's not yours, you know.'

Rose frowned as she answered: 'What isn't?'

'Your body. Your youth.'

'Well whose is it, then?'

Mr Martin chewed his pencil. 'Time,' he said. 'It belongs to Time. This' — he held up his sketchpad, the line-drawn facsimile of Rose's naked body — 'that's gone. That's in the past now.'

'I'm still here as far as I can tell,' Rose chirped, and the audience laughed.

'But you've changed, you see.' Mr Martin resumed sketching — the actor adding superfluous strokes to the pre-drawn study. He pointed his pencil to the light glowing through a gap in the curtains. 'That sun, which feels so good against your back, it's slowly breaking you down. So is the food you eat, the air you breathe. That's what Time does. That's what life is.'

Rose moved her hand through the shaft of orange sunlight. 'You sound . . . old.'

Mr Martin harrumphed a shallow laugh. 'Well, I earned the privilege.'

Faye stood, stretching her hands above her head, her breasts rising on her ribcage. A knowing smile crossed her mouth as she rotated left and then right, presenting her youth to her lover, showing him her disdain for Time.

In rehearsals and previous shows, Rose would sit sideways on Mr Martin's lap now. Lace her hands around his neck and kiss him. 'I'll share it with you,' she'd say.

And when Mr Martin asked, 'What?' Rose would answer, 'My youth, as she took her teacher's hand and placed it on her thigh.

Now, however, on the second night in the Brixton Playhouse, Faye straddled Gareth, her bare legs parting as they went to either side of his hips. She laced her hands around his neck, and when she kissed him, she let her tongue trace the space between his lips.

'I'll share it with you,' she said.

'What?'

Give it your fucking all.

'My youth,' she said, taking his hand and placing it on her right breast.

The audience had always responded at this point; a rumble of scandalised amusement. And Faye was gratified to hear that response

156

amplified this evening, not simply in numbers, but by the depth of its effect.

Some laughed, others drew breath; the producer tapped a note into her phone.

* * *

In the third row from the back, slouched low in his seat behind a heavyset man and his wife, Alistair leaned incrementally to his left for an unobstructed view of the unfolding scene. This was new.

He imagined the view from the actor's perspective. Imagined the weight of Faye on his own lap, the touch of her skin under his hand. His body felt what his mind imagined; releasing chemicals, elevating his heart rate and rerouting his blood. After all, it's not like she could get any more pregnant.

In a few days they would be in Ljubljana on an expense account, and they would have an opportunity to be alone in some capacity. They had important things to discuss and decide. But in his capacity as a professional persuader, Alistair had learned that it was prudent to establish a dialogue in advance of the big presentation. Like seduction, persuasion is a process best begun early and developed slowly. One he intended to begin this evening. He had bought flowers — twelve red roses from a vendor by the tube station. But approaching the theatre, Alistair had sensed this was too much and had stuffed the blooms into a gum-stuck and fag-burnt litter bin.

On stage the actor squirmed out from beneath Faye and went through his routine of dilemma and fear and frustration. *You don't know the fucking half of it, mate.*

He and Sally should have been in counselling tonight, but Sally had said she needed to work late and Alistair didn't feel inclined to argue the point. After all, what could they possibly discuss with Joyce that wasn't laughable in its triviality?

What makes Alistair laugh?

What makes Sally smile?

Name one thing you'd like to change.

It would be like tending to a squeaky hinge while the house burned around them.

The sessions took place in an office — a discreet, brushed-steel plaque above the buzzer — four tube stops east of their own. There were counsellors closer to home, but they had worried about being recognised. Or, worse, finding a pair of familiar faces in the small waiting room.

Sitting on those squashed-together seats, waiting with the other unhappy couples, Alistair would assess his peers in matrimonial discord, looking for the tell-tale signs of a marriage in worse repair than his own. And he invariably found them — an expression of disdain, an unironed shirt, bloodshot eyes, an absent wedding band.

Last week, Sally had been waiting inside when he arrived, the chair beside her occupied by a woman with tired eyes and bitten nails. Sally looked up when Alistair walked into the lobby; she said hi, but made no move to stand up and greet him. To kiss his cheek. Al caught the eye of

158

a young man looking at him and the man quickly looked away, an apologetic smile on his lips, as if Alistair and Sally were the couple against whom this man could measure his own advantage.

That evening, Joyce had given them each a colourful bracelet of plaited cotton. The kind of thing kids exchange in the playground. The bracelets were deliberately loose so they could be easily slipped on and off. 'Whenever you find yourself saying or thinking something negative about each other,' Joyce had said, 'I want you to switch the bracelet to the opposite wrist.'

Sally had asked why — the single word betraying her frustration. Or boredom, or exasperation, or all of the above. He was losing her. And losing the will to fight for her.

When Sally messaged him last week — *We need to talk* — he thought it was over. He carried the idea home with him like a weight slung from his neck. As the tube rattled north, he imagined himself pleading and reasoning; but at the same time he saw himself receiving the news with resigned and quiet dignity.

When Sally had told him this was about Faye, about her being pregnant, it was almost a relief. His immediate reaction had been to hug his wife, but Sally had wriggled out from his arms, swapping the cotton bracelet from one hand to the other before picking up her wine glass. She asked Alistair what they were going to do, but cut him short when he attempted to point out the obvious answer — accusing him of looking for an 'easy way out', a 'selfish way out'.

'I'm thinking of you,' Al told her, and again

159

Sally's bracelet travelled from one wrist to the other.

'You're thinking of yourself!'

'I'm thinking of us both.'

'And who's thinking of Faye?'

'She can think for herself. She's got Mike. And anyway, who says I'm not thinking of her. Do you think she *wants* this? None of us *want* this, Sally.'

Sally switched the bracelet again.

'Will you stop doing that!'

'What?'

'That. The bracelet thing.'

'Fine. Fine!' Sally pulled the bracelet off her wrist, rolled it into a ball and dropped it into the bin. 'Happy now?'

'Sal, we're in this together.'

Her hand went to her wrist, and finding nothing there she topped up her glass instead. Alistair walked over to her and quietly, gently, took hold of her free hand. The bracelet around his own wrist looked more incongruous than ever, but he felt that to remove it now would be to concede the end of their marriage. Maybe it was inevitable, but he wasn't ready to give up nearly seven years of marriage just yet.

Tonight should have been session nine. Next week he would be in Ljubljana, and — optimist, fantasist, delusional fool — he had rescheduled the appointment for the week after. Perhaps by then they would know what they were dealing with.

The play moved through its final beats; Mr Martin exiting through the window, Faye exiting

160

stage left, leaving behind the sketched evidence of her transgression. Applause rippled through the theatre, the patrons in the front rows rising to their feet, and the rows behind following in a wave towards the rear. Alistair stood with the rest of the audience and added his applause to theirs.

Faye (wearing a dressing gown now) and the new actor returned to the stage — the latter via the window, which drew a fresh round of laughter and applause. They held hands, bowed, and allowed the appreciation to wash over them.

Alistair drilled his eyes into Faye's, willing her to notice him, but Faye's attention had locked on to someone — a woman — in the front row. Faye appeared to be mouthing something to her, nodding and indicating a door to the side of the stage. A friend maybe, or a journalist.

Faye and the actor bowed once more and left via opposite sides of the stage. As they did so, the audience relaxed, some retaking their seats, others pulling on coats and moving towards the aisles. As the crowd thinned out, the woman who Faye had acknowledged from the stage gathered her own coat and bag, went over to the stage door and knocked. A scruffy man opened the door from the inside, words were exchanged, the man nodded, beckoned her inside. Before stepping over the threshold, the woman glanced over her shoulder and Al got his first look at her face.

Sally stepped through and closed the door behind her.

17

'What the *fuck*, Mike! What the *absolute fuck*!'
'Kim.'
'Je-*sus*, Mike. How *could* you?'
'Kim, will yo — '
'I mean, seriously, how *the fuck* could you?'
Kim was moderating her volume, but was in every other sense screaming through the monitor. Her face filled the screen as she leaned forward, her features animated with colliding anger and exasperation. Kim's top teeth pushed into her lower lip, preparing for another four-letter assault, but she inhaled deeply, held the breath and shook her head as she exhaled.
'I'm sorry,' Mike said. 'I know it's disappointing.'
'Do you? Do you really? Easy to say, Mike, but if you had even half an idea how much this is going to break your daughter's heart . . . '
'It's *work*, Kim. You of all people should understand that.'
'Don't bring me into it. Don't you dare. You're unbelievable. Literally, unbelievable.'
'I told you — '
'And I told you. You are un-believable. I don't believe you.'
Kim sat back from the monitor and pushed her curly hair behind her ears. That hair had been the first thing Mike noticed about his ex-wife: wild, erratic, dark, impossible to fathom.

And how like the woman.

Someone knocked on a door, and Kim turned from the monitor to answer a muffled query.

She was taking the call in what could have been her bedroom, although it was hard to see much beyond her face and hair. Mike had messaged in advance to warn her he was going to have to postpone Jojo's visit. Kim had immediately launched a salvo of aggressive, threatening and hurtful judgements and declarations that Mike felt all the more fully for their truth. He'd hoped Kim might have calmed down in the hours since, but Mike was — as had been pointed out several times today — an idiot.

Kim reached forward and rotated the laptop, and by the time the pixels had reaggregated he was face to face with Brendan — Kim's husband, Jojo's stepdad.

'Hey Mike, how's things?'

'Shit Brendan, thanks for asking.'

'Yeah, Kim mentioned. The Joje is going to be disappointed, man.'

Joje? The Joje?

'Work, Brendan. You understand, right?'

'Well, you can't have the wagon pull the pony, Mike. Doesn't get you anywhere.'

'Talking of, shouldn't you be pulling teeth?'

Brendan smiled his wide and perfect smile. 'And miss the Zingers?'

'The . . . oh, Jojo's T-ball thing?'

'Semi-finals, man.' Brendan mimed the action of smacking a baseball into orbit.

'Bren took the afternoon off,' Kim said.

'Benefits of being my own boss,' Brendan

163

added, and again with all thirty-two impossibly white teeth. 'I mean, some things you can't put a price on, right?'

'Well, don't let me keep you, Bren.'

'Right.' Brendan walked towards the monitor, then leaned in to kiss Kim on the forehead. 'We should leave in fifteen, hon. Take it easy, Mike. I hope you manage to sort things out.'

'Sure.'

Brendan flashed ten fingers then five at Kim as he backed out of the room. 'Fifteen minutes.'

'I'll be less than five,' Kim said. She waited for the door to close, then leaned in. 'So why don't you tell me what the fuck is going on, Mike?'

Mike took a breath and looked around his own bedroom, at the framed pictures of Jojo on the chest of drawers. At the arrayed bottles of Faye's perfume, the inventory of make-up and associated paraphernalia, the scattered earrings and tangled necklaces. The NHS leaflet: A HEALTHY BABY STARTS WITH A HEALTHY YOU.

He turned back to his ex-wife. 'It's going to take a little longer than five minutes.'

'Tell me.'

He told her.

'What in the name of *fuck*, Mike!'

'Let's not go through that routine again.'

'Routine? Seriously? Mike, how does . . . Sally? I . . . I just . . . No words, Mike. I have no fucking words.'

'It happened.'

'Yeah, it damn well did, didn't it. How, though?'

'We were pretty drunk.'

164

'I get drunk, Mike, but I don't fuck the neighbours.'

'No, Kim. You just fucked your dentist.'

For a moment, Mike thought the screen had frozen; he was about to check when Kim tucked a stray lock of hair behind her ear, formed something like a smile and said: 'How long?'

'Ten, eleven weeks. Ish.'

'The poor girl.'

Mike nodded. 'Yep. It's worst for her, I think.'

'No shit, Mike. Where is she now?'

'Brixton. She's . . . the play moved to Brixton.'

'The naked thing?'

Mike nodded.

'Jesus. That's going to take more than a minor script amend.'

Despite himself, despite the sensation that his lungs, his heart, his guts were fossilising inside him, Mike laughed.

'Is she going to keep it?'

'I don't know. I don't think so.'

'Big decision,' Kim said, blowing at her fringe. 'And you don't know whose . . . '

Mike shook his head.

'I never liked Alistair,' Kim said. 'I never knew what Sally saw in him.'

'He speaks fondly of you.'

'Really?'

'Really.'

'So what do you think?'

'About Al?'

'About the baby. About . . . God knows; pick a place to start.'

The permutations made his temples throb. 'I

hope it's not mine, I suppose.'

'You suppose?'

'Well, I doubt we'll ever know. Unless she has it. And then it's too late, isn't it?'

'You want her to have a termination?'

That word — harder and more brutal to Mike's ear than all the alternatives. It was impossible for him to consider the question without thinking about Jojo.

When he and Kim had walked up the aisle and said 'for better or for worse', Jojo had been there too, although neither of them knew it. Not for sure, anyway. Babies were in their future, and Kim had come off her pill a month before the wedding. They had assumed it might take months to get pregnant, but in reality, it had taken weeks, maybe days. When Kim and Mike celebrated their first wedding anniversary they had celebrated it with their four-month-old daughter.

He recalled the paper gifts they gave each other that year. Kim had made an origami bird, and he, in an accident of symmetry, bought tickets to *Madame Butterfly*.

'Things that fly,' Kim had said — the irony gestating slowly over the following unhappy years.

He knew now that he and Kim never should have married. So, the question he has asked himself is this: if he had never proposed, if Kim had become his ex instead of his wife, how then would he have reacted to the news that she was pregnant? Would he have wanted her to terminate that inconvenient pregnancy? The idea that he might have done has moved him close to tears, and he has thanked the God he doesn't believe in that he never had the option.

So, what of this thing growing now inside Faye? If she has the baby and the child turns out to be his, will he not look back five years from now and again thank God that things progressed the way they did? But the question is disingenuous and built on a teetering stack of guilt and assumption. In five years, Jojo will be eleven. Who knows where Mike will be and who he will be with, but it won't be with Faye. So if she does choose to end this pregnancy, won't the Mike of five years from now be very glad that she did? No use pretending that he won't.

'I don't know what I want,' Mike said.

'What about Sally?'

Mike stared at the transmitted image of his ex-wife. 'I don't know. She's gone dark.'

Kim pushed both hands into her hair. 'Dark?'

'She's not answering my calls.'

'Good Christ, what a fuck-up.'

'Thanks, Kim.'

'What will she do if it's Al's baby?'

'How do I know? How would I know, Kim? I just told you — she's not answering my f . . . she's not answering my calls.'

'I was always jealous of her, you know.'

'Of Sally?'

'Of the way the two of you were together.'

A knock echoed through the speakers as Brendan rapped on Kim's door. His voice followed behind, telling her they had to leave in five minutes.

167

'So, what now, Mike?'

'I thought I could come to you.'

'Excuse me?'

'Maybe make it a surprise for Jojo.'

'And when were you planning on doing this?'

'Next weekend, weekend after. I mean, I could come this weekend, if you like.'

Kim laughed. 'Well I don't like, Mike. I do not like one little bit. For a *start*, Mike, your girlfriend is pregnant. You can't just fuck off and leave her on her own because that's what suits you this day of the week. And actually, no — for a *start*, your daughter, who you haven't seen in months, will be devastated. Devastated, Mike.'

'Hold the hell on, will you. For one th — '

'Don't give me that bullshit. Whatever it is, don't give it to me. Faye needs you and Jojo needs you, so man the fuck up, Mike. Okay?'

Mike nodded.

'Okay?'

'Okay.'

'Are you and Faye still sleeping in the same bed?'

'What's that got to do with anyth — ?'

'Two minutes!' Brendan called from outside the room, sounding a little agitated.

'I can tell the time, Bren!' Kim took a breath, tucked her hair behind her ears again.

This minor discord between his ex-wife and the man who'd taken her away was hardly a silver lining to the dark cloud of Mike's life. But in the absence of any other relief, he would take any scraps of light available.

'It's got to do with where you sleep while Jojo

takes the spare room,' Kim said. 'Because she's arriving in three days, Mike — so wash the sheets, buy some food and sort it the fuck out.'

Mike nodded. 'Give her my love, will you?'

'I always do.'

Kim blew Mike a kiss and snapped the laptop closed.

18

Sally had spent the last ten minutes sketching fairies. Marking them out in crayon on thin sheets of A4 paper — flying, sheltering beneath leaves and sitting on polka-dotted toadstools. The proportions were a little off, she thought, but the children were impressed nevertheless.

'You're even gooder at drawing than Mummy' Ada, the youngest of the Johara children at a few months over five, was colouring in the fairies' dresses with great care and surprising precision.

'I'm sure that's not true,' Sally said.

'Is very true,' said Mrs Johara, the staccato rhythm of her knife uninterrupted as she diced an onion at the chopping board. 'Cows draw like donkeys. Donkeys draw like ... what is *jalahastha*?'

Ada put her little hand in the air as if they were in a classroom. 'Hitopotamus! Hitopotamus!'

Maisey, the older of the pair by around two years, laughed. 'She means hippopotamus!'

Ada's features contracted with fast anger. 'That's what I said. You're rude! Mamma, Mais — '

'Girls!' Samna's voice rose steeply. In the following beat of silence, Sally saw the woman's back lift as she drew a slow breath. 'Don't bicker-bicker, girls. Be nice.'

'I used to go to classes,' Sally said, an image of

170

her and Mike in the basement life-drawing classes flickering across her mind.

He had called, several times, in the last few days. But Sally hadn't answered. She wanted to hear his voice; hear him tell her everything would be okay, but she knew that he couldn't. So instead of accepting his call, she had stared at her phone, at his name across the top of the screen, waiting for the ringing to stop.

'Why? Were you bad at drawing?'

It took Sally a second to pick up the thread. 'Actually,' she said, 'I was quite good. But I wanted to get better — I thought I might draw anatomy books one day. Maybe I still will,' she added, although this was more to herself than to anyone else in the kitchen.

'What's 'natummy'?'

'*Anatomy*,' Sally explained, 'is . . . it's how the body works. What people look like inside.'

'Inside!'

'Sure.' Sally pointed at a plump crayon love-heart on Maisey's sheet of paper. 'See that heart? Well, *your* heart' — tapping a finger against the girl's chest — 'your heart doesn't really look like that at all.'

'Mine does!' protested Ada.

Sally shook her head. 'Here,' she said, finding a clean sheet and selecting a purple crayon, 'I'll show you.'

As a junior GP, Sally had loathed and dreaded home visits. Nine times out of ten they were depressing affairs — alcoholics who had dropped off the radar, befuddled old dears who had failed to redeem or renew their prescriptions, victims

171

of domestic abuse, the depressed, lonely, lost and suicidal. But in recent years, it had come to feel like one of the more rewarding aspects of the job. People could diagnose themselves online now and frequently did, appointment times were being squeezed, budgets cut. In the community, though, a doctor could intervene in a way that wasn't possible from behind a desk.

Ostensibly, she had come to visit Nadeem Johara, who she hadn't seen since referring him to the oncologist three months ago. He would be under the care of a skilled and efficient multi-disciplinary team now, including his specialist, radiographer and cancer nurse. A counsellor, too, if he wanted one, but she doubted this jovial man did. His wife Samna, however, might be a different matter.

Mrs Johara had, in fact, been in to the surgery five weeks ago, bringing in the youngest with an unexplained rash on her chest. The rash was nothing: a harmless patch of dry skin that could have flared up for any one of a thousand reasons from a hot bath to a change in washing powder. More concerning was Samna. Bags under her eyes, chewed nails, a reflexive wince whenever Ada's voice rose beyond even a moderate volume.

Samna had declared herself to be 'good good', but the pretence was as plain as the rash on her daughter's chest.

When Sally had knocked at the door, Samna had answered wearing an apron. The woman was surprised to see the doctor standing on her doorstep, having forgotten all about the scheduled visit — 'Head like a teabag,' she had said,

172

making Sally laugh. Samna beckoned Sally inside, apologising and explaining that Nadeem was upstairs, sleeping. She had offered to wake her husband, but Sally insisted this wouldn't be necessary. So, while Mrs Johara continued cooking, Sally had taken off her coat and joined the children at the kitchen table where they had been busy drawing angular cats, happy snails, stick figures and wonky rainbows. Initially shy and cautious, the girls had warmed to 'Doctor Sally' by the time she had finished her first wide-eyed pixie.

Samna shook a jar of spice into a wide pan, the sharp scent cutting through the heavier aromas of onions, butter, meat.

'Is he still taking his statins?' Sally asked now.

Samna used her knife to gesture at an array of pill packets and bottles, lined up beside the kettle. 'Eats more tablet than food,' she said.

'Mummy says Daddy rattles,' Ada said. 'Is that true?'

Sally smiled at the girl. 'Well, he's certainly taking a lot of medicine. What do you think? Do you think he rattles?'

'It's just a joke, isn't it?' said Maisey. She was copying Sally's anatomically correct heart now, complete with chambers, valves and fat vessels.

'That's right. It's just a joke.'

'Do you have to draw hearts to be a doctor?'

'You do,' Sally said, although she wondered if this was still the case.

When she had studied for her degree, her papers had been written by hand, the diagrams painstakingly drawn and shaded with pencil, annotated with black ink and a ruler. Now, with everything done on computers, perhaps the students simply cut and pasted their images from the internet.

'Daddy has cancer,' Ada said, as if announcing that her father had just bought a new pair of shoes.

Sally nodded. 'I know, sweetheart.'

'He said he'll be okay, though,' Maisey added. 'Didn't he, Mummy?'

Mrs Johara ha-hummed an answer, a high, clipped sound that was trying to be optimistic. Sally saw the woman's back convulse under the effort of restrained tears.

'Can you draw a pancass?' the youngest child asked.

'I can,' Sally said. 'But they're rather ugly things.'

'Is Daddy's an ugly thing?'

More than you know, little one. 'Well, it's certainly a naughty pancreas, isn't it?'

Ada laughed. 'Put it on the naughty step.'

Samna made a small, pained sound through closed lips.

'Are you okay, Mummy?'

Still with her back turned, Mrs Johara nodded. After a second, she said, 'Girls. Go upstairs, quietly please, and change out of your school uniforms.'

'But I want to draw a panc — '

'Now, please.'

The girls scraped their chairs back from the table and dawdled off in the direction of the hallway. As their footsteps hammered up the

174

stairs, Mrs Johara turned from the stove, wiping her eyes with her sleeve.

'The house is normally tidier,' she said, the last word stretched thin as it gave way under the insistent pull of her tears.

Sally went to her. She took the wooden spoon from Samna's hand and steered her to a chair at the table.

Mrs Johara regarded the crayon drawings scattered over the table, idly running two fingers along the sweep of a murky rainbow.

'They're good girls,' Sally said. 'Very bright.'

Samna nodded and allowed herself a small smile. Her tears continued, as slow and undramatic as thawing ice. 'He's going to die, isn't he?'

'I haven't seen his notes. People can survive, some people . . . '

Samna looked her in the eye; the silent request for honesty as clear as anything she might articulate.

Sally nodded. And Samna understood, dropping her head and shaking it slowly.

'How are you?' Sally asked. 'I came to see how you are.'

Samna shook her head. 'When he sleeps,' she said, 'when he sleeps in the daytime, I already . . . I already miss him, you know.'

Sally felt the pressure of tears behind her own eyes, but commanded them back.

'You are married.' Samna nodded at Sally's left hand.

Sally turned the hand over, touching her thumb to her wedding ring. 'Almost seven years.'

'Eleven,' Samna said. The tears continued to leach from her eyes, but she allowed herself a smile. 'But maybe not twelve. Not thirteen.' She picked up a crayon, and began fattening one of Ada's small love-hearts. 'The girls,' she began, but her mouth twisted inwards and the tears came harder now.

Sally took hold of her hand. 'They're young.'

'Already I miss him,' Samna said. 'Already so much.'

As a doctor, Sally had been in this situation and others far more desperate and depressing, countless times. Children dying, both suddenly and with cruel slowness and great pain; patients reduced to drooling shells by dementia; families destroyed by addiction and violence and abuse. And she had hardened. She remembered being on the hospital wards a decade and a half ago, crying silently in the staff toilets. And later, training as a GP, seeing the purple bruises on a teenage girl's back and ribs where someone — the girl would not say who — had punched her so hard they had left imprints of their knuckles. That night Sally drank too much with friends, buying round after round in a display of reckless ostentation, boasting about the value of her job whilst belittling those of her friends — lawyers, bankers, consultants. She had vomited in the night and cried over her breakfast. At work that morning, smelling alcohol on Sally's breath, a senior GP had gently sent her home. The woman hadn't said she understood, but Sally had felt that she did. What else wasn't said, but intuited, was that this was the only time such behaviour would be tolerated. And you harden. Her profession nurtured a disproportionate level of depression and alcoholism, but though she had felt the pull, Sally had, for the most part, learned the trick of partitioning her life from those that passed through her surgery.

Maybe that's why she felt Mrs Johara's grief so profoundly now, because she was removed from the protective indifference of the surgery's cream walls and bright fluorescents. In the cluttered kitchen with the accumulated marks and scuffs and bashed corners, the tragedy was amplified rather than muted, and Sally sensed it as keenly as the impregnated aroma of spice and bodies and family life. And her own tears insisted. Or maybe she simply stopped fighting them.

Sally heard one of the children, Ada perhaps, squeal with laughter in an upstairs room. Samna went to rise from her chair, but the sound of her husband's low incanting voice stayed her.

'The giant,' Samna said, smiling.

Mr Johara grumbled something to his children, his rhythmic voice gaining volume before gathering into a deep roar that drew excited shrieks from both girls. Their footsteps drummed the ceiling as they fled across the upstairs floor.

Sally watched Samna as she stared up at the ceiling, as if she could see through the layers of wood and plaster to where her husband now climbed slowly out of bed and plodded heavily after the young girls. *She loves him*, Sally thought. And she envied this woman; she envied

177

the noises and smells and scuffs of this small house, crowded with life and love and latent grief.

'Samna,' she said now. 'How are you coping?'

'I cope,' Samna said. 'I just . . . ' She measured her breath, taking a second to compose herself and master the threatening tears. 'I just cope.' Mrs Johara shrugged peaceably: *What else can I do?* 'I cope.'

'You can come and see me,' Sally said. 'If you feel like it's too much, if you're struggling, you can come and see me.'

'Thank you, Doctor.'

'Sally.'

Samna smiled. 'Sally.'

'Promise me, Samna. You'll come and see me.'

Samna patted Sally's hand before standing and returning to the stove. She reignited the gas ring, then measured out rice from a glass jar into a stainless-steel pan.

'You can eat?' Samna asked, glancing quickly over her shoulder. 'With us?'

Sally indicated her watch. 'Oh, thank you, thank you, but I should . . . ' She nodded towards the door. 'I should go.'

'The girls would like it, I think.'

'That's very kind.' But still not committing.

'Nadeem,' Samna said, nodding towards the ceiling. 'He doesn't eat so much. It's nice to eat with someone, I think.'

'Are you sure?'

Samna nodded. 'I would like it very much.'

'Okay, but I wash up.'

Samna smiled and nodded again.

19

Alistair snored gently as he slept next to Faye. The low, satisfied moan was a vaguely soothing sound, and anyway, better that than anything he had to say. To ask, suggest or insinuate. The sour smell of last night's alcohol seeped out of his pores, and Faye turned her head to look at the black sky through the opposite window.

The film was 'in the can', as they liked to say, and Faye's involvement in the project over. She wished she could say the same for her involvement with this man. But there were still questions to be answered, courses of action to be decided.

'Toss a coin,' Al had said with respect to the latter. They had talked about it before he succumbed to sleep, Al smiling through a thin veneer of impartiality. 'If you don't like the outcome, you'll know what you want to do.'

As if it came down to heads or tails. To carry this child or to end its life.

Both awful, both impossible, one unavoidable.

He had arrived late on Monday evening, with one day's shooting already completed. For a whole day, Faye had entertained the possibility that he might not show — the thought blossoming like a clear space behind her sternum, expanding by degrees with every passing hour.

But when she went down to breakfast on

Tuesday morning, the waitress informed Faye that her friend was waiting, indicating a small table for two in the far corner. Faye's heart sank as Al waved to her across the bright room.

Alistair had been unexpectedly relaxed and charming, standing to greet Faye then kissing her cheek lightly before fetching coffee and fresh orange juice. Over breakfast, he had enquired only about her flight, whether her room was comfortable, and how the previous day's shoot had progressed. His enthusiasm for the commercial had been infectious, putting Faye somewhat at her ease, and after ten minutes, Alistair had excused himself, saying he'd only just landed and needed to take a shower before joining her on set later in the morning.

Having covered off the more technically demanding aspects of the production on Monday — those involving elaborate rigs, zoned-off streets and stunt drivers — Tuesday's schedule was given over to the few shots that required some degree of acting, rather than merely sitting and periodically checking the rear-view mirror. Faye had worried that Alistair might — as he had at the casting — feel compelled to interfere from the wings, driven by a need to demonstrate control perhaps, or out of redirected hostility for Mike.

But Alistair had sat quietly at the back of the room, keeping out of Faye's eye-line and, as far as she could tell, out of the director's ear. When they wrapped a little ahead of schedule, Alistair had clapped along with the rest of the crew, hanging back while she kissed cheeks and accepted compliments.

He intercepted her as she walked off set, the client at his elbow.

'We thought you might like to join us for supper?'

Faye looked from Alistair to the client, polite, expectant. This was Karl's show and, as she was sure Alistair understood, refusal would be awkward. Imprudent, too.

'What about . . . ?' Faye had indicated the room, the crew, the agency, her co-star.

'Small restaurant,' Alistair had said, wincing apologetically. And then, in a stage whisper, 'Terribly expensive, too.'

Faye glanced from the wider room back to Alistair. 'I'd hate them to think you're playing favourites.'

Al laughed. 'They'll get over it. And anyway, we're friends — they know that.'

The client smiled ingratiatingly. 'I thought you were excellent today, Miss White.'

'Faye. Thank you.'

Closure wasn't the word. After all, Faye might be carrying the man's child. But perhaps this was an opportunity to build some kind of rapport.

'No pressure,' Alistair said then, 'if you'd rather . . . you know . . . '

'Well, so long as it's terribly expensive,' Faye had said, 'I'd love to come.'

She glanced at him now as he dozed beside her, unaware that she was holding her breath for fear of waking him. Maybe he had a drink problem, she thought. Not an alcoholic, necessarily; rather that alcohol turned him into a bit of a prick. Some claimed that drink revealed the 'real you', that a person demonstrated their true character from behind a glass, but Faye didn't know if that was true. As if we lived our lives affecting a pretence that dissolved in red wine. Alcohol was mood altering, in her experience, but not necessarily character revealing. It made the meek bold, the joyous tearful, the enamoured aggressive, the faithful flirtatious, the hostile genial. It lowered inhibitions, no argument there, but a person's inhibitions could define them as much as any other trait. Many a morning Faye had woken with a dry mouth and a sore head, wondering just who the hell had filled her skin the night before. Not a problem she had this morning, however. Despite Alistair's efforts to the contrary.

Last night's waiter had introduced, with studied detachment, a new wine with each of the six courses, detailing its origin, delineating tasting notes, and explaining exactly why it complemented, for example, the translucent slices of lightly peppered beef. He would fill Faye's glass first, and at the end of the course clear it away, untouched, before uncorking the next bottle of special reserve whateverorother.

Every time, Alistair would clink his glass against hers. More than once he slid the glass towards Faye's hand. The teasing becoming by degrees less playful and more insistent.

'Just a sip.'

'Just a taste.'

'Live a little.'

'Never have I ever,' holding eye contact as he

clinked his glass against hers once again, 'met an actress who didn't like a drink.'

'Maybe you haven't met enough.'

Alistair laughed a little too loudly. 'Oh I've met more than enough, thank you. Believe you me. More than enough.'

Sensing an awkward moment, Karl had interjected. 'I'm sorry Mike couldn't make it, Faye.'

'Yes,' said Faye, 'he'd have liked to be here. But this man . . . ' She turned to Alistair, patting his arm affectionately. 'This man works him *too* hard. Don't you, Alistair?'

Al put his arm around Faye's shoulder, pulling her towards him and kissing her on the temple. 'How else am I going to get you to myself?'

Karl laughed. 'You have to watch this one, I think.'

Al shrugged, opening his palms to the table. 'Guilty as charged.'

Faye laughed along with her hosts; and it was the finest piece of acting she'd done all day.

When the taxi arrived to take them back to the hotel, Faye quickly installed herself in the front seat. She had anticipated some remark from Alistair, and would, in fact, have preferred any amount of facetious commentary to his looming silence from the seat behind her.

The layout of the hotel was such that Karl accessed his room via a lift immediately beside the reception desk, whereas Faye and Alistair had to pass through the bar area to take a lift at the rear of the building. Alistair invited Karl for a 'nightcap', but he declined and the three said their goodnights and *gute Nächte* before heading their separate ways.

As they entered the bar, Alistair took gentle hold of Faye's elbow and used his eyes to ask again if she would join him for a drink. Sensing her hesitation, perhaps, he said, 'We should talk, don't you think?'

Alistair was the first four letters into drunk by now, his eyes glassy and his tone precarious. But he was right; they should talk — and if not now, when? Moreover, if she declined the drink, she would have to step inside a small lift with this man, and the idea made her feel claustrophobic.

'Sure,' she said. 'But cut that 'just a sip' shit, okay?'

Alistair showed her his palms. 'I'll drink for both of us.'

You have been all night. But there was no sense in antagonising him.

The bar was relatively quiet, and they took their drinks to one of three booths across the empty laminate dance floor. Alistair waited for Faye to sit, and then, instead of sitting on the opposite side of the small table, slid onto the bench seat beside her, effectively trapping her in the corner.

Alistair tapped his glass against Faye's. 'So . . . good health, I suppose.'

Faye nodded, using the straw to stir the ice-cubes in her soda water.

Alistair took a sip of his beer. 'Karl was right — you were good today. Really good.'

'Thank you. It's a good script.'

Al nodded. 'Took a long time to get to it. We

briefed the department in the summer, must have been through . . . God, forty, fifty scripts. More probably.'

'Tricky client?'

Al laughed lightly. 'Tricky Mike. Given the chance, Karl would have likely bought most of the scripts your boyfriend — is that what he is? — anyway, he'd likely have bought most of the scripts Mike rejected.'

Faye ignored the snide incidental. 'Rejected why?'

'That's his job. Creatives, particularly the youngsters, they fall in love with their own ideas — it's what drives them, I suppose. But they get carried away, don't see the flaws and the pitfalls. That's where Mike comes in, with the tough love. It kills him.'

Faye swivelled sideways in her seat, turning to face Alistair and using her knees to create a little distance between them. 'How d'you mean?'

'He just wants to write ads and keep everyone happy. He hates telling anyone they've got it wrong. That they're making a mistake.'

Faye nodded. 'Is that what you're telling me now then?'

Alistair shrugged. 'It depends what you're planning on doing.'

'I don't know. I honestly don't know.'

Sally had, in a less oblique yet more compassionate manner, asked the same question four nights previously. Sitting in a bar across the street from the Brixton Playhouse, Faye fiddling with a Diet Coke, Sally drinking a large glass of red.

185

'Will you keep it?' Sally had asked.

Faye said she hadn't decided. 'But probably not.'

'Can I give you some advice — as a friend?'

Faye remembered the first time she'd met Sally, how she had instinctively felt that they could have been good friends. She felt the same way now; they *could have* been. But everything had changed since Brighton. Everything had changed because of Brighton.

'I have no *ethical* problem with abortion,' Sally had said. 'It's your body, your life, your choice. But it can fuck you up. I see it all the time — women dealing with guilt and depression and regret.'

'Not everyone though.'

Sally shook her head. 'No, not everyone. Just don't . . . don't rush into a decision. Okay?'

'I'll have to do something soon, though, won't I?'

'Do you remember in Brighton?' Sally said, and Faye's eyes narrowed in a pained wince. 'That thing you said,' Sally went on. 'It became kind of a joke: You only regret . . . '

' . . . the things you didn't do.'

'Yeah, well it's not true, Faye. It's a long, long way from true.'

'Evidently.'

'Let's talk in a few days? Let it . . . you know, sink in.'

Faye had promised that she would, but the only thing to have sunk in was a deep sense of uncertainty and confusion. Looked at from the right angle, everything was a thing you didn't do.

Acceptance or refusal, restraint or indulgence, an abortion or a pregnancy.

Sally's concerns had felt genuine and sympathetic; not at all like her husband's contrived and self-serving agenda.

Sitting in the hotel bar, Alistair regarded her with forced sincerity: 'You've got a lot of potential, Faye. They're already working on a follow-up script to this one — who knows, maybe it'll be a continuation. Same characters, same cast.'

'What are you saying?'

'I'm not saying anything. Just . . . you have a lot of potential. Things are happening for you *now*.'

Faye sipped her water. And *God, for a good measure of something stronger . . .*

'What does Mike want you to do?'

Faye shook her head. 'He hasn't said. Whatever I choose to do, he'll support me, is what he said.'

'Even if it's mine?'

Faye shrugged and shook her head slowly.

Alistair leaned forward, extending his hand slowly towards Faye's stomach, but stopping short of touching her. 'Can I?'

The gesture and request so surprised Faye that she found herself nodding assent.

She tensed as he placed his hand on her belly, laying it gently against the thin fabric of her dress. Something changed in his expression and Faye relaxed, softening the distance between this man's palm and the life that lay beneath.

'It'll be okay,' Alistair said.

Faye placed her hand on top of his. She nodded. 'Yes.'

The sound of approaching voices echoed across the room; a mixture of laughter, singing and loud conversation. Faye leaned forward to see their director walking into the bar, Jody and another member of the crew in tow.

'Company,' she said, and Al turned to see Jody walking towards their table. He removed his hand from Faye's belly a second before she arrived at the booth.

'Not interrupting anything, are we?' Jody asked.

'Not at all.' This from Alistair. 'The more the merrier, right?'

'Bruce is getting the drinks. Anyone?'

'I'm good,' Alistair said, raising his pint.

'Ditto,' said Faye, half standing. 'Just need to use the ladies, actually.'

Alistair slid out of the booth to let her past. He held her eyes: *Everything okay?*

Faye nodded, squeezed his arm. 'Be right back.'

At the bar, she stopped to kiss cheeks with Bruce before continuing towards the toilets. Once around the corner and out of sight, Faye walked past the ladies towards the lifts. The lift was four floors up and rising, so she took the stairs, walking at first and then breaking into a run.

In her room, Faye went to the curtains and looked out on the lights of Ljubljana, her own reflection ghosted over the city. Her heart was slowing from her rapid ascent up the stairs, but she still felt discomfited by the conversation with Alistair, and she found herself approaching the minibar as if on autopilot.

She selected a miniature bottle of Hendrick's gin, and a bottle of tonic, placing them on top of the fridge while she undressed and began removing her make-up. In the bathroom, she rinsed a glass under the tap, took it through to the bedroom and added first the gin then the tonic. She held the glass to her nose, smelling the astringent botanicals and feeling the gentle tickle of bubbles against her top lip. No ice, no lemon, but it would do the job well enough.

She carried the glass over to the window and placed the cool tumbler against her cheek, listening to the effervescence and coming slowly to a decision. Or coming to recognise one that had been made for some time.

She brought the glass to her lips and felt the first sip seep into her mouth, cold against her teeth, lively against her tongue.

When someone knocked on the door — one rap followed by another — Faye did well not to drop the glass. She turned slowly from the window to the door, holding her breath as she did so. Perhaps, she thought, the knock had been delivered upon another door at an adjacent room. But even as she formed the thought, she knew it was false. The person on the other side of the door knocked again.

Carefully, Faye placed her drink on the small desk, grateful now for the absence of tinkling ice-cubes which might otherwise betray her.

'Faye? Faye.' The second utterance of her

name not a question but a command.

Of course Alistair knew she was in here. But he didn't know she was awake, didn't know she hadn't jammed foam plugs into her ears and swallowed a sleeping pill.

She held her breath as she crept towards the door.

'Faye.' No knock this time. 'Faye, it's Alistair.'

Could he sense her consciousness? Her proximity?

She braced her hands against the frame, pushing up onto her tiptoes to bring her eye level with the spyhole.

Alistair. Fish-eye distorted, looking left and right along the corridor. He crossed and uncrossed his arms, removed a cotton bracelet from one wrist then placed it on the opposite hand.

Turning his back on the door, he bounced on his toes as if in impatience or deliberation. After half a minute, he rotated back towards the room, regarding the door as if he could see through it to Faye on the other side, balanced on the balls of her toes, forehead resting against the wood, afraid to move for fear of making a sound.

Alistair moved closer to the door, leaning likewise into the wood such that Faye could no longer see his face, only the check pattern of his shirt in extreme close-up. She felt — or fancied that she did — his weight pushing against the door. Heard the timber and the hinges flex.

Quietly: 'Faye.' At a volume she couldn't be expected to hear if she weren't right in front of him. 'Faye? Faye?'

How long could he stay there?

How long *would* he?

He straightened abruptly, banging his fist hard on the door so that Faye felt the force of it through her scalp.

And then he was gone.

Faye poured the gin down the sink, brushed her teeth and slept more soundly than she might have predicted. Perhaps she had found closure after all.

Alistair had been perfectly pleasant at breakfast, to the point that Faye wondered if he had any recollection of banging on her door the previous night. He had been drunk, for sure — although not, she thought, to the point of amnesia. But for all Faye knew, Alistair had continued drinking in his room until the minibar was empty.

She turned to him now, dozing in the seat beside her on their return flight home. The 7.15 from Ljubljana to London Heathrow hit a pocket of turbulence and Alistair stirred, muttering something quietly but not yet opening his eyes.

As they finished breakfast at the hotel this morning, Alistair had passed Faye a folded sheet of paper.

'What's this?' she had asked, reluctant to open it and see for herself.

'Upgrade. You're travelling business class. With me.'

'I was fine in economy.'

Alistair shrugged. 'Gold card. If I don't use 'em, I lose 'em.'

191

It was an early flight, and Faye had decided she would sleep through it, but in the event, Alistair had been out before they left the runway.

He rubbed his eyes now, yawning theatrically. 'Did I sleep long?'

Faye checked her watch. 'Couple of hours, more or less.'

Alistair winced. 'Think my hangover's arrived.' He reached up and pressed the attendant call-button above his head. The flight attendant arrived and Alistair ordered coffee and a bottle of water.

'Got any painkillers?' he asked Faye, after the attendant had politely declined the same request.

Faye had a box in the overhead compartment, but why should she go to any effort to ease Alistair's suffering? She gave him her best sympathetic smile. 'Sorry.'

★ ★ ★

The flight attendant brought Alistair's drinks, and he gulped down half the water in one go.

'Last night,' he said, his head turned away as he regarded the still-dark sky outside.

'What about it?'

'We were talking about the script. About Mike.'

Faye made a noise indicating she remembered.

'When we started out,' Alistair said, 'I'm talking . . . fifteen years back, we were working together on a newspaper brief. Mike had written this script, very smart, very funny. And he was excited as hell about it, we both were. We'd win

192

awards, get promoted, get a pay rise. That's how it works, you see.

'We presented it to Malcolm — creative director at the time. And he sat through Mike's pitch with not a flicker. Asked Mike if he had anything else — any more scripts. And Mike said, 'No. Nothing as good as this.' And Malcolm says, 'Well, I hope you brought a sleeping bag.''

Alistair laughed at the memory. 'Brutal. You can't get away with that now, HR'd be down on you like a tonne of shit. Your Millennials need their hands holding and their noses wiped. Not then, though. So, Mike starts in, telling old Malcy why the script is good, why it's fresh and surprising and whatever. So Malc listens to him, lets Mike say his piece and then he says to him, camp as Christmas: 'You have to kill your darlings, *darling*.''

Alistair turned to Faye now. 'You ever heard that expression?'

'Sure.'

'Cliché, really. But there you go. Mike walked out of there fucking livid. Ranting on about Malcolm being an old fart, how he was stuck in the past, wouldn't know a good ad if it fell on his foot and all that shit. But . . . we had a couple of pints, Mike went back to the office, worked all night and wrote something better. And that did win awards, and we did get a pay rise. And now, Mike is the man in the big office.'

Faye didn't know if Alistair had made his point or if indeed there was a point to be made. She watched him add milk and sugar to his coffee before taking his first sip.

'Did you eat yet?' Alistair asked, and Faye shook her head.

Alistair adjusted his watch, winding it back an hour to London time.

'Reason I was a day late,' Al said, 'is we've got a big pitch coming up. Had the creative review Monday. Got this young team working on it, too cool to comb their hair or pull their jeans up. Anyway, they've got half a dozen concepts. Not bad, but . . . ' He wavered his palm to represent mediocrity. 'So Mike tells them to go back to the drawing board. And it was just the same: them telling Mike why what they'd done was good, how clever and cool it was, how many awards it would win and all that blah. And you know what he said to them?'

'Kill your darlings, right?'

'Almost,' Alistair said. 'He told them to kill their *babies*.'

Alistair let the words hang in the recycled air, his eyebrows raised as he waited for a response. Faye said nothing.

'History repeats,' Alistair said, turning again to the window.

Faye counted to five, found a measure of composure and then thought fuck it. 'There's no need to be a prick.'

Alistair turned to regard her, a look of amusement playing about his lips. 'None of this was my idea.'

'But you did it anyway. We all did it anyway.'

'Why?' Alistair asked, his voice level. 'Why did *you* do it?'

Some form of spite, is what she had suggested

to Sally. A kind of petty revenge for what she had witnessed through the kitchen window. Maybe that was true; maybe it was just a crazy thing to do.

'Maybe I'm just a slut,' she said to Alistair.

He looked hurt. 'That's not . . . that's . . . I wasn't saying that.'

'Well what are you saying, Alistair? Because all this' — she gestured uselessly — 'it's bullshit.'

Faye was moderating her volume, but Alistair glanced about the business-class compartment all the same.

'What do you want me to say?' Faye asked. 'That I did it because I'm attracted to you? Because I want to be with you?'

Alistair clenched his lips together, took a slow breath through his nose and let his mouth relax into a small, resigned smile. He shook his head.

'I don't know what's going on with you and Sally,' Faye said, 'but . . . '

'We're fine. We'll be fine.'

You just bang on women's hotel doors at midnight. And what would Sally think about that? What would she say if I told her? But it wasn't Faye's place to tell tales; she didn't understand what was happening in her own life, so how could she presume to interfere in anyone else's?

'We've had a rough patch,' Alistair continued. 'But we're working on it. This, though . . . ' He waved his hand in the direction of Faye's stomach. 'No one wants this.'

He reached between his feet and took hold of a leather attaché case. Unzipping it, he removed a white envelope printed with a blue and red Travelex logo. Alistair passed the envelope to Faye. 'I'm not trying to be a prick.'

The envelope was unsealed and Faye lifted the flap, revealing a wad of fifty- and twenty-pound notes.

'What is it with you and envelopes full of money?'

Alistair laughed. 'That's a grand.'

'And what am I supposed to do with it?'

They both knew the question was redundant.

'There's a clinic on Weymouth Street. If you're less than fourteen weeks pregnant ... ' A pause.' ... it costs just over seven hundred quid.'

'You said there was a grand.'

'After fourteen weeks — fifteen to eighteen weeks — it's nine hundred.'

Faye looked from Alistair to the envelope.

'After that,' Alistair said, 'we'll need to talk again.'

Faye held up the envelope. 'Does Sally know?'

Alistair shook his head.

'What if I don't? What if I don't want to?'

'Then you're really going to need it, aren't you? And a lot more besides.'

'Fuck, Alistair.' Faye deposited the envelope inside her bag. 'Fuck.'

20

Mike worried that he'd overdone it with the sign.

Princess Jojobee!!!

The surly chauffeurs and taxi drivers clutched their scrawled placards as if they declared the holder's crimes, rather than the names of arriving passengers. Standing among them with his oversized, multicoloured, heavily glittered poster, Mike felt highly conspicuous and wholly unwelcome. As if he were mocking these men and their profession. Passing travellers, on the other hand, appeared to appreciate Mike's efforts — laughing, taking pictures, blowing kisses.

At least the sign was big enough to hide behind — almost an arm's span in width and more than a head deep. In the last week, he'd spent more time working on this sign than he had on billable client projects.

After trying upwards of two dozen typefaces, he'd settled reluctantly on Brush Script. Personally, he disliked the font — he wouldn't allow any of his art directors to use quaintly looping letters, but then, none of them had ever had to design a welcome card for a princess-obsessed six-year-old. Besides, it worked well with the stars and love-hearts.

And then he saw her.

Even at fifty yards, Mike could see that she had changed more than he'd gleaned from their transatlantic Skype sessions. Waist-high to the flight attendant, Jojo had become long in the leg and arm. And although Mike couldn't explain how, she walked differently now; confidently, and without the tottering uncertainty he remembered, or thought that he did.

The flight attendant saw Mike first, offering a quick wave and then directing Jojo's attention to her waiting father. In his imaginings, Mike had seen Jojo run towards him, shrieking 'Daddoo!' as she launched herself into his arms.

Now, she stopped in her tracks, pushing sideways into her chaperone as if for reassurance. The woman bent and said something to his daughter, pointing again at the ridiculous sign. It was too big to hold and wave simultaneously, so Mike set the placard down and extended his hands towards Jojo.

Still holding the attendant's hand, Jojo stopped a pace short of her father. 'Hi Dad, Kathryn has got two dogs and a cat called Whiskey. It's like a drink.'

Mike nodded to the woman and mouthed the words *Thank you* as he opened his arms to Jojo. 'Do I get a hug?'

Jojo shrugged: *If you want.*

Mike wanted, and so he pulled Jojo to him, feeling her weight and warmth and the cotton texture of her hair. 'I missed you,' he said into her ear, and was surprised to find himself on the edge of tears.

'You're squashing me, Daddy.'

Mike relaxed his embrace and Jojo wriggled free. She pushed her hair behind her ears, looking in that moment like a perfect reproduction of her mother.

'So,' Mike said, 'what shall we do now?'

Jojo shifted her weight from one foot to the other. 'Daddy, I need a wee.'

★　★　★

It was late evening when they arrived at Mike's flat, but Jojo's body was still on New York time. And it had an appetite. Mike watched his daughter scoop up a forkful of macaroni cheese, amazed that the child he had created could achieve this simple yet infinitely complex task. Jojo had been four when she moved out with her mother, still unable to tie her laces, still in need of someone to wipe her bottom. And here she was, slim-fingered and dextrous. Becoming her own confident and capable person.

'You're doing it again, Daddoo.' Jojo bugged her eyes to make the point.

Mike smiled at the casual wit of it.

'I'm sorry, Jojo. I've missed you is all.'

'Where's Faye?'

'She's at work.'

Since returning from Slovenia five days ago, Faye had been quiet and withdrawn. His work and her play put them on a different clock for the majority of the week. Most nights, Mike would go to bed alone, waking in the morning to find Faye sleeping beside him. Or waking in the night to find her restless with the heat and

199

hormones of her advancing pregnancy. Their mornings were clumsy with inhibition, but at night — in the concealing dark — they would lie in bed, talking with ease about their days; talking around and glancing past the issues unresolved.

They talked about Jojo — her birth, her absence, her impending visit. The timing was a disaster, but the anticipation of time with his daughter — of holding her small warm hand — had lifted his head. And in the way that a background hum can become most noticeable after it has ceased, the improvement in Mike's mood revealed a creeping depression that had been closing around him. Faye, too, had been energised by the prospect of the little girl's visit. Several times, she had spoken to Jojo through the screen of Mike's laptop, developing a small rapport and growing affection, and both were excited about finally meeting, as Jojo had put it, 'in the skin'.

Faye wanted to buy something for Jojo, and last Sunday she and Mike had taken the bus into town to pick out a dress or maybe a scarf and gloves.

They returned in a taxi several hours later, the boot and back seat stuffed with bags from a variety of shops. Disney bedding and pyjamas, a glow-worm night light, a stack of DVDs, things to make and do and read and watch — tea sets, puzzles, games, books and films. They filled the cupboards and refrigerator with a dozen types of breakfast cereal, bagels, peanut butter, jam, chicken nuggets, waffles, French fries and ice-cream. That night, Mike and Faye had watched *Mary Poppins* together, eating fish-finger sandwiches off their laps and drinking chocolate milkshakes through bendy straws. Faye had fallen asleep before the end, with her head resting on Mike's shoulder, but Mike sat through the last act, crying as Mr Banks took his children to fly their kites. Up in the atmosphere. Up where the air is clear.

'Is Faye's job doing acting?' Jojo asked now.

'That's right,' Mike said.

'Like on TV?'

'She's in a play. Like at the theatre.'

'We did a play in school. I was a tree.'

'Did you have lines?'

'Just brown tights and a green jumper and some paper leaves.'

'You didn't have any words to say?'

Jojo shook her head emphatically. 'It wasn't a talking tree.'

'Right, of course. What was your play called?'

Jojo shrugged her loss in the face of this clearly obscure question.

'What's Faye do in her theatre?'

'She's pretending to be a schoolgirl.'

Jojo's eyes went wide. 'Like me?'

Mike laughed. 'Not exactly, babes. A bit older.'

'A teenager?'

'That's right.'

'Is she a teenager?'

'No, Faye's twenty-seven.'

'That's lots younger than your birthday'

'A little.'

'Mum says she's young enough to be your daughter. But I think that can't be right because

201

I'm your daughter and not nearly even seven almost.'

'Yes. Silly' — *fucking* — 'Mummy.'

Jojo giggled.

'Right, let's finish that macaroni and we can have ice-cream.'

Jojo lowered her fork. 'Really? Daddy Brendan doesn't let us have ice-cream or sweets. Well, hardly never. I had some jelly beans at Eloise's birthday party.'

'When was that?'

Jojo shrugged. 'Can't remember. A while ago.'

'There's a jelly bean shop in London. We could go.'

'Maybe Faye could come?'

'We'll see, sweetheart. She might be busy.'

Mike smiled and wondered if the insincerity would be apparent to a nearly almost seven-year-old. Stupidly, he had allowed himself to imagine Sally might spend some time with him and Jojo during her short visit. Sitting in his office, fiddling with Princess Jojobee's sign and gazing out over the Thames, Mike had seen the three of them — him, Jojo and Sally — posing for photographs at Madame Tussauds; at the zoo, throwing apples to obliging chimpanzees; slowly rotating over the capital in the London Eye; sitting three abreast on the tube home, Jojo dozing between him and Sally, a look exchanged over her head that said: *Soon*.

He'd messaged Sally, asking if she'd like to 'play tourists' with him and Jojo, but Sally had politely declined — *I'd love to, but* — with a non-specific excuse about being busy. Maybe she was. Probably she wasn't, but Mike understood, nevertheless. Everything was in the air, uncertain, confusing. Everything was fucked.

'*Daddoo?*' The inquisitive, mildly irritated intonation suggesting Mike had missed some question or statement.

'Sweetheart?'

'What's Faye's play called?'

'*A Still Life.*'

'What's it about?'

'Oof, Jojo, that's a tricky one. Er . . . life, I suppose.'

A look: *Huh?*

'Having it all — your life — having it all ahead of you. Or behind you.'

Nope, still not getting it.

'It's about . . . I think it's . . . maybe it's about appreciating what you have. Or maybe that you never really can. Until it's gone.'

'Like an ice-cream?'

'Yes, baby. Just like an ice-cream.' Mike stacked Jojo's dishes on top of his own and carried them across to the sink. 'Right,' he said, standing beside the fridge like a game-show host beside a velvet curtain: 'I've got vanilla, strawberry, chocolate, chocolate orange, chocolate hazelnut, white chocolate, and mint choc chip.'

Jojo laughed, showing a large gap where she had lost her front two baby teeth.

'Say them again!'

Mike said them again. 'So, what's it going to be?'

'What do you think, Daddoo?'

Mike went to the cutlery drawer and counted out seven teaspoons. 'I think we should try them all.'

★ ★ ★

After supper, Mike unpacked Jojo's bags while his daughter showered. He wanted to join her, to wash her hair, to stand under the water with her, the way he had done when they still lived under the same roof. He wanted to see his baby girl's naked and shower-red skin, to towel her dry and blow a raspberry on her protruding belly. But it felt somehow inappropriate now, and the realisation of this fact made Mike feel hollow.

When Jojo emerged from the bathroom, self-swaddled and trailing steam, Mike went to warm two cups of milk while his daughter changed into her pyjamas. It was close to ten now, but a couple of hours off bedtime by Jojo's body clock, and Mike thought they might settle down in front of a film for an hour or so. Ten minutes later, he knocked on her bedroom door. When Jojo didn't answer, he went in and found his little girl foetal and sleeping on top of the covers, one corner of blanket pulled over her shoulders.

Mike lifted Jojo from the bed, feeling the surprising weight of her as he held her to his chest. Pushing the blankets back with his foot, Mike sat on the edge of the bed, then lay on his side, bringing his girl with him, her head beneath his chin, the smell of strawberry shampoo coming off her still-damp hair.

Mike woke in his own bed some hours later. He checked the clock — 3:04 — but Faye's side of the bed was empty.

After dozing beside Jojo for thirty minutes or so, Mike had jolted awake with Jojo's hair snagged in his stubble and his right arm fizzing with pins and needles. After carefully and reluctantly climbing out of the bed, he had tucked Jojo in before transferring himself directly into his own bed. Faye hadn't yet returned from the theatre, and Mike had considered waiting up for her, but it was as if his cells had taken on his daughter's fatigue. He didn't even remember falling asleep.

He slid his hand across the sheets to where Faye's bottom would have been and felt her residual heat trapped beneath the duvet. Dogs were barking somewhere in the street, and this must be what had roused him from a deep slumber. Several of them, by the sounds of it — barking, howling, yipping, yowling in a terrible cacophony. And then . . . a mumbling voice (male), a horse whinnying, a cat mewling. Music.

Mike found them in the living room, Jojo and Faye snuggled together beneath a blue blanket. *101 Dalmatians* on the TV. The animals relaying their message from Regent's Park to Hampstead and the Suffolk countryside around the ramshackle De Vil house: *Fifteen Dalmatian puppies — stolen.*

'Fifteen spotted puddles stolen,' Mike said,

mimicking the confused old colonel.

Faye and Jojo turned to see him, the former grimacing an apology.

Jojo pointed at the TV. 'That's what the old doggy said.'

Mike nodded. 'The Twilight Bark.'

'Have you seen it before, Daddoo?'

'I've seen it with you.'

Jojo turned back to the movie.

'Didn't hear you come home,' Mike said to Faye.

'You were deep,' Faye said, smiling. 'Snoring like an old bloodhound. Did we wake you?'

Mike nodded. 'What's this? Movie night?' He folded himself into the sofa, so that Jojo was bracketed between them. Jojo pressed herself against her father's arm — a silent acknowledgement — then listed sideways against Faye.

'Slept on the flight, apparently,' Faye said over Jojo's head. 'Walked into' — a miniscule hesitation — 'our room, about an hour ago. Said, 'Hello Faye, was your play good? Can I have something to eat please?' Just like that, like it happened every night.' Faye threaded her arm around Jojo's back and pulled the girl to her in a slow hug. 'She's *wide* awake.'

'And what about you?'

'I'll cope. Wasn't really sleeping anyway.'

Jojo didn't take her eyes from the movie, mirroring, Mike thought, the drowsy puppies watching the black and white TV in the De Vil mansion. 'Faye? We're going to Madame Tooso's tomorrow. Do you want to come? They have wax people.'

Faye kissed the top of Jojo's head. 'We'll see,' she said. 'I have . . . things . . . '

'And then we're going to Paul's cathedral. He was a sai — '

On screen, Jasper hurled a bottle at one of the puppies and Jojo flinched in shock, leaning now towards her father.

Mike became aware that Faye was staring at him. She held her bottom lip between her teeth, as if unsure whether or not to say the thing that was apparently on her mind.

Mike lowered his voice. 'You okay?'

Faye shook her head. Whispering now: 'When are you taking Jojo to see your parents?'

'Day after tomorrow.'

Faye nodded. 'Okay, we'll do it then.'

'Do what?'

She mouthed the word across the space between them.

'Are you sure?'

Faye nodded, a gesture made slow and heavy with resignation.

21

The room smelled of steel; of glass and white tiles. It smelled of the widescreen monitor, the probe, the tasteful prints on the pale walls. It smelled of nothing and the stench of it was close to overwhelming.

Sally squeezed Faye's hand. 'Okay?'

Faye let her eyes slowly close. When she opened them, she was still in the room, still lying on the bed with her belly exposed.

The doctor was holding a small syringe. 'You'll feel a little scratch.' And she pushed the needle into the skin above Faye's navel.

A cold pinch, the plunger sliding down inside the syringe's barrel. Her skin dragging around the needle as the doctor withdrew it. No blood this time.

The doctor pulled Faye's jumper down over her stomach. 'The anaesthetic will take a moment to work. I'll pop back in a few minutes.'

Faye nodded and the doctor left the room, closing the door behind her.

And what did she make of this situation? Of Sally and Faye and the two men sitting apart in the private waiting room — one of them soon to be revealed as the father. Five to seven days, they said it would take. When she had taken their blood, had the doctor noticed the wedding ring on Alistair's finger, the absence of one on

Mike's? Was she judging them or had she
become immune to the inherent scandal of it all?

* * *

When Faye and Mike had arrived, they had been
informed that the 'other party' had already booked
in and would Mike and Faye like to join them, or
would they prefer to be kept separate? When they
entered the room, Alistair and Sally had stood to
meet them. The receptionist lingered a moment
— perhaps to reassure herself that chairs were
not about to be thrown — before quietly backing
out of the room. Alistair and Mike had nodded
mute acknowledgement, while Sally went to Faye,
taking both of Faye's hands in her own, and then
pulling her into a hug. Faye held the embrace a
moment longer than she might have done, buying
a handful of seconds before disengaging and
facing Alistair, who was loitering in her periphery. He kissed her once on the cheek but they
didn't hug.

'Well,' Alistair said.

And everyone mumbled their own non-
response to this non-statement.

Alistair offered a packet of mints around, and
everybody took one. As if to do otherwise would
be to break ranks and declare oneself isolated.

They stood at the corners of a misshapen
square, sucking their mints, waiting.

When the nurse came in and asked which of
the gentlemen would like to go first, Alistair
stepped forward. The remaining three sat. Sally
asked after Jojo, and the mood lightened a little

when Mike told her about the late-night Disney session.

'Fifteen spotted puddles,' Sally said.

Mike smiled and nodded a short laugh. 'That's what I said.'

'We went to Madame Tussauds,' Faye interjected.

Sally turned to look at her. 'The waxworks?'

Faye wondered why she had felt the need to blurt out this piece of information. 'I had the day off, so . . . ' She nodded in Mike's direction. 'Jojo invited me, didn't she?'

'I've never been,' Sally said. And then, 'She's with your parents now?'

Mike nodded. 'They're having an early Christmas.'

'Cute.'

'Yeah, she's as excited as . . . well, as if it were Christmas Eve, I suppose. I'm going back later today, after . . . you know, after this.'

'Sure.'

There was an expensive coffee machine on a low table, next to a glass bowl filled with candy-coloured coffee pods. The paternity test cost just under a thousand pounds, so Faye guessed they could afford it. She made herself a cup for something to do.

The nurse returned with Alistair and took Mike away.

'So,' Alistair said, taking a seat between them. 'Here we are.'

Faye's bag was at her feet, inside it the Travelex envelope stuffed with fifty- and twenty-pound notes that Alistair had given her. She had considered using the money to pay for the test, but Mike had settled the bill at reception and the moment was gone.

'Here we are,' Faye said.

And how far would one thousand pounds take her?

When they checked in, the receptionist had given Faye and Mike consent forms to sign while she took photocopies of her passport and Mike's driving licence. She could walk out of this room, excuse herself to the toilet; after five minutes or maybe ten, about the time the others would begin to wonder what was keeping her, she could be in a taxi to the airport. But then what? She'd still be pregnant, and there was no running from that.

Sally cleared her throat. Alistair shuffled his feet. 'How long — '

'Five days,' Faye said. 'Five to seven days. So . . . '

'From Wednesday.'

The doctor walked into the room. 'Faye White?'

'That's me.'

'This way please.'

Faye turned to Sally. 'Will you . . . will you come with me?'

They followed the doctor along the corridor to the room that smelled of cold metal and neutral colours.

★ ★ ★

Faye turned to Sally now. 'How long has she been gone, do you think?'

'Three and a half minutes,' Sally said.

'I need to pee.'

'You and me both. Hold it, though, it'll make the scan easier.'

'I didn't realise they . . . ' Faye nodded towards the monitor.

'They need to see where they're putting the needle.'

Faye glanced at a steel dish she had been trying to ignore. On it lay a large syringe, the fat barrel marked in increments counting up to fifty, the needle as long as a kitchen skewer.

'And check you're not having twins,' Sally said.

'Fuck me. I hadn't thought about . . . fuck me.'

'Listen, Faye . . . are you sure about this?'

Faye nodded.

'Of course. But you understand the risks, right? One in — '

'One in a hundred. You already said.'

After resolving to determine the baby's paternity, Faye had gone on the internet looking into prenatal paternity testing. The NHS website outlined the procedure — blood taken from the mother and potential fathers, fluid withdrawn from the womb to harvest the baby's DNA. Largely painless, apparently, but looking at the savage needle, that was hard to believe. The small but not insignificant risk of miscarriage was outlined, too.

Awful, of course, but at the same time a chance — one in a hundred — that all this would go away.

Yesterday, as they strolled past the rows of celebrity effigies, Jojo had held Faye's hand. Small and warm, sticky with sweets and fidgety with life. In the evening, Faye had washed the child's hair in the bath, while Mike 'cooked' fish fingers and chips for supper. And it was impossible not to think of the thing growing inside her belly. Safe in its amniotic sac, incapable of knowing the risks its mother was contemplating for the sake of a name.

Before Faye left for the theatre that night, Jojo had kissed her on the lips, wishing her good luck and goodnight all in the same breath. Maybe because she sensed Jojo was expecting it, Faye had then kissed Mike goodnight too, and it had felt in that moment that they had gone back in time. Or to another time, where things were different and they were happy. When Faye returned home, she had checked on Jojo before taking off her coat. Kissing her in the middle of the forehead. Her own father had called these kisses 'dreamers', and under her breath, Faye wished Jojo sweet dreams before kissing her again and leaving the room.

In the Harley Street clinic, Faye said to Sally: 'We're here now,' and Sally nodded: *It's okay.* 'How long has she been?'

Sally looked at her watch. 'About ten hours, I think.'

Faye exhaled slowly, forced herself not to look again at the long needle.

'Why now?' Sally asked. 'What changed?'

Faye regarded her belly. '*A Still Life*,' she said. Then, registering a look of something like panic on Sally's face: 'The play.'

'You mean . . . but you're not showing. Not really.'

'Enough for the director to notice, though.'

'Oh shit. Really?'

'Had a chat after Sunday's show.' Faye couldn't help a small laugh. 'It must have taken him five minutes to get to the point. Anyway, eventually, he said he'd noticed I was maybe a bit 'fuller'.'

'That's the word he used?'

'On the money, right?'

'God, Faye.'

'Well, it's not like I hadn't been expecting it. And anyway, he deserved to know.'

'You told him you're quitting?'

Faye shook her head. 'I told him I was pregnant.'

'So, you're . . . what?'

'I don't know. I'm meeting him again next week.'

'But' — gesturing at the room, the monitor, the fierce needle — 'you're here. Why are you here?'

'It's . . . I need to know. Whatever I do, I need to know — whose I'm keeping, or whose I'm . . . '

Sally took this in for a moment. 'What does Mike think?'

'We haven't talked about it, not in practical terms. But if it's his . . . who knows? Seeing him with Jojo, it almost seems . . . I don't know.'

Sally nodded. 'But if it's Alistair's?'

Faye shook her head. 'I don't think I . . . '

'It's still a life, Faye. It's still a — '

'Don't. Don't you do that to me. I . . . not you, okay. Don't you — '

The doctor knocked gently on the door before entering the room. 'How are we?'

Faye looked unsure.

Sally said, 'Can you give us a moment?'

'Well, we have other . . . there are other — '

'They can wait,' Sally said. 'Make them a cup of that . . . fancy coffee, or something.'

'I don't think th — '

'Five minutes,' Sally said. Her tone had softened, but even so, it was clear this was a statement, not a request. 'Just give us five minutes.'

The doctor left, leaving the door ajar. Sally closed it then went back to sit beside Faye.

'I'm sorry. I just . . . I'm sorry. It's your choice.'

Faye drew a deep breath. 'What if . . . what if the baby's not right, Sally?'

'What do you mean?'

Faye looked away, looking at the stark walls as she spoke. 'The drugs. We . . . I . . . I did a lot of drugs that night. I drank a lot.'

Sally took hold of Faye's hand. 'Sweetheart.'

'Not just then,' Faye said. 'But . . . weeks.'

'What are we talking about? More drugs?'

Faye shook her head. 'Only drink, but . . . I got pretty drunk a few times, maybe three or four times. More maybe.' Her free hand went to her stomach.

'I don't think you've got anything to worry about. You're young and — from what you're telling me — its not ideal, obviously, but . . . it's a few drinks. I don't think you need to worry too much about that.'

'But you don't know, do you? If I've hurt the baby?' There were tears in her eyes. 'You don't know that?'

'Not one hundred per cent, no. But honestly, Faye, I really don't think — '

'Will the test show it? If there's a problem?'

Sally shook her head. 'Not at this stage. Not that, anyway. They can test for Down's, cystic fibrosis, some others . . . genetic conditions. Do you want them to check?'

'Would you?'

Sally shook her head. 'I — '

The doctor didn't knock before entering, this time accompanied by a female nurse. 'Ready?'

Faye nodded. 'As I'll ever be.'

The nurse switched on the monitor as the doctor pushed Faye's top up to her ribs, exposing the creamy skin of her stomach. 'It's a little cold,' she said, picking up a bottle of gel and applying a layer to Faye's stomach. 'Let's see what we've got here, shall we?'

The screen filled with a swirl of grey, streaked and dragged like smudged chalk on a blackboard. As the doctor moved the probe, a dark empty space appeared on the screen, and for a moment Faye thought she was seeing an empty womb, a phantom pregnancy, and how she felt about that she didn't have time to decide. The space — like a black jelly bean against the shifting grey — appeared to blink, once, then a second time, revealing the life at its centre. No tests were needed — Faye understood immediately that this baby was perfect. Lying on its back, knees drawn to its chest, she saw the child in profile — yes, a child, not a foetus, not this fat-bellied thing with chin and nose and forehead, and wisps of white bone. And now an arm, a hand and surely these must be fingers held in front of its face. Something beating in the centre of its chest. The doctor moved the probe, and the baby appeared to separate into two parts, the illusion of the head coming away from the body before everything blinked out of view and the screen was filled with grey.

The doctor passed the probe to the nurse. 'Okay,' she said to Faye. 'The baby looks healthy and it's in a good position.'

She picked up the wicked syringe. 'It's okay, you won't feel anything.'

'What if it hits the baby?'

'That's why Jane's here' — nodding at the nurse — 'she's going to help me see where I'm going, while I take the fluid. Okay?'

Faye nodded and the nurse moved the probe into position. Again, the smeared greys and whites, the black jelly bean of her womb, and her baby curled up in one perfect peaceful piece.

'Here we go.'

Faye focused her attention on the monitor. Sally squeezed her hand and she felt a firm downward pressure against her abdomen — like a finger pushing into her gut.

'Relax your stomach, Faye.'

Easier said than done, but Faye took a breath and relaxed the tension in her muscles.

The syringe entered the top right corner of the screen, pushing the layers of grey tissue ahead of it, then stopping as it met the resistance of Faye's uterus. Another push and the needle broke through, the acutely angled tip so white in the black space it appeared to flash. This was where the baby's feet were, and the child drew them into his own belly now as if retreating from the threat.

Sally whispered in Faye's ear. 'There's another option.'

Faye flicked her eyes towards Sally.

'And we're done.' The doctor placed the syringe on the tray, and Faye noticed the tip of the needle was smeared with blood.

'Is everything . . . ?' Faye turned to the monitor, but it was a uniform black now.

'Baby's fine,' the doctor said, pulling off her gloves. 'They'll give you a leaflet at reception.'

Sally was still holding Faye's hand. 'What other option?' Faye asked.

'Tonight,' Sally said. 'We can talk tonight.'

22

Alistair and Sally held hands, their chairs separated by a low table on which sat a box of white tissues. So far unused this session.

You can't go back to the way you were, Joyce had told them eight sessions ago. But who was she to make such definitive prohibitions? What authority did this night-school counsellor have to tell him and his wife of nearly seven years what they could and couldn't do?

Perhaps Al had believed her for a while. And then, two days ago, over lunch in a shabby café, Sally had said the words. 'What if we could go back to the way we were?'

'You seem happy,' Joyce said.

Sally answered: 'We are. I . . . ' She squeezed Alistair's hand. 'I think we are.'

Nine sessions now. Nine hours of introspection, accusation, guilt and tears — but they had come this far and they were still together. Side by side and holding hands. The sessions had spanned more than three months — a short or a long time, depending on your perspective. A single season, a quarter of a year, maybe one hundred days.

A lot had happened. But in the context of almost seven years married, perhaps these events loomed less large. After all, it was not their actions, but the consequences — unforeseen and dispropor-tionate — that had pulled everything out of shape. A moment's weakness, not a grand-scale betrayal.

You could blame any number of things — blame the drink, the drugs, the slow attrition of life and age and accumulated disappointments; blame complacency, blame Mike and Faye, blame work, blame time. Isn't it how we move on that counts? Isn't it the way we pick ourselves up that defines our character? And what of seven years from now? And seven again, looking back on twenty years of marriage — down that line of sight, won't this one autumn seem as insignificant as a single fallen branch, dropped leaf or windblown seed?

Maybe, with the gift of distance, the events of that day in Brighton will prove to be the best thing that ever happened to them. Forty-eight hours ago, the idea would have seemed absurd. But as Alistair could testify, a lot can change in a short space of time.

They went for coffee, the four of them, after the test. Faye opposite Al, Sally opposite Mike. The exact formation they had taken around the kitchen table in Brighton, Alistair with his wife to his left and his old friend to his right. He almost said as much, if only to get a reaction. He and Mike had talked haltingly in the waiting room; about Jojo, about the shoot, but they hadn't talked about the reason they were there. What, after all, did they have to say to each other? Their friendship was over now; in a few days the results of the paternity test would propel them along separate trajectories, and they need never speak again outside of the office. And even then, Alistair felt it would be best for all concerned if Mike moved on.

They had sat around the table, not talking, and Alistair had contented himself with sitting back and watching the other three fidget with their coffee cups. Mike stealing unreciprocated glances at Sally. Sally watching Faye with something like professional — or maybe maternal — concern. Faye looking past them all, staring at an inert wall-mounted TV, as if it were projecting some show only she could see.

Sally had looked from Faye to Alistair and smiled; mouthed the words: *You okay?* And those two mute words of concern and solidarity had felt as warm and intimate as a kiss on the lips. *Yes*, he nodded, *I'm all right.*

It lifted him, this further display of the gradual . . . softening, warming . . . returning, maybe, of his wife.

For weeks and months, he had felt Sally drifting away from him, their frayed moorings pulled tight to the point of breaking. They had been sleeping in separate rooms more often than not, an arrangement that had happened insidiously, without discussion or confrontation. Over the years, and with increasing frequency and casualness they had learned the habit of taking to separate beds when one or the other had had too much to drink, or needed to work late or rise early; a cough or cold would be reason enough for a night alone in the comfortable loft room; frequently, Sally would exile herself when her monthly cycle nudged her into hot fretful sleep.

Maybe two weeks ago, Sally had taken the spare room for some reason Alistair couldn't recall, and perhaps none had been given. A night or two later she was still there, and had taken some items — her bedside clock, her good pillow — from their shared room to the spare.

There had been no hostility in the house, and some mornings they would eat breakfast together, talking amiably and easily. One adding milk to the other's tea, the other placing the breakfast bowls in the dishwasher, some of the old synchronicity remaining as they moved about each other in the well-grooved patterns of their life together.

But drifting nevertheless.

And then this weekend, Alistair had felt the tension slackening slightly. Sally had suggested a walk on Sunday and they had wrapped up against the cold and strolled as far as the river. They talked slowly and with long pauses, and for a while, they held hands. Sally's fingers laced through his, feeling both familiar and conspicuous at the same time. When Al had gone up that evening, Sally was asleep on her side of the bed, her clock, pillow and water glass returned along with his wife. Nothing said, but still a feeling that this commonality was fragile.

Sitting in the café after the test, the silence between the four was drawing the attention of the girl behind the counter, and Al felt obliged to comment on the weather and the shortening days purely for the sake of appearances.

Faye had reached into her bag then, withdrawing a white envelope, and for a second Alistair thought it was the money he had given her on the flight back from Ljubljana. His stomach lurched, and he felt everything fall apart — the delicate peace between him and Sally shattering at his feet.

'They gave me this,' Faye said, placing the envelope flat on the table.

The envelope was plain white, no tell-tale Travelex logo. Even so, Alistair could feel his pulse beating in his temples.

Mike asked the question, and Faye answered by pushing the envelope into the middle of the table. 'The scan,' she said. 'The baby.'

Mike looked at the envelope as if trying to see through it. 'A picture?'

Faye nodded. 'Anyone want it?' Turning her eyes on each of them in turn.

Mike looked at her, his mouth open but forming no words.

Faye turned to Alistair, something defiant in her eyes.

Alistair fared better than Mike by a single declarative letter. 'I . . . '

Faye shook her head. 'Thought not.'

She stood from the table. 'I have to go.'

Sally put her hand on the envelope, resting it there for a second before handing it to Faye. The two exchanged a charged flicker of eye contact before Faye gathered up her coat and turned to the door.

'Wait,' Mike rose to his feet. 'I'll walk you to the train.'

The four muttered a crisscross of vague goodbyes, and then Alistair and Sally were alone.

Sally, who had the day off, had suggested lunch, and Alistair, who was largely at liberty to come and go as he pleased, had accepted. It was raining, so rather than venture out into the cold, they ordered bacon sandwiches in the café, something they hadn't done for years.

After the waitress had cleared away the plates, Sally's hand had drifted to the centre of the table, where, thirty minutes previously, Faye had placed the hidden picture of her twelve-week-old baby.

'What if we could go back to the way we were?' Sally had said.

They ordered more coffee and Alistair had phoned the office saying he wouldn't be in for the rest of the day.

In their counsellor's office now, Joyce leaned forward in her chair. Smiling, as if her clients' happiness was down to her guidance, her wisdom. 'It's good to see you turning a corner,' she said. 'It's good to see you smiling. So, tell me about last week?'

Sally looked at Alistair, and Alistair nodded. She squeezed his hand again before saying to Joyce: 'We're thinking of adopting.'

Caught momentarily off guard, Joyce's hands came off her knees and her mouth opened as if to clap and coo delight, or maybe express shock. She caught the gesture though, closing her mouth and sitting back in her chair. 'It's a big decision,' she said.

'We've discussed it before,' Sally said. 'Years ago, when we found out we couldn't . . . you know.'

'I see. And what stopped you then?'

They were silent for a moment, Joyce waiting,

her eyes moving slowly between her two clients.

'It was me,' Alistair said. 'I . . . '

Sally turned to him. 'The timing,' she said. 'After everything we'd been through, the disappointment.'

Alistair understood that Sally was saying this to protect him, and he touched the back of her hand with his thumb. *Thank you.*

She was partially right; they should have waited longer after their final round of failed IVE But Sally had been so broken and desperate and lost that Alistair would have agreed to just about anything to make her happy. They had attended open days, counselling and interviews; they had been vetted psychologically, financially and professionally. They had been told they were perfect candidates for adoption, but despite it all, despite the look on Sally's face, Al had been unable to go through with it. Part of it was fear; children of abusive parents, of drunks and addicts, damaged in many cases but to an extent unknown.

Part of it, too — the bigger part, in truth — was a coldness he couldn't shake and an excitement he couldn't summon. Worse because he could identify the lack — the feeling in his bones after the first time they made love with the intention of making a life. A cellular exhilaration that had dimmed with each successive failure until there was nothing left. An adopted child — someone else's abandoned baby — would be a consolation, a replacement, for the one they had been unable to create, and Al hadn't believed he could ever see beyond that. So he had said no, had denied his wife the one thing that would make her happy again.

But now, Sally had given him a chance to right that wrong.

'I don't want you to be like Mike,' Sally had said in the café, Alistair still reeling from Sally's suggestion. 'Do you remember what he was like after Kim left him?'

He had taken this as a thinly veiled threat of divorce.

'Having Jojo taken away from him,' Sally said. 'It ruined him, Al.'

'Right. But Jojo was . . . he'd lived with her for four years at that point. It's not the same thing as . . . ' He nodded over his shoulder, at the private clinic across the street.

'Did you see how hollow he looked today? That tragic early Christmas thing his parents are doing today, because he can't watch his daughter open her presents on the real day. I wouldn't wish that on you. I'd hate that for you.'

'This is for me? This . . . idea?'

Sally tidied up the packets of sugar in the ceramic dish on their table. 'It's for us.'

'We don't even know whose it is.'

'We will. Soon.'

'Even then, we don't know what Faye's going to do with it.'

'I don't think she knows either. But if we . . . ' a back and forth gesture with her hands, 'I think she might.'

'Have you asked her?' Sally didn't answer, and Alistair recalled watching her slip through the stage door in Brixton two weeks or a million years ago. 'Sally. Have you asked her?'

Sally raised her head and met his gaze. 'Not yet.' A beat. 'Tonight.'

'Jesus.'

'Well, when else? Five days from now it might be too late. This' — Sally tapped her index finger on the centre of the table — 'this could be . . . this *is* our last chance, Alistair.'

A final chance to have a child. A final chance to stay together.

'What makes you think she'll agree?'

Sally shrugged. 'You get a feel for these things, and . . . ' Sally trailed off, resumed worrying the sugar packets.

'And?'

'Money,' Sally said. 'We'll offer her money.'

Alistair nodded, then signalled to the waitress that they were ready to settle their bill.

Sally met Faye that evening, and they discussed the proposition that Faye had been anticipating. The uncomfortable business of compensation had been mentioned but — for now at least — in nothing more than speculative terms.

Faye hadn't said no.

It was illegal, to financially incentivise a mother to hand over her baby; what the penalties were, Al didn't know, but he doubted they would be severe. And besides, if they were careful, no one would ever know. His major concern at this point had been the effect on Sally if the scheme fell through. In response to this small sliver of hope — Faye not telling them to fuck right off — Sally had become invigorated, speculating endlessly on what might be. As part of the scan at the clinic, they had dated the foetus and if the pregnancy went to term it would be born in the middle of May. A gorgeous name for a girl, Sally had said last night. She had drifted off then, but Alistair could see the images behind her eyes, of Sally and her little girl. Or a boy, it didn't matter; it would be Sally's baby.

And it would be his.

Less than a week ago, Alistair had given Faye £1,000 to terminate her pregnancy, and now they were on the verge of offering her a great deal more to keep it. And the startling fact was, Alistair didn't feel at all bad about this profound and unexpected shift. He felt lighter and more optimistic than he had all year. Sally's tentative happiness was infectious.

Mike didn't know, of course. It had been a stipulation of Faye's. Until she knew who the father was, and until she had decided what happened next, there was nothing to be gained from telling him. Al found he didn't care; either way, Mike lost and either way he would find out soon enough. After this weekend, they all would.

'You say the timing was wrong,' Joyce said. 'What's changed now?'

'Everything,' Alistair said. And again, Sally squeezed his hand.

23

'What's an otherstudy?'

'Understudy,' Faye said. 'And the answer to that particular question will cost you two jelly beans.'

'What colours?'

'One blue, one pink with speckles please.'

The kitchen table was a mess of colour; scattered jelly beans from a tipped carton the size of Jojo's head and half a dozen jars of nail varnish from the same shop and the same palette. Jojo picked out the requested beans with her right hand while Faye continued to apply 'Berry Blue' varnish to the thumb of her left.

'Feed me,' Faye said, leaning forward.

Jojo laughed as she popped the sweets into Faye's open mouth.

'So, an understudy? Well, it's like a reserve. No, do you have supply teachers?'

Jojo shook her head. 'I don't know what that is.'

'If your teacher is sick, they bring in a spare teacher, right? From the spare teacher factory.'

Jojo laughed. 'There isn't a factory.'

'Well, maybe I made that bit up. But you've had a spare teacher, right?' Jojo nodded. 'Well it's like that. A spare actress.'

'In case you're sick?'

'That's right.'

Mike was concentrating on a jelly-bean

portrait of the Little Mermaid, but he looked up now, catching Faye's eye. Whatever happened next, Faye would soon need to take a break from the play. Around a week if she had a termination, or a permanent departure if she didn't. Mike flashed her a quick smile and continued applying mint-flavoured scales to Ariel's tail.

'You're not sick, are you?' Jojo asked. 'Like Granddad?'

Mike cleared his throat.

'No, sweetheart, nothing like that.'

'Like what then?'

'It's for just in case. That's all.'

'What flavour's this one?' Jojo held up a black jelly bean.

Faye's mind flashed to the scan of her womb, the smeared greys and whites, and at their centre, the void shaped like a black bean. The appearance of her child inside it, lying on its back, arching its still-forming spine and flexing its separating fingers.

'Liquorice,' Mike answered. 'Or grape. They all look the same to me.'

Faye winked at him, mouthed the word, *Racist*. 'Right,' she pinched Jojo's index finger. 'What colour shall we paint this one?'

'Orange sh . . . What does that say?'

'Sherbet. Orange sherbet.'

'That one. What's her name?'

'Whose?'

'The otherstudy.'

'Ah, that's Florence.'

'If you're not sick, why is Florence being you tonight?'

Faye laughed. 'Practice. In case I explode' — *and I just might* — 'or if I get sick from eating too many jelly beans.'

'Good point,' Mike said. 'I think we should clear these away, Jojo, and have a bath before supper.'

'But my nails . . . '

'After they're dry, then.'

'Can Faye do bath time, Daddoo?'

'If it's okay with Faye?'

'It'll cost you a red,' Faye said.

Jojo smiled and popped a jelly bean into Faye's mouth.

Daddoo. Faye smiled at the moniker, as she did every time Jojo used it. And Mike was a good daddoo, too; attentive, patient, playful. His daughter's bags were packed now, and this would be their last night together for many months. Mike was doing his best to conceal the sadness, but his smile wasn't quite up to the challenge.

Faye hoped Jojo's stepfather (an understudy in his own right) was even half as devoted to this little girl. *Could he be?*

Could anyone other than a child's natural parent love it in the blind fathomless way of shared blood? The child inside her was still a half-formed thing, but already Faye understood what that love might feel like. 'Unconditional' was the word people used, and although its definition was simple enough, the concept had taken on dimension and weight in Faye's mind. In her gut. This no-questions devotion growing apace with the child forming itself out of her material. Could anyone other than a mother

231

project that level of love?

Could Sally?

Faye believed that she might come close. Maybe maternal affection was a thing that flowed from the child, that the infant demanded and stimulated. Faye had heard of women who lactated in response to the suckling of children not their own. Maybe love could work the same way — a child would draw from you what it needed to thrive and flourish.

Faye had not been entirely surprised by Sally's proposition. When Sally had held Faye's hand in the clinic and whispered, 'There is another option', Faye had understood the intimation. There had been earlier hints too, but these had only become clear in retrospect. Sally's unsolicited counsel, her gentle urging away from the idea of abortion. Faye had thought Sally's concern had been for her, Faye, but she saw now that it was for the baby. For the child Sally had never been able to bring into being. And that was okay. It was natural and sincere, and — yes — Faye believed that, given the chance, Sally could love this child to the limit of her ability. Whatever that limit was.

But that could only happen if the child was Alistair's, and that was a less certain thing.

'Are you Daddy's wife now?' Jojo looked from Faye to her father then back.

'I . . . What makes you ask that, Jojo?'

Jojo shrugged. 'Mummy and Brendan are married.'

'That's . . . different,' Mike said. 'They've been together longer.'

Jojo nodded, the answer appearing to satisfy her young logic. 'And they have had a baby.'

Mike and Faye turned to each other simultaneously; Mike smiled, Faye cringed, Mike laughed and then Faye was laughing too, snorting, gasping and crying with the awful fucking irony of it all.

'Did I do a joke?'

Mike kissed the top of his daughter's head. 'Yes, baby. You really did.'

'Phew!' Faye fanned her face with her hand. 'And about time too. About . . . bloody time.'

★   ★   ★

'She told me she loved me.'

Mike turned to face Faye, lying on her side, face half sunk into the pillow, just inches from his own. Her breath smelled of toothpaste and jelly beans.

'And what did you say?'

'I was washing her hair, and she just said it. It's nothing to a kid, is it? They think it, they say it. None of the coyness or bullshit that we deal with. She just pushed her hair out of her eyes, and . . . ' A tear swelled in the corner of Faye's right eye, held in place by the bridge of her nose. Another tear followed behind, dislodging the first so it rolled off her face and into the pillow. 'And she said she loved me.'

Mike used his thumb to wipe Faye's cheek.

'And I told her I love her too. Because . . . maybe it's hormones, I don't know . . . because I love her too. I feel like I do.'

'Thank you.'

'I'll miss her.'

Mike nodded. 'Me too. It's been nice.'

The duality was unintended, but it registered all the same. Beneath the blankets, Faye felt for Mike's hand.

'What if it's yours? If it's ours?' She pulled Mike's hand towards her, holding it against the gentle swell of her belly. Relaxed and soft.

Mike stroked her stomach, a movement of millimetres. Faye inhaled and for a moment they were as still as sleep. A thought lay between them, projected and received.

We could be a family. Could we be a family?

Fatigue and warmth and something else stirred Mike's thoughts, making them hard to discern and hold on to. A week ago — or was it two? — the future had been Sally. But then . . . Faye's belly moved beneath his hand, rising and falling with her slow breath. The future was less clear now; it was forming inside Faye's womb, made with his blood or with Alistair's, the answer just days away. Faye could stop this child, regardless of its paternity, but Mike didn't believe that she would.

What if it's yours?

There would be no Sally in that future; why would she give herself to a man — a fickle and unreliable man — already divided between two children from two different women. They hadn't spoken since Faye's revelation; they had barely communicated, Sally neither picking up his calls nor responding to his texts with more than a handful of careful, efficient words. It was clear that Sally — always the quicker, wiser, more perceptive — had already seen, understood and rejected the possible futures available to them now.

And if instead, Faye carried his old friend's child and brought it kicking and shitting into the world? Sally would leave Alistair, of course, but what of her and Mike? Two weeks ago they could have made it, buoyed up with old love, stubborn optimism and selective memory. But everything had changed now; the story was shameful and ugly and they had each played their part. There was no Sally and Mike, not any more.

Faye moved towards Mike, or maybe he moved towards her. Their faces came together now, nose to nose, close enough to feel the heat coming off the other's lips. The warmth of their breath. Mike's hand slid from Faye's belly to the contour of her hip, drifting over and behind to the small of her back. With gentle pressure he pulled her against him and her hand moved now, mirroring his and making the embrace symmetrical and secure.

'Maybe we . . . '

The remainder of the sentence stopped against the lips of the other, the contact becoming a kiss, Mike shifting his weight so that his head was above Faye's. Her hand moved to the back of his neck and his body responded.

Mike wondered if Jojo would walk into the room now, stopping this thing from progressing any further. He held his breath and hoped that she would. He exhaled slowly, and hoped she would not.

235

Faye whispered, 'They said . . . at the . . . ' The word — *clinic* — would kill this. 'They said I . . . we shouldn't. Twenty-four to forty-eight hours, they said.'

'How long has it been?'

Faye smiled. 'Too long.'

She kissed him, sliding her body beneath the expectant weight of his. 'Be gentle.'

24

Alistair moved on top of Sally, his body
— heavier than she remembered — pressing
down on her chest and hips. He propped himself
up with his right arm, grunting at the effort of it,
running his free hand from her face to her throat
to her breast, dipping his head to kiss her there,
to take her nipple between his lips, his teeth.
Sally felt him harden between her legs; she
closed her eyes and willed the memory of Mike.
But the memory was ill formed, failing to
coalesce against the reality of her husband. It
was as if he had been keeping track; totting up
the nights in separate beds, or under the same
sheets but facing in different directions, and was
now addressing the deficit. Alistair pushed
himself inside her, and Sally worked back
through the calendar — three times now in nine
days.

Before this, before Brighton, before the
counselling even, how frequently would they
make love? Weekly might be a good guess,
possibly more. Friday nights after a bottle of
wine. Sunday mornings following a long lie-in.
The odd surprise, the spontaneous and self-
congratulatory midweek romp, a well-timed
caress that led to the bedroom. Holidays and
weekends away. Anniversaries and birthdays.
Weddings, too, often proved an aphrodisiac. She
remembered Mike's wedding now, how she had

drunk herself insensible — so no whoopee that night.

Sally remembered how her organs had reacted — with happiness and envy — when Mike told her he was going to be a father, the baby due less than nine months after the wedding. The little life coming to them without effort or setback. Too easily, maybe.

Years ago, when Alistair had closed the door to adoption, Sally had considered that she might leave him and adopt on her own. Fear had stopped her, but she was a different person now. And if the child inside Faye wasn't Al's, Sally would move on without him.

Alistair shifted his weight forward and pressed his face against her neck. His breathing came faster now as he gained tempo. Sally repositioned her hands; Alistair's back was damp with perspiration. She lifted her hips to meet him, giving volume to her own breath, a gentle moan at the start of each exhalation to signal encouragement. Convincing enough, and she felt Alistair tense, felt him hold his breath as he attempted to hold back his climax.

'That's it,' Sally whispered, digging her fingers into his buttocks, urging this thing to be over.

She had looked into the logistics and legalities, called agencies. Adoption would be straightforward if the kid was Al's. If they all agreed, the process could happen within a few months. Added to the six months of pregnancy Faye still had to go, there could be a child in a cot at the foot of their bed just nine months from now. The term of a full and natural pregnancy. And this

— this could be its conception.

'Fuck me,' Sally said now, and the effect was instantaneous.

Alistair bucked harder on top of her, driving himself into her with short fast strokes, pausing, tensing, rearing up from the waist as he shuddered to climax. Then rolling to the side, his already soft penis sliding out of her.

Alistair sat on the side of the bed with his back to her, and Sally heard the wet snap of him removing the condom. 'You know I love you?' he said.

Sally sat up and put her hand around his shoulder, leaning her torso against his broad back. She kissed his neck, and then his cheek. 'I love you too.'

Alistair put his hand to Sally's face, pressing it softly against his own. She closed her eyes, listening to his breath, the slowing of his heart . . .

She was in a doze when Alistair stood and walked quietly through to the bathroom.

As she listened to him pee, Sally opened her bedside drawer and found the box of antidepressants Mike had entrusted to her almost two years ago. 'Meant for someone else,' she thought, and wasn't the same true of her, or Mike, of the unborn baby growing inside Faye.

And now, in the semi-darkness of the room, through half-closed eyes, she could see the image of Mike before her. Sitting on the edge of the bed and holding her hand the way he had in Brighton, before they made love. Before it all turned bad. They had been so close to being together.

'More than anything,' is what she wanted to whisper to Mike in this stolen and imagined moment. But it's not entirely true. The baby is the thing she wants more than anything, and if it must be one or the other, then it will be the child. She has considered every scenario and eventuality, including one in which Mike is revealed to be the father — in which Sally gets to have it all.

'What do you think?' she whispered to Mike.

But Mike wasn't there and he didn't hear.

Just as well, Sally thought. This idea is too complex and awkward and counter-everything; too sprawling to hold in your head, too jagged to pass through your mouth.

For now it is. The results are due any time in the next three days; maybe they will bring perspective.

In the bathroom, Alistair flushed the toilet. Sally popped one of the oval pills out of its blister strip and swallowed it with a small sip of water.

25

Unhampered by sentiment or pretence, Jojo had been giddily excited about returning home. To her mother and Brendan, her sister and friends and T-ball and ballet and life without Mike. 'Home.'

It had been a little after 6 a.m. when they'd checked in at the airport, but the woman at the desk had made a fuss of Jojo despite the early hour — admiring her candy-coloured fingernails, asking about her trip, listing the in-flight movies — as she scanned in £65 worth of excess baggage. An extra suitcase filled with new clothes and books and dolls and souvenirs and jelly beans. A teddy, too, for her baby sister; a box of Earl Grey tea for Kim. Nothing for Brendan, he'd taken enough from Mike already.

It was good, of course, that Jojo was happy — better than a hysterical 'Don't make me go, Daddoo' crying jag — but, yeah, a few tears would have been appreciated. And now she was gone — not yet airborne, but on board. Waiting. And already he could feel her absence, as if they were connected by invisible wires that would pull a part of him loose as her plane left the ground.

Faye held his hand as they stared out over the runway, reading his thoughts and answering by resting her head against his shoulder. They had watched Jojo through the large glass window, walking across the tarmac and ascending the steps into the gigantic plane. They had waved — Mike and Faye — but Jojo hadn't seen them. The doors had closed, the steps were withdrawn.

Last night, as Faye slept beside him, he had climbed out of bed to look in on Jojo. Being deliberately noisy, or, at least, not deliberately quiet. If he accidentally woke her, then they could have cuddled up under a blanket and watched one last film. *Chitty Chitty Bang Bang*, he'd thought, the flying car and foreign lands cranking up the emotion between Daddy and his little girl — maybe they'd cry a little, but he would comfort Jojo and tell her again how much he loved and missed her. But Jojo hadn't stirred, even when he kissed her firmly on the forehead, even when he whispered, 'I love you, Jojobee', even when he shook her shoulder.

Faye had volunteered not to come, to give Mike these final hours alone with Jojo, but he sensed she wanted to be there, to say her own tearful goodbye at the departure gate. And Jojo, too, would want Faye to see her off. So he had loaded a sleeping Jojo — still in her pyjamas — into the child seat, and Faye had waited with her in the car while Mike brought down the bags.

Eight days ago, he had bought a kite, thinking they might fly it like the born-again Mr Banks had done with his children. But they never had; a combination of time and weather conspiring against them. As he'd packed the boot of the car, Mike had placed the kite on the back shelf, imagining even then that they might stop en route to the airport and send the thing up. But as they drove through the quiet streets of Putney, it

242

was as dark as midnight and the dashboard thermometer had the outside temperature at a bitter four degrees.

One more thing he had failed to do.

Faye yawned.

'What now?' She asked, still staring ahead at the restless aeroplane.

She was talking about last night, but Mike had no answer to that question. He sighed. 'I'm presenting you,' he said.

Faye hesitated for a second before remembering. 'The commercial. When?'

'End of the day, but I have to go in after . . . ' He nodded out of the window. 'Stuff to catch up on.'

'Have you even seen it yet? The commercial.'

'Jody emailed me a rough cut.'

'And?'

'It's good. You're good.'

Faye nodded. 'Well, present me well.'

'You can count on me.' An internal wince; everything now was open to interpretation. Everything could be taken two ways. 'You on tonight, or is it the *otherstudy*?'

Faye smiled at the shared joke. 'The other-study,' she said. 'I could cook supper. If . . . if you wanted?'

Mike nodded, smiled. 'That'd be nice, but you . . . '

Reading his thoughts again, smiling: 'I may be a lousy cook, but I can drive a microwave. I'll get a ready meal. A nice one.'

Mike laughed. 'Sounds good. What will you do today?'

'Sleep. I'm going to go home and sleep. All day if I can.'

Outside the window, the aeroplane rotated into position at the end of its runway. A striped orange and white windsock caught the breeze.

Mike turned to Faye. 'When's the last time you flew a kite?'

'What? Not since I was . . . God knows, why?'

'I'll tell you on the way home.'

'Well aren't you a man of mystery.'

Jojo's plane began moving, rolling slowly forward. It was hard to get a sense of the acceleration that he knew Jojo must be feeling against her chest and belly, but the tail of the plane dipped towards the tarmac, the nose lifted and the craft floated clear of the ground. Rising gently and shrinking away from him, the plane disappeared to nothing. The invisible cables yanked tight against his guts, and Mike felt they might just pull him to his knees.

26

They had flown a kite, and it had pulled through into her dreams. Trees and cloud and unspooling twine. A deep sleep, uninterrupted by noise, bladder or her subconscious mind. Faye laid her hand on the clock and the numbers glowed in the darkened room; she had been out for almost four hours. She lay back in the warm bed, closed her eyes and dozed, one foot in the waking world, the other dangling over the precipice of sleep, her thoughts as shifting and shapeless as smoke.

They'd driven back from the airport in something like silence. As if Jojo had reminded them how to communicate, but had now taken that knack away. Entering London, they had hit rush-hour traffic; the cars and bikes and pedestrians, all eyes ahead and heads down. Mike had parked in Putney and they bought coffee from an Italian deli, assembled a kite on the heath. Was that real or part of the dream? Real, she thinks; in a dream it would have been less sombre, more colourful. They had left the house before sunrise, but the day had begun now, albeit in mist and grey and monochrome. Maybe Mike had thought it would be a joyous thing, a romantic thing even, but the kite was as reluctant to fly as the commuters were to arrive at work; the hunched figures shortcutting through the park, feeling ridiculed by these two fools and their uncooperative kite.

They had made love. Moving slowly and silently so as not to disturb Jojo. So as not to disturb themselves. No one initiated it, it had simply happened. Briefly, Faye considered the possibility that it hadn't in fact happened, that her dreaming mind had imagined his face against her face, his body against her body, his cock hard and hot inside her. But it was real and her skin remembered.

Fifteen minutes or more had passed — the simple mathematics eluded her — and when Faye drew the curtains now, the day was bleeding colour and fading to grey. She needed to pee, but something held her in front of the window. A certainty that when she left the bedroom she would see mail piled at the base of the door. Perhaps it was nothing more than dread; she would step into the hallway, there would be nothing, and she would forget the idea had ever occurred to her. Or maybe her sleeping mind had registered the flat ka-clink of the letter box, the slap of paper on the white tiles. Two envelopes to this address; one bearing Mike's name, one Faye's. Another on the doormat, or halfway through the letter box, at Alistair and Sally's house. The sky changed before Faye's eyes.

A slow imperceptible shift from one thing to another.

To an early dusk, the roads and pavements not yet flowing with the commuters who would soon be returning to their homes and families and lives, whether happy or sad or hovering between both.

Walking the steadily darkening streets, Faye had no destination in mind. She simply moved, wrapped against the damp cold, her bag heavy with the weight of the brown and as yet unopened envelope. It would yield a name, but not an answer. Faye would still be pregnant; hard decisions would still need to be made. 'Flip a coin,' Alistair had said.

But while she walked, all the potential outcomes and impossible choices were held in check, contained inside the brown envelope, contained inside her bag. And so, Faye kept walking.

Christmas was looming. The supermarkets were pushing big tubs of chocolates and the local Tesco was doing two for one on Baileys. 'Tis the season of make up or break up, Faye thought, and wondered whether she and Mike would be unwrapping their surprises together or alone.

He and Al would be at work; 'presenting you', Mike had said. Sally would be behind her desk, administering good news and bad.

★ ★ ★

Her feet were sore and she had a dull pain in her belly. A stitch, probably, from all the walking — she had no watch, but it was fully dark now and the roads were clogged with traffic. She hadn't eaten since eleven and felt unsteady on her feet.

Faye sat on a bench and realised she was back where she'd been earlier this morning — maybe seven hours ago — flying a kite and watching the dots of aircraft in the morning sky. The bench was wet beneath her.

She felt again the twinge in her side, the dampness across her buttocks and her heart lurched with sickness and dread. Afraid now to move, to know, Faye slid her hand beneath her coat, feeling the wetness on the seat of her jeans. She counted to five and then to ten — *please, no* — and brought her hand out from beneath her. Just water. The bench was wet from a day's rain, nothing more. The pain in her side — a stitch — was subsiding and she felt relief seep down from her scalp and across her back and chest. Just water.

She opened the envelope, two sheets of paper, each bearing her name and that of a different 'alleged' father. The word — *alleged* — reeked of accusation and Faye felt that judgement was extended to her as well as the men. Columns of numbers, words — *locus* and *allele* and *polymorphism* — which meant nothing to Faye. Probabilities, too — 0 and 99.99999%. One man had been ruled out as the biological father of the 'tested child'. Another 'could not be excluded'.

99.99999% was a little way short of absolute, but with one alleged father excluded from the reckoning, Faye figured it was close enough.

27

Faye loomed large in the room. The child clutched to her chest, the father looking on like he was the luckiest guy in the whole wide fucking world.

The car manufacturer's logo and strapline faded up bottom and centre. 'Drive Your Life'; a platitude and a nonsense. Not Mike's finest work, but, considered in personal terms, possibly his most ironic.

The director aimed a remote at the giant plasma, freezing the action for maybe the tenth, twelfth or fifteenth time in the last two hours. Mike knew the beats of the commercial by heart now: Faye at her bedroom mirror, her face reflected in the apartment window, her eyes framed in the car's rear-view and wing mirrors, her image distorted across the windscreen. It was a commercial of reflections, an accidental visual theme that only now occurred to Mike. Even the ending: Faye regarding her child, her affection mirrored in her on-screen husband's eyes.

The final item on the agenda was music, and they were now running the half-minute commercial against various tracks, each colouring the narrative with a different mood, the score lending drama, pace, warmth, humour. As Faye's silent image waited, Karl compared notes with the director and producer, deciding what would be the tone attached to this slice of contrived life. Mike knew that the lazy acoustic track would overlay the emotion that the camera had failed to capture, but he lacked the enthusiasm to give breath to his opinion. The meeting had gone on long enough and he had no desire to prolong it.

He looked again at Faye and her thirty-second family; the handsome husband, the perfect child. His eyes drifted to Faye's belly, to the unseen presence gate-crashing this commercial, insisting itself into their lives. Soon it would be identified as either his or Al's, but regardless of the child's paternity, regardless even of whether it was born or edited out of existence, it would change them all profoundly and forever. Mike glanced across the room and saw Alistair regarding the same image, reflecting Mike's own expression, thinking the same thoughts or shades of such. Sitting back in his chair, one arm crossed over his chest, he was a study of silent reflection — his right hand cupping his face, thumb against cheek, two fingers lying over his lips as if to contain the ideas he was contemplating. Al had been largely quiet throughout the presentation, allowing the producer to run the meeting and only commenting when addressed directly. It seemed to Mike now that this must be harder for Alistair than it was for him. Mike's thoughts were tinged with optimism; there were wisps of hope or consolation in every outcome for him now; but the same could not be said for Alistair.

The paternity results and subsequent decisions would bring relief or heartache and no in-between. Even the former providing only a temporary reprieve, a brief stay, before Sally and Alistair's marriage crashed to its inevitable conclusion. Al had been seduced, cuckolded and betrayed, and there was more hurt in store. No matter how you cut it, there was no happy-ever-after freeze frame for Al.

Perhaps sensing this scrutiny, Alistair turned away from the screen and regarded Mike. He sent a small smile across the boardroom then tilted his chin towards the image of Faye looking down on them, her advertising smile disguising, they might imagine, her deeper feelings of admonition, exasperation or despair. Mike matched Alistair's smile — they understood each other, and each laughed behind a closed mouth, acknowledging the joke and the absurdity before them.

Al's phone went first, the generic ping of an incoming message. And in that moment of shared prescience, even before Mike's phone echoed Al's, they both understood that the time had arrived.

Al picked up his phone and Mike reached for his own.

Mike took in the short message with a single glance. Then read it again — the simple statement and request. Across the table, Alistair was staring intently at his own phone, motionless until he drew a long breath, then placed his phone on the table and turned to Mike. It was done.

The meeting continued around them. Faye stared down from the screen.

Mike looked again at the message:

251

We need to talk.

Can you come home?

Eight words — so simple and yet so difficult to assimilate. He glanced at Al, and Al nodded in confirmation. Someone pressed a button and the commercial began again. Mike stood from his chair and left the room.

As he walked back to his office, the ground felt uneven beneath Mike's feet. As if the building was being buffeted by the uneasy Thames, as if — *wishful thinking* — this whole thing was simply a bad and confused dream.

He thumbed his phone into life, reread the message and hit Faye's number.

Her phone went straight to voicemail. He tried a second time and a third, each with the same result. He was about to try Sally when Alistair arrived.

He stood in the doorway of Mike's office, his own phone clutched in his fist. 'Can I come in?'

Mike nodded as he pulled on his jacket. 'I have to . . . sorry about . . . ' He nodded along the corridor. 'I needed to get out of there.'

'Yeah. Was that . . . ?' His eyes going to Mike's phone.

'Faye, yeah.'

Al held up his own phone. 'Sal. I guess they talked already.'

'Looks like.'

'So . . . congratulations, I suppose?'

Mike looked hard at Al, searching his face for signs of spite or bombast, but he found none. Only sincerity.

'I'm sorry,' Al said, 'about the way things

252

. . . about the way everything went, the way it all . . . you know.'

Mike nodded: *I understand. It's okay.* 'I need to go. Faye . . . we've got some talking to do.'

'Sure. Of course. Give her my . . . give her a hug from me.'

'I will.'

'Listen, if you want to talk about this' — Al nodded in the direction of the meeting: Faye looping through her perfect life with her perfect child and perfect husband — 'I'll make up some excuse and we can get a drink somewhere.'

Mike shook his head. *There's nothing to say.* 'Thanks, but . . . I really need to go.'

'Another time,' Alistair said.

'Yeah. Another time.'

⋆   ⋆   ⋆

We need to talk.

Can you come home?

On the train, squashed in among the returning commuters, Mike read and reread the message. Holding his phone close to his chest, shielding it from prying eyes that would surely read between these two short lines. As if a tired banker or schoolteacher would read the eight words over Mike's shoulder and know what they had done in Brighton, and how that night had now played out . . .

He put the phone in his pocket. Took it out and again read the message he knew by heart. Checking again the sequence of words and the order of the sentences. Reading it in tones of warmth, urgency, accusation, trepidation.

It never occurred to him that the child might not be his, and in the days to come — the message still lodged in his phone — Mike would ask himself why. How had he missed the deliberate absence of any tone at all, the careful ambiguity, the implied apology? He had missed it, he would come to conclude, because he hadn't wanted to see it.

He would wonder, too, at Al's attitude in the minutes after the news had dropped. At the conciliatory tone Mike had interpreted as well-meaning sympathy. And maybe this was partly true, although not for the reasons Mike had first assumed. He would come to understand that Al's mollifying attitude was born out of something closer to guilt. 'I'm sorry,' Al had said, knowing the news — unimaginable to Mike — that was waiting at home for his old friend.

'Congratulations', too. Mike taking this as confirmation of his — Mike's — paternity. Not understanding until days later that Alistair was instead congratulating Mike on having escaped any consequences or responsibility.

But these were deliberations for another day; heading home now, in a state of nervous ignorance, Mike concentrated on Faye and the baby he mistakenly believed to be his. He forced himself not to think about Sally, because he didn't know what to think about Sally. Or, more accurately, *how* to think about Sally. How to hold that disappointment in his mind while *his* child was flexing its legs inside Faye's belly. That was the future he'd been handed. He had to focus on Faye now, on the baby. And he couldn't do that looking backwards.

He held his mind against a single possibility, seeing the good. Understanding how time would make this outcome the only one there had ever been. He counted down the stops, the carriages emptying as the train travelled south, disgorging passengers to their empty flats or houses full of family.

He read the message again, his attention narrowing to the final word. *Home.*

Not, *Can you come back to the* flat? But: *Can you come* home?

At his station, Mike walked past the flower vendor then doubled back and nodded to the amaryllis, their livid petals evoking images of flesh. One bunch seemed mean and thin, so he bought a second. Carrying them towards the house, though, the twin bunches seemed too much and Mike considered discarding one but at the same time knew he wouldn't. He would explain this floral angst to Faye and they would laugh about it, it would become an anecdote and amaryllis would become their flowers. To be bought on Faye's birthday, the child's, maybe anniversaries too.

Fumbling for his keys, Mike laid the flowers on the doorstep.

★ ★ ★

He was carrying flowers.

For a moment, it was as if he hadn't seen Sally, although his eyes had passed over her, taking her in before continuing on to Faye. Sally watched his expression shift, from nervous expectation to confusion. His hand dropping slowly, lowering the flowers from his shoulder to his hip, his smile slipping at the same speed as he took in the situation before him.

Sally's stomach clenched against the curdling emotions. Fear, guilt, elation, heartbreak. She wanted to stand and hug Mike, to tell him she was sorry.

She watched him scan the papers on the coffee table; the official letter with its 'alleged' fathers and revealing percentages; Sally's notepad, scrawled with dates and underlined numbers; the black and white scan of the twelve-week-old baby; the sealed brown envelope.

They were all on their feet, although Sally didn't remember standing. Mike placed the flowers on the bookshelf, as if unsure right now what to do with them. He went to Faye, kissed and then hugged her. He turned to Sally, said, 'Hey,' kissed her cheek.

Mike unbuttoned his coat, but didn't yet take it off. 'So,' he said. 'What's going on?'

Faye sat back down on the sofa, but Mike made no move to follow. Sally felt that whatever she did now would be an act of allegiance or solidarity. She sat. And still, Mike remained on his feet. Sally attempted to read his thoughts, to discern what he had seen and what he under-stood, but she found nothing.

Faye gathered the papers into a thin sheaf. 'Sally and Al,' she said, pausing, hoping perhaps that Mike would join the dots and spare her from saying what needed to be said.

Something near his feet caught his eye, and Mike bent to retrieve it.

'Jojo must have left it,' he said, placing a red hair clip on the table.

'The baby,' Sally said. 'Me and Alistair, we're going to . . . we're going to take it. Take care of it.'

Mike turned to look at Sally; he looked almost amused in his incomprehension.

'Adoption,' Sally said. 'We'd like to . . . to adopt the baby.'

'You can't.'

'It's what I want,' Faye said. 'I can't . . . ' Her hand went to the scan on the coffee table. She picked it up and placed her index finger against the image, against the child's round belly. 'But I can't keep it either. This way's best for everyone.'

There was an urgency to Mike's voice when he spoke. 'What about me? It's my baby too.'

Sally's hands went to her mouth and Mike caught the gesture. She tried to take it back, to recover her composure, but realisation was dawning behind his eyes now. Mike stared at Sally and she shook her head slowly. 'I'm sorry.'

'What?'

Faye stood and went to him, taking hold of his hand as she spoke. 'It's not. It's not your baby.'

Mike took his hand from hers, took a backward step away from her. His eyes went again to the coffee table and the tidy stack of papers. The brown padded envelope that could only contain cash.

Mike pointed at this now. 'How much?'

Faye: 'It's not about that.'

'No?'

'No. It's about the baby.'

'It's Alistair's,' Sally said. 'It's his baby. It'll be ours.'

'How much?' Mike said again.

'Mike,' said Faye, 'don't turn this into — '

'What? Into what, Faye? I thought you . . . ' His eyes went again to the pregnant envelope. 'I thought you were . . . '

Faye shook her head, trying but failing to fight the tears. 'Please don't.'

Mike picked up the brown envelope, weighed it in his hands. His lip curled as if the thing he were holding was foul and contaminated and he dropped it back onto the table.

'You're *selling* your baby?'

'It's not like that.'

'Well it sure looks like it.'

'You bastard. You bastard!'

'Really? I'm the vic — '

'Mike,' Sally interjected, her voice sharp. 'Don't be a . . . ' She trailed off.

Mike looked at her like she was worthless. 'You know this won't save your marriage, don't you?'

'Mike, I know this must be . . . confusing.'

'I'm not confused. I was. But . . . ' He shook his head. 'I'm not confused at all.'

Mike turned to leave the room, stopped and turned to Faye. 'I think it would be best if you weren't here when I get back.'

'Mike, please. Where will I . . . ?'

'Not my problem. Spend some of that money

on rent somewhere.'

'It's late,' Sally said. 'Why don't w — '

He turned to Sally. 'Here's an idea: why don't you move her in with you? Put her in the spare room before you turn it into a nursery.'

Sally held his gaze. 'You're better than this.'

'Yes. I know.' Then to Faye, 'Two hours.'

On the way out, Mike slammed the door so hard it made Sally flinch.

28

The space felt womblike. Enclosed and softly lit, the walls painted a deep maroon.

Faye closed her eyes and held her hand to her stomach, feeling its subtle convexity and warmth. Whether or not she was 'showing' remained a subjective issue. Not that it mattered any more. She had the lapel badge now — *Baby on Board* — declaring her 'condition' to anyone who cared to know. She hardly needed it, but Sally had insisted.

Faye removed her top and then her trousers.

There was a visible groove running around her belly where the waistband had cut into her skin, the buttons leaving two stacked circles beneath the deeper indentation of her navel. They looked like pale traffic lights, showing nothing, neither stop nor go.

If she didn't want to walk on stage looking like a magician's assistant who had been sawn in half and neatly put back together, she would need to wear something looser fitting before leaving for tonight's performance.

Seeing Faye for the first time, an audience member might see the gentle swell of her stomach as nothing more than a few pounds of padding. Maybe they wouldn't notice at all. But give it two weeks, give it four, and the audience would start questioning the script — wondering why the art teacher had missed what was so evident to the paying guests: *The girl is with child, sir.*

Faye huffed a small laugh.

'Okay in there?' A shop assistant's voice on the other side of the changing-room curtain.

'All good,' Faye answered. 'Just . . . all good.'

All good.

The crew knew now. Her co-star, Gareth, had seemed genuinely happy for her, saying: 'Children are a gift.' Telling Faye she would make a 'wonderful mother'.

(But I won't, will I? I'm giving that gift away.)

No one had said anything, but her revelation had compromised the performance. Gareth kissed her differently now, handling Faye delicately — as if she might break or go into premature labour all over his chinos. She might have been able to pass this off as simple paranoia, except she saw her suspicions mirrored in the director's eyes.

But it would be over soon. She had just over one week left before taking her final bow on the Brixton stage.

And then what?

Then the role of happy expectant mother. A twenty-six-week run playing for an audience of two. Faye pulled on the maternity trousers and inspected her reflection; she looked more pregnant now than before. She slipped out of the trousers and sat on the low bench.

Faye wondered how long she could stay in this small cubicle before the shop assistant called security. Or an ambulance. They must be on permanent red alert, she thought; all these pregnant women bending and straining within a confined space. And if the physical effort wasn't enough to induce labour, the price tags just might.

'Do you have them in the next size up?' Faye asked.

'Sure. Same colour?'

'Yes. Maybe the coral too.'

'Coral and taupe, both in a fourteen. Perfect.'

It was a long fucking way from perfect, but it should be good for another five, maybe ten minutes of seclusion.

She had a flat now, but was in no hurry to be there. A one-bedroom pad within sprinting distance of Al and Sally. Not big by any stretch of the imagination or estate agent's tape measure, but it felt empty nevertheless. Eating a meal for one in front of the TV, sleeping on the left side of the double bed, eating her cornflakes alone at the kitchen table (the sad acoustics of single spoon and bowl). Faye felt that if she sat still for long enough, she might simply fade out and vanish.

She had paid the rent and deposit from that heavy envelope full of twenty-pound notes. Sally and Al could pay the landlord directly, of course, but it would be better — they had decided — if their financial involvement remained hidden. 'No paper trail,' Alistair had said, relishing the role, it seemed, of covert operative.

For two nights after Mike accused her of selling her baby, Faye stayed and cried with Sally and Al, sleeping in the loft room of their immaculate five-bedroom house.

The room had been decorated tastefully with simple prints and solid wood furniture. A chest of drawers stuffed with neatly folded summer clothes; a low table bearing a stack of magazines: *Elle Decoration, Homes & Gardens*; a leather armchair in which to read the magazines or contemplate life. That first night, recalling Alistair's behaviour in Slovenia, Faye had pushed the armchair up against the bedroom door.

The bed had been made up with clean sheets, and despite her unease, Faye slept for more than ten hours. It was after nine when she woke, but Alistair and Faye were waiting for her down-stairs. They picked up the previous night's conversation, making plans and arrangements but not once mentioning Mike. Alistair made Faye breakfast of coffee and scrambled eggs whilst Sally juiced oranges. Once Faye had eaten, Sally handed her a box of vitamins and a jar of folic acid. As she washed down the tablets with fresh orange juice, Faye had felt the walls closing in on her, pressing against her back and elbows and knees, compressing and confining her. Recalling the sensation now, the cubicle felt uncomfortable, oppressive, hot — less like a womb and more like a cell.

'Okay in there?' The voice on the other side of the curtain again.

'Great.'

The assistant passed the clothes through the curtain and Faye dropped them into a heap on the floor.

Contrary to Mike's suggestion — or accusa-tion — her room at Sally and Alistair's would not become the nursery That would be the room next to the master bedroom, and standing in the stark space as Sally — glass of wine in hand — had talked colours and layout and late-night feeds, Faye felt not like she had sold her child, but that she had handed over possession of herself. But that's what Faye did. She gave herself to others. To producers and directors and writers, to the audience, to a brand, to the highest bidder. She remembers that Saturday morning in Brighton. Puking into the toilet and feeling like a thing passed around. And here she was again, passed from Mike to Alistair and Sally, who had now installed her in a one-bedroom box close at hand; both things — Faye and her flat — rented for as long as they were needed.

Faye became aware of the shop assistant — fidgeting, clearing her throat — on the other side of the curtain. Maybe she had identified Faye as an imposter, trying on clothes that were beyond her means. A shoplifter, in fact, shoving pairs of two-hundred-quid slacks up her jumper. Faye picked up the coral trousers and pulled them on, making a good deal of noise about it and agitating the curtain with her elbow for the benefit of the shop girl.

She had phoned and texted Mike, but he hadn't replied. Sally had done likewise with the same result. Only Alistair had had any contact with him — a letter of resignation waiting on Al's desk when he arrived at work two days ago. Mike hadn't been in the office since and wasn't, according to Alistair, answering emails. His contract required him to work three months' notice, but Mike had suggested in his carefully worded letter that it might be more 'discreet' if he took those months as paid leave. Alistair had recognised the implied threat and had been offended only that Mike thought it necessary.

Faye hoped Mike would use the time well. Take a holiday, perhaps. Maybe visit Jojo in the States. Faye hoped so, and at the same time she felt a pang of absence for the small girl they had briefly shared. Like a family.

You're selling your baby. His face made ugly with disdain as he said the words.

When Sally had first suggested the idea, Faye had said no.

The evening after the test, Sally had come to see her in a bar across the street from the Brixton Playhouse. She had spelled out what Faye had already guessed: that she and Alistair wanted to adopt the baby if it turned out Al was the father. Sally told Faye about their failed attempts to have a child of their own, both naturally and through several expensive and futile cycles of IVF. Years of heartache that felt like loss. But now, after all the blood and drugs and time and scans of an empty womb, they had the chance to be the parents they had always dreamed of being.

And Faye had said no. They were asking her to spend six more months carrying a child she would never raise. She would have to quit the play, would be out of work for who knew how long. She doubted (and how quickly she had been proven correct) that she would be able to remain living with Mike. And even then, what was to say Alistair and Sally wouldn't break up or change their minds. Then what?

Sally had been careful with her choice of words, avoiding 'pay' and all its derivatives, although she came close; stumbling towards and swerving away from the grubby word several times. Saying instead: *We'll make sure you're looked after, we'll take care of you, we'll make sure you're comfortable, Faye.*

Using words like 'selfless' and 'noble' and 'blessing', Sally talked about surrogacy as if she'd memorised a brochure. But careful syntax or not, it was clear that this blessing would be paid for.

Sally had asked Faye how much she might hope to earn in a year. Writing down the number in her notebook, Sally had suggested Faye's answer was low, doubling the sum and underlining it in clean black ink. And still these figures were nothing more than hypotheticals. Also, Sally had said, you need to think about transport and accommodation and 'peripherals'. Never articulating a number, but instead writing a column of them in her notebook. The numbers were added, a total circled at the bottom of the page. And Faye would need to book a lot of commercials to get anywhere near a number like that.

And again, she said, 'No.'

'Think about it,' Sally had said. 'Please.'

How long after that meeting, Faye wondered now, had Sally waited before going to the bank to withdraw five thousand pounds in twenty-pound notes? Faye would bet it all that Sally had taken out her card the very next morning. Certainly there had been no time after Faye had called her from that damp park bench, reading the letter that identified Alistair as the father.

Sally had made Faye read it again, checking and double-checking the names and numbers. 'Have you talked to Mike?'

'Not yet. I wasn't sure.'

'About what?'

'About . . . anything.'

It was after five by then, the banks long closed, and Sally had arrived at Mike's flat within thirty minutes of Faye hanging up.

They had hugged and cried and gone over the results again. Sally began talking about 'next steps', taking a diary from her bag, uncapping her biro with her teeth.

'There's another clinic,' Faye said, turning over the tell-tale letter to reveal a handwritten phone number. Beneath it a date and a four-figure sum of money.

'But . . . ' Sally was shaking her head, the pen cap still between her teeth. 'It's Alistair. It says it's Alis — '

'They have an appointment in two days' time,' Faye said. 'I could be back on stage within five days.'

'What?' The blue plastic cap dropping to the floor. 'You mean . . . Faye? You don't mean . . . you can't. Faye, you can't . . . '

Sally had become distraught, pleading through tears for Faye to 'let this baby live'.

Faye didn't say no this time, moved as much

by Sally's sincerity as by her words.

She made tea. And when she returned to the living room, the brown envelope was sitting on the table — Faye didn't need to ask what it contained.

'I haven't said yes,' she said.

'It's not much,' Sally said. 'But you'll need things. Clothes.'

Faye picked up the envelope and immediately replaced it on the table. It weighed as much as a thick paperback novel and must have contained enough cash to buy a new outfit every day for the next six months.

Her mind turned to another envelope full of twenties, this one from Sally's husband. This one to *not* 'let this baby live'.

Hadn't, in fact, her whole life been reduced to a succession of variously stuffed envelopes? 'Services rendered', Al had said, passing her that first package of cash in a stairwell, not yet understanding the implications of his words. Another envelope containing the image of her unborn child; one more holding the name of its father. Faye herself, just one more fat white wrapper around another item soon to be delivered.

'What does Alistair think?' Faye had said to Sally.

'This is our chance to be a family. To be happy.'

'Aren't you in counselling?'

'Yes. Because of *this*; because we couldn't have a baby. But now we can. We're in counselling because we want to make it work.

Alistair wants to make it work.'

It felt like the truth.

Sally looked again at the letter, face down on the coffee table, a phone number scribbled on the back. She turned it over, showing instead the irrefutable evidence of Alistair's paternity. Of a life. 'I don't believe you want to terminate this baby.'

Faye shook her head.

'You just have to keep it safe for us. Just keep it safe, and then we'll look after it and love it and give it everything it needs. Everything it wants.'

'How do I know you won't change your mind? That Alistair won't change his?'

The expression on Sally's face was all the answer Faye needed. Sally would take this child, and she would do it with Alistair or without him.

'We'll look after you too,' Sally had said, and Faye wished she hadn't.

No matter how Sally justified the arrangement, with words like *appropriate* and *fair* and *extraordinary* and *compassion* and *friendship* and *love*, this had become transactional and it made Faye feel cheap. Mike's words rang inside her head, and they hurt all the more because they rang with truth.

But what had happened had happened, and what would happen next was already in motion. Sally and Alistair and even Mike were concerned only about themselves, about what they wanted and what worked for them. But no one was thinking about Faye.

These people had their homes and cars and

expensive furniture. Wine deliveries and organic vegetable boxes. They had people to clean their toilets and iron their shirts. Italian espresso machines, reclaimed parquet floors, numbered prints on the walls. They had careers and pensions and money.

Faye had none of those things. She had herself and a half-formed baby, and they both needed taking care of.

There were, of course, commercial opportunities for pregnant actors. The advertising industry loved a woman with child — the big-domed belly in the bath, the bewildered couple in antenatal class, the mum-to-be practising yoga, the late-night motorway breakdown, the early-morning suburban dash. Building societies, roadside recovery, home insurance, sofa warehouses and purveyors of everything from bubble bath to washing machines. Yes, they loved a ripe mum, glowing with health and expectation. Less so the single mum, tired, bewildered and deflated in every sense of the word. Faye was facing a narrow and rapidly closing window of opportunity, so when Sally asked again, Faye said yes.

She took their money because what else was she supposed to do?

The woman on the other side of the curtain said, 'And how is everything in there?'

'Everything is peachy.'

Faye pulled on her trousers, dragging them up over her widening hips and sucking in her stomach as she fastened the buttons.

'And how are the trousers?'

'I'll take them.'

'The coral or the taupe?'

'Fuck it,' Faye said, emerging from the cubicle. 'I'll take them both.'

29

'This won't save your marriage,' Mike had said.

But he might have been wrong about that. No marriage was perfect, but you worked at it. Isn't that what they said? Well, she and Al were working at it. And it would be different now; they would have a focus outside of themselves. Less than half a year from now they would have a child.

Not long. Not long to make the arrangements, prepare a room, prepare themselves. They needed bottles, nappies, a monitor, a child seat for the car. The list went on. Probably they should attend antenatal classes, but when Sally had suggested it, Alistair had . . . not bristled, but retreated. The idea was still new to him. He needed time.

But time would move on regardless. The surgery was close to a thriving high street, and Sally had spent each lunchtime this week browsing paint samples, baby clothes, night lights and mobiles. Yesterday she had purchased a pair of white baby mittens, barely big enough to take three of her fingers.

In yet another boutique baby shop now, Sally stopped in front of a sturdy cot. Resting her hand on the side, she let her eyes lose their focus and imagined the cot full of warm and hungry life.

As the other shoppers and expectant mums

moved around her, Sally pulled the black and white picture of Faye's baby from her coat pocket. She studied the profile she knew so well, wondering, would this be a son or a daughter? She didn't care, but hoped for a girl — it would bring a balance. If the baby was a boy, wouldn't nature incline him towards his father, towards his own biology? But a girl, Sally and a girl would share their own nature — the thing that made them female buried deeper in their code than simple paternity.

'Natural oak.'

Sally turned to the woman who had appeared at her side, a short, ruddy-faced lady somewhere in her fifties — Iris, according to her name-tag.

'Excuse me?'

'The cot, love. Natural oak.' She pointed at the picture in Sally's hand. 'That the little one?'

Sally nodded and slipped the picture back into her pocket.

'When are we due?'

'Not . . . not for six months. May.'

'You're not showing much, are you?'

'Not yet.' She put a hand to her stomach, over the thick wool of her coat. 'Maybe a little. Awful morning sickness, though.'

Iris took Sally's wrist. 'Sniff a lemon,' she said, winking as she imparted this secret knowledge. 'Three, I've had. Works every time.'

'Okay, I'll get one.'

'Get a bag.' Someone across the shop floor caught Iris's eye. ''Scuse me, love. Just wave if you need me.'

Sally thanked Iris and watched her shuffle over

to a woman who looked like she might give birth at any point in the next five minutes.

Mike had accused Faye of selling her baby. And by extension, Sally of buying one. The thought didn't trouble her. She wasn't buying the baby; she was saving its life. Sally felt maternal and imagined she felt it in her belly and breasts. Felt already the layers of affection and compassion being laid down inside her. The formation of a protective urge, too, that was close to anger in its intensity. Did these other mothers feel the same way? Did the men who were holding their hands?

She had wondered what might happen if the child had been revealed to be Mike's. They had been so close to happiness. Just a few weeks ago, huddled together on a park bench — charged with optimism and resolve and heat. Love, really. A simple fact of life, as real as the baby — unknown and unsuspected at the time — that was to come between them.

Sally would feel the lack of him like damage. But, like a scar, it would fade.

In the real world, we don't get to have it all. She saw the truth of this every day from behind her desk. Samna Johara had not come in to the surgery, but Sally had again gone to visit the family. Drawing fairies, gently counselling Samna, eating at their table. Samna Johara had two beautiful girls, a husband she loved as much as he loved her. Everything Sally had ever wanted for herself. But a year from now, Samna would be raising those girls alone.

At times in her life — standing on a train

platform or at the edge of some high and spectacular view — Sally had felt the perverse compulsion to tilt forward, give in to gravity and be gone. She read, but can't remember where, that vertigo is a manifestation of this same glitch — a fear that we may temporarily lose control and inflict permanent harm upon ourselves. But we shake our heads, we step back from the edge and we walk on.

Depression, too, she feels may be something like a precipice — something we can tilt into or step back from.

Mike had said the baby wouldn't save her marriage. But Sally thought it could. And she thought it might also save her.

She waved across the shop floor to Iris, at the same time reaching into her handbag for her purse.

30

Mike had been born at 3.21 in the morning. 'Like a countdown,' his mother would say: 'Three, two, one, and there you were.'

And here he was: nine hours into his fortieth birthday, pacing and wondering if it was too early to start drinking.

A card from his parents stood on the mantelpiece. 'Warm wishes on your birthday, son'. A baby polar bear huddled between two adults. Inside: *Our winter baby! Can't believe you're 40. Love Mum and Dad.* The card was one of five. One from an aunty on his mother's side, one from a friend he never saw, another from the Indian takeaway at the end of his street.

The fifth card, and the first he had opened today, was from Jojo. A hand-drawn picture of Mike and Jojo on the front, each labelled in case of any ambiguity: Jojo and Daddoo. Jojo in a stripy dress, her hair a mad brown scribble, her cheeks and lips bright red against pink skin. Mike outfitted in a shirt and tie, his face dotted with stubble, his mouth a ten-tooth grimace of impossible happiness. The figures had been set against a scratchy black backdrop dotted with — Mike had counted them — forty yellow stars.

Happy Birthdey Daddoo, I love you to the wide world and infinitey.

And I love you to the wide world and infinity too, baby.

A little riff she had developed in the past several months, reciting it — he supposed — every night to Kim and Brendan. Declaring it to Mike on their transatlantic calls.

She had said it to him minutes ago — *Bye bye Daddoo, love you to the wide world and infinity* — and if Mike concentrated hard enough, he could still hear the echo of it in his empty flat. He would have preferred it if she had called later, giving him something to look forward to (a reason to stay sober), but Jojo had a busy Saturday ahead of her — T-ball, swimming, homework, a party, a sleep-over — and so she had wished her father happy birthday through a mouthful of Cheerios. She had asked after Faye and Mike had lied, saying she'd had to go out to the shops. Jojo had been disappointed and made Mike promise that Faye would be there next time she called. So he had lied again and said that she would.

In the days immediately after Mike had kicked her out, Faye had texted and called, but he had ignored and then deleted the notifications. Erased her voicemails without first pressing play. But when the messages stopped arriving, Mike had missed them.

There was a mark on the wall where Faye had thrown the mug. He'd bought filler to smooth out the damage, sanded it flat and retouched the paint. But if he squinted, he could still see the evidence — *how did this happen?* — of her time in his life.

It had occurred to him that Faye might try again today, but it was possible — likely, in fact

277

— that she had forgotten it was his birthday. Sally would know, but she, too, had stopped trying to make contact. Perhaps, with ten days passed, she had moved now from contrition to indignation. And perhaps he wouldn't blame her. With little else to occupy him, Mike had replayed the scene over and over again. He fell asleep watching himself accuse Faye of selling her baby. He woke to the hurt in Sally's eyes when he told her that adopting the child wouldn't save her marriage. Perhaps two hundred times he had rerun the short and bitter exchange. Seeing the sense of it and the stupidity. Seeing compassion, seeing selfishness, seeing desperation and sadness and hope and heartbreak and inevitability. He had wished the child were his and then thanked God that it wasn't. He blamed everybody, but most of all he blamed himself.

Ten years ago today he had let Sally walk away with Alistair, and if you wanted to talk about blame, why not start there? Hadn't all this been set in motion that night? The dress code had been 'anything black', a piece of whimsy at the passing of Mike's youth. But looking back over the mess and disappointment of the last decade, the contrived irony of that night had come to feel like a blunt truth.

He remembered what Sally had been wearing — the biker jacket and adidas — and how he had wished he could vanish everyone else out of the basement bar, leaving just the two of them alone and together. But he'd been with the banker (her name now eluding him), and it had seemed to

Mike that every time he put himself next to Sally, the banker would position herself between them. And then Alistair had introduced himself to Sally, the pair of them finding a cosy table in an alcove, effectively pulling off the trick that Mike couldn't — that of making everyone else disappear. And then they too had vanished, leaving Mike alone in a room full of drinkers dressed in black.

'Happy birthday,' he said to himself now, his voice swallowed up by the empty room. 'Happy birthday,' he said again, louder this time, trying to force an echo from the walls. His voice sounded flat, not his own, and the bricks absorbed it without comment. He said it again. He shouted it: 'Happy birthday, Mike!'

There was no drink in the house, but there was an off-licence five minutes down the road. Mike pulled on his coat, checked for his wallet and headed out.

31

'Mimosa?'

It was barely midday and there was little that Sally wanted less. But Alistair was already taking down the good champagne flutes from a shelf above the sink, holding them to the light, polishing them with a tea towel that itself needed washing. He was trying so hard, but Sally felt his effort — the flowers, the breakfast in bed, the hot bath — like a tight band across her chest. Maybe a drink would help.

She smiled, showed Alistair the gap between her thumb and forefinger. 'Small one.'

As Al removed the blue foil collar from the bottle, she realised with a jolt of something like panic that this was the same brand of champagne they'd drunk on the train down to Brighton. Just a handful of hours before she'd made love to Mike and Alistair had impregnated Faye.

Alistair popped the cork and the sound of it echoing off the kitchen walls made Sally flinch. The bottle foamed slightly, and, seeing that Al intended to suck the bubbles from the bottle-neck, she quickly turned her head.

Alistair had bought lilies, as he always did. Sally couldn't remember, but assumed that at some point in the past ten years she must have expressed a preference for the pale, funereal blooms. Or perhaps reacted with excessive gratitude when once presented with a bunch. But the pollen stained and she had always found them somehow aloof.

Regarding the tall stems now — looking through them — Sally recalled, again, Mike bringing flowers home for Faye. Believing the child was his; thinking, perhaps, that he and Faye would be a family.

It was his birthday today, but neither she nor Alistair had mentioned the fact. That the man who had brought them together was turning forty. On his own for all anyone knew.

It was the first clear thought that had passed through her mind on waking. Ten years ago today, she had set out determined and confident that she and Mike would be together. But instead, she had come home with Alistair.

The morning after, her black clothes in a heap on the bedroom floor, he had asked, 'What would Mike make of this?' And Sally, finding the bedroom too small for Mike's name and Alistair's presence, had gone out to buy bread. This morning Alistair left her in bed while he went out for juice. The question — *What would Mike make of this?* — as uncomfortable now as it had been then.

As soon as Alistair left the house, banging the door closed behind him, Sally climbed out of bed and began looking. There were old suitcases, boxes and zip-up storage bags. Stuffed under beds, at the back of cupboards, in low corners of the loft. Winter, summer and holiday clothes, archived when they should have been discarded. Old fancy dress, dubious jumpers, painful shoes.

And a black leather biker jacket, a little creased, but weren't they all a decade on? It fitted well.

After showering, Sally dressed in a pair of black cotton trousers, black vest, black roll-neck sweater. Then Alistair came home and gave her lilies. As he always did.

'Happy anniversary.'

Sally turned and accepted the champagne. They clinked and drank.

Alistair put down his glass and smiled with what looked like sincere affection. Sally noticed a wet stain on the front of his shirt — orange and flecked with pulp — and the muscles in her neck contracted into hard cables as she willed herself not to turn away from him.

He said, 'You look as beautiful today as the first time I saw you.'

Sally laughed, a hard sound that was too loud and too abrupt.

'You do.' His voice sounding hurt at this braying rebuttal.

'Thank you.'

She should play it back to him, she knew: *And you look as handsome as the first time I saw you.* But Sally felt that her voice . . . *the first time I saw you* . . . would betray her.

Because it wasn't meant to be him, it was meant to be Mike.

Alistair leaned in and kissed her. 'I was thinking. We should do something special for our . . . you know, proper anniversary. Our wedding anniversary.'

Sally's skin flushed and her chest drummed with palpitations. 'Special?'

Al tilted his face to the ceiling and swallowed the last of his mimosa in one gulp. Glass still in hand, he held his fist to his mouth, cheeks inflating against a contained belch of champagne bubbles.

'Top-up?'

Sally shook her head. She had barely touched her drink, but she took a sip now as Al refilled his own glass. 'Get away,' he said. 'Somewhere hot, romantic and disgustingly expensive.'

'But . . . Faye, she'll be . . . '

'Faye will be fine, she'll be barely seven months.'

'What if she needs us?'

'Sal, she'll be fine. And this is likely our last chance, for a *long* time, to be alone. Just the two of us. We deserve it.'

'I . . . I don't know about deserve.'

'You do, Sal. You've been amazing.'

Sally shook her head. 'Not true.'

'You have. This whole thing, in your position, I . . . I don't know.'

Sally took a sip of her drink, and then another.

'Honestly, Sal. If anyone could justify wanting to . . . not wanting this baby, it's you. But . . . but you're a better person than me.'

'I'm not. I'm . . . I'm selfish and stupid and . . . ' tears standing in her eyes, ' . . . and I don't deserve anything.'

Alistair took hold of her hand. 'You're a good person.'

'Stop saying that!' She pulled her hand out of his. 'Stop telling me what I am! Stop telling me that. Just . . . just please stop.'

She took a deep breath, clinging to what remained of her composure, teetering on the border between telling him everything or nothing. It felt that either option would be equally destructive.

Alistair's hand went to the bracelet at his wrist, frayed now, but still clinging on. He rotated it around his wrist, caught himself and stopped.

'I'm sorry,' Sally said. 'I'm a mess of hormones. I'm confused; I'm frightened.'

'Hey, it's okay. It will be okay.'

Sally nodded. 'I need . . . I think I need some space.'

Alistair flinched.

'No, no. Just . . . *literally*, I need some space, some air. I need to . . . to walk.'

She was already standing.

'Do you want me to come with you?'

Sally kissed him lightly on the lips. 'I'll be fine.'

Alistair followed her through to the hallway, hovering at her shoulder as she pulled on her boots.

'You'll be back?'

'Of course.' Sally picked up her keys and handbag. Checked for her wallet.

Alistair touched his watch. 'When . . . ?'

'I don't know. Couple of hours. I might get some lunch, go to the shops. I don't know.'

'I booked a table.'

'For lunch?'

He shook his head. 'Supper. That Italian you like. Seven-thirty.'

She took the biker jacket down from the rack.

Too thin, really, for this time of year, and the leather creaked as she wound a scarf around her neck. 'If I'm not back by then, I'll see you in there.'

Alistair took the lapel of the jacket between his finger and thumb. 'New?'

Sally nodded. 'Yeah.'

She kissed Alistair once more, and stepped out into the afternoon.

32

Faye's first thought was that the baby was kicking, a sensation she had been both dreading and anticipating. But it didn't feel like a kick; too sharp and too deep. It came again, with more force this time. The woman serving her coffee must have seen Faye wince and asked if she was okay, her eyes flicking towards the badge on Faye's lapel: *Baby on board.*

Faye excused herself to the toilet, leaving her coffee on the counter.

Blood in her underwear. How much — a teaspoon or a table-spoonful — was hard to tell; her pants were black and the blood had soaked into the dark fabric. Faye put her hand to herself and it came away sticky with more blood — darker, surely, than it should be.

Still in the coffee-shop toilet, still with her pants around her calves, she called Sally. The phone rang half a dozen times then went to voicemail.

'Sally,' keeping her voice low so the customers on the other side of the door wouldn't hear her drama. 'Can you call me? It's . . . there's blood. I don't know what to do.'

After hanging up, she called again, and then again.

33

Sally was waiting at his front door. Sitting on the stone step, hunkered down inside her scarf.

'You'll catch cold.'

Sally looked up, taking in his tired eyes, the stubble, the blue plastic bag in his hand. 'Happy birthday.'

Mike nodded. 'Yeah, something like that. How long have you been here?'

'Don't have a watch. But I've lost all feeling in my bum.'

'Should have called.'

'Don't have a phone.'

'Like the old days, hey?'

'Yeah, something like that.'

Mike stubbed out his cigarette and extended his hand towards her. 'I always liked that jacket on you.'

She nodded, took his hand. 'You should have said.'

'Yes. I should.'

He pulled Sally to her feet, bringing her face level with his own. Each regarded the other from this intimate distance, thinking the same thoughts, resisting the same impulses whilst hoping the other would not.

'Let's go inside.'

In the kitchen, Mike placed the bag on the counter and two bottles clinked against each other. He shrugged. 'It's not every day you turn forty.'

'Will you pour me a drink?'

He cleaned two glasses and poured them each a good measure. They tapped their glasses together and drank. Mike glanced at the bottle, as if about to pick it up. He hesitated for a second, left the bottle where it stood and walked through to the living room. Sally picked up the bottle and followed.

Mike took the armchair, and Sally sat in the corner of the sofa closest to him.

He emptied his pockets; keys, lighter, phone. Turned his phone to silent, set it face down on the table and settled back into the chair.

34

Faye could feel the panic threatening to swamp her.

She concentrated on breathing, improvised a pad with a folded-up hand towel, pulled up her underwear and washed her hands. She wiped a smear of blood from her phone and tried Sally again with the same result. No answer.

She scrolled through her contacts to Alistair's number; he might be with Sally. But if he wasn't . . . she didn't want to face this with only him. After all, wasn't this — this crisis, this blood — wasn't this what he had wanted all along?

There were other people she could ring, but she found her finger hovering over Mike's number. Probably he was the last person she should call, but he was still a part of this. She had called him a bastard, but he wasn't. He was hurt and confused, shocked. But he wasn't a bastard.

She called him, counted the rings, measuring her breath against them from one to seven. But Mike didn't answer. She left a message and hung up.

And then she called Al.

35

Mike tilted his glass towards the front door. 'How long were you going to wait?'

Sally smiled awkwardly. 'I've got keys. Faye's keys.'

'Right. I'm . . . I acted like a dick.'

'You had every right. It's crazy. It's crazy and it's fucked up.'

'But you're still going ahead with it.'

Sally nodded. 'Yes.'

'How's Faye?'

The flowers he had brought home that night stood in a vase on the bookshelf, vibrant and oblivious. Mike had been waiting for them to die, rather fancying the image of wilted stems and shed petals. But the amaryllis had proved irritatingly resilient.

'Nervous,' Sally said. 'Confused and lonely, I expect. You should call her.'

Mike looked at the thin layer of whiskey in the bottom of the glass, rotated it around the inside of the tumbler then set it down on the table. 'Alistair said that when you slept with me — that night — he said you only did it because you wanted to get pregnant.'

Sally winced.

'Was he right?'

Sally shook her head, but she was silent for a while before answering. 'I slept with you because I wanted to sleep with you. Nothing else. But after . . . afterwards, I wondered if . . . ' She shifted on the sofa, looked Mike in the eye and smiled. 'I hoped, you know? I really hoped.'

Mike picked up his glass and drained the end of his drink. Sally's glass was empty too, and he refilled them both.

Sally looked at the glass but didn't pick it up. 'It's why I came today, I suppose.'

'To . . . what?'

Sally was crying, and she used the heels of her hands to draw back the tears. Mike went to stand, but Sally shook her head and held up one hand indicating he should stay where he was.

'Sal?'

'Okay.' This said to herself more than to Mike. 'At the end of our second year at uni, there was a time when . . . when everything was good. We saw a lot of each other — I think it was our best time.'

'That and the few weeks you were in London. Before you found a flat.'

Sally picked up her glass and took a long sip. 'But that summer, when we were, what? Twenty?' Mike nodded. 'You were travelling somewhere.'

'Greece.'

'Right, and I went back to my parents. I had a summer job at a hospice.'

'Sure.'

'But when I came back, when we came back . . . '

'We'd lost our way.'

Sally nodded. She was crying again, the tears coming more freely now.

'You came to find me at the library,' she said. 'After we got back. We sat on the grass, do you remember?'

'I remember. You didn't seem particularly pleased to see me.'

Sally shook her head in acknowledgement, or confession. 'There was so much I wanted to tell you, but I . . . ' something like dread, perhaps, in her expression, ' . . . it was too hard.'

'I took you for granted.'

'It's not your fault.'

'I'm sorry,' Mike said. 'I should have tried harder. I — '

'I had an abortion.'

Mike stared at her.

'Two, three weeks before. At the end of the summer holidays. I . . . an abortion.'

He stood up from the chair, walked two paces away from it then doubled back and sat down again. 'But you can't . . . you can't get pregnant.'

'Not with Al. Maybe not with anyone now.'

Mike went to form a question but something — fear of the answer, perhaps — stopped him.

'It was yours, Mike. And I'm . . . ' She screwed her eyes closed but the tears found their way through. She folded her arms across her chest then immediately released them as if even this scant self-comfort was more than she deserved. Her face was a torture of grief and failed restraint, her voice coming through in a thin whisper: 'It was yours. They scraped it out of me and it was yours.' She bit the knuckle of her fist, her forehead pulling into wrinkles with the effort.

'Stop it!' Mike jumped out of his seat, grabbed Sally roughly by the wrist and pulled her hand from her mouth. 'Stop it,' he said, quietly now. 'Stop it.'

Mike sat beside her on the sofa, pulling her to him and stroking her hair while she cried with her head against his chest.

Sally's breathing slowed and for a long time they sat quite still.

'I know what it feels like,' she said, 'to be pregnant. But I . . . twenty-fourth of August. Every year. I regret it more every year.'

'Why did you do it?'

'I had my studies, my degree. Everything mapped out. Doctor Stevens. Mum said I was stupid, that having the baby would ruin my life.' She shook her head at the irony of this — if that's what it was.

'Did you know? When we were together?'

'I didn't find out until I was home. I was about six weeks by then. Told Mum a few weeks after that.'

'You should have told me.'

Sally nodded. 'I should have. I worried you'd be angry. Talk me out of it, or into it. I don't know.'

'I would have come down.'

Sally laughed, 'That too, But . . . ' All the humour left her face then. 'I told my parents I didn't know who the father was.'

'You didn't have to do that.'

Sally shrugged at this. 'I suppose that I still thought we might one day be together. I didn't want them to hate you.'

She was still sitting with her head against his chest, Mike's arm around her waist. 'I'm sorry,' he said, meaning it on more levels than he could pick apart. 'I'm sorry for everything.'

Sally took hold of his hand, running her thumb slowly across the backs of his fingers.

'When Mum took me to the clinic, I was hoping there'd be protesters. I thought, if there were protesters screaming at me, that Mum would take me home. But there was no one.'

'It must have been . . . ' Mike shook his head.

'The machine makes a noise,' she said. 'You can hear it happening to you. To the . . . '

'I wish I could have been there with you.'

'To stop me?'

'I don't know. Just to be there. I should have been there.'

Sally turned to face him. 'The things we didn't do.'

Mike put his hand against her cheek and kissed her. When their lips touched they were twenty years old.

★ ★ ★

In the bedroom afterwards, neither of them spoke, each knowing that no words would be the right words. Everything they needed to say they said with their bodies; a head on a shoulder, lips to an ear, fingers laced together.

And then a slow inhalation, signalling that this time was over.

They let the words return slowly as they dressed. Trivialities at first — the darkening sky, the temperature — easing the way for the heavier commentary on what they'd done and become. But even this was only touched upon. They had missed each other, they would continue to miss each other. They would be friends forever, but this — the unmade bed, the taste of each other in their mouths — this was over.

'Are you sure?' Mike said.

Sally nodded. A weight of reluctance made her head heavy, but she nodded.

'I . . . ' The words insisted: 'I don't want to let you go.'

Sally took hold of his hand. 'You already did.'

They moved from the bedroom to the living room, the transition significant and understood. The tumblers of whiskey remained where they had been left and brought to mind the tears and revelations, not just of today but of the last year and the previous twenty. Mike took the glasses through to the kitchen.

When he returned to the living room, Sally was pulling on her boots and the impression of her teeth was still visible on her knuckles.

Sally looked up. 'What time is it?'

Mike picked up his phone to check. 'It's . . . '

He froze. The screen was full of stacked messages from Faye and from Alistair. His eyes flicked from one to the other, taking in the repeated words, *blood* and *bleeding, baby* and *hospital.*

'Mike. *Mike.* What is it?'

Mike held a hand to his mouth. 'Faye. Something's happened to Faye.'

Sally was on her feet. 'What? Tell me? Is she okay?'

'I don't know. She's been bleeding. They're at the hospital now, her and Alistair.'

'Who are you calling?'

'Taxi. I'll text Faye and Al on the way, let them know we're coming.'

'Is the baby okay?'

Mike held up his hand. He spoke into the phone, requested an immediate cab for the hospital, gave the operator his address and hung up. 'Five minutes.'

'The baby, Mike?'

Mike shook his head. 'It's just happened, about . . . give me a second.' He read the messages again, in sequence and more carefully this time. And then played the voice message from Faye — frightened, breathless, her words broken up and wet with tears.

'Some blood,' he said. 'They got to the hospital maybe fifteen minutes ago.'

'Fuck. Fuck, Mike. While we . . . while we were — '

'There's nothing we could have done, Sal. Come on, we'll meet the cab outside.'

'If we . . . they'll know. If we go in together, they'll know that we . . . I don't even have my phone. Jesus, Mike. This is so fucked up.'

'Maybe you should go home; I'll go on to the hospital.'

'No, I need to be there. What if I go and you st — '

'Sal, slow down. You said yourself, you haven't got a phone. How did you even find out about this?'

'Shit. *Shit.*'

He passed Sally her jacket, shrugging into his own at the same time. 'We'll get your phone on the way.'

Sally glanced at the watch she wasn't wearing.

'It'll add five minutes,' Mike said. 'Less.'

'Maybe it would be best if you didn't . . . if you stayed?'

Mike stopped fastening his jacket. He looked past Sally to the ghost of damage on the far wall. *How did this happen?* The question as incisive now as it had been redundant all those weeks ago.

He remembered making love to Faye two days after the test and wondered if they had induced some kind of damage. He remembered, less than twenty-four hours later, accusing Faye of selling her baby. And giving her two hours to move out of his flat. And after all of that, she had called him, asked him to come to her. *I need you, Mike. Please.*

Sally read the expression on his face. 'I'm sorry. I . . . was being selfish. Again. You should be there. Faye would want you there.'

'What about . . . ?' *all this.*

'We'll say we met in reception.'

'Do you think they'll believe us?'

'Would you?'

Mike continued fastening his coat. 'No. But I'd *want* to.'

'Well, I suppose that'll have to do.'

36

Al was holding her hand as they opened the door to the private room. Faye was lying on a hospital bed, Alistair on the far side, sitting quietly beside her as a nurse typed something into a PC. Both Faye and Alistair looked as if they'd been crying.

'Come in, come in.' The nurse stood up as she beckoned Mike and Sally into the room.

Sally was first through the door, going straight to Faye and taking hold of her free hand, so she was now connected to both Sally and Alistair. 'Are you okay?'

Faye nodded and Sally muttered 'Thank God' under her breath. *Thank. God.*

'Nothing to be too concerned about,' the nurse said. 'Placenta's a little low, but that's not unusual. We'll need to keep an eye on it, but the scan's good, the little one's good. It's all good.'

Sally brushed a stray lock of hair from Faye's face. 'I'm sorry I wasn't there for you. My phone was at home.' She turned to Alistair. 'I'm sorry.'

Alistair's eyes flicked towards Mike who was still only a single step inside the room. He looked back to Sally. 'Are *you* okay?'

'I got home and you weren't there. Turned on my phone and . . . '

'We met in reception,' Mike said.

Faye looked at him now, something behind her eyes as she glanced to Sally and then back to Mike. She smiled. 'Hey.'

'I'm sorry for being a massive dick.'

'Oh!' The nurse passed Mike on her way to the door. 'Cosy in here, isn't it? I'll leave you all alone for a minute.'

Mike approached the bed and Sally moved out of the way, stepping around to the other side, next to Alistair. Faye reached out for Mike's hand. 'I don't blame you.'

He leaned in and kissed her forehead. 'I blame me. But . . . I'm just glad you and the baby are okay.'

Faye grimaced.

'What?' Sally's voice was quick and taut. 'I thought the nurse said . . . '

'I don't know if I can go through with this. I . . . I don't even know what *this* is.'

The room seemed to amplify the silence, drawing it out and pushing it against their ears like a dense liquid.

Sally spoke first. 'What are you talking about . . . through with what?'

Faye shook her head. 'I don't know. Any of it.'

'Faye, we *talked* about this.'

'You talked. Mostly. But I' — reacting to Sally's expression — 'It's okay. I . . . I'm not accusing you . . . but . . . I'm the one on the hospital bed.'

'The nurse said you were fine.'

'And what if this happens again? What if . . . ' She looked at Alistair and then at Sally. 'What if . . . '

'Us? We're fine.' Sally turned to Alistair. 'Aren't we? We're fine.'

Alistair put his arm around Sally and nodded.

'We want this. *I* want this.'

Sally leaned her head against Al's chest. 'Nothing's changed, Faye.'

Mike felt like an intruder in the room, but he understood that he should stay by Faye's side to bring balance, to lend her mute support, if she wanted it.

Alistair spoke quietly. 'We could . . . the money,' he said, 'we could arrange to . . . '

Mike watched Sally as her husband spoke; her expression one of surprise and gratitude and affection.

'It's not about the money,' Faye said.

'No,' Sally agreed. 'It's about the baby.' Her eyes found Mike's for the space of one heartbeat before she turned back to Faye.

One heartbeat but he read it clearly: *It was about the baby Faye was carrying and the one Sally had failed to take to term.*

Sally said to Faye: 'It's about our commitment to the baby.'

Faye turned to Mike, asking the silent question. *What should I do?*

'You need to rest,' he said.

'God yes.'

'I'm sorry,' Sally said. 'It's been a . . . a mad day. A long day.'

Nobody denied it.

Something occurred to Alistair and he levelled a slow finger at Mike. 'Isn't today your birthday? I mean, it is, right?'

Mike nodded. 'The big four-O.'

'No!' Faye sat up straight. 'Oh my God, Mike. I'm so . . . Why didn't you say something?'

He laughed. 'When?'

'Babes.' Faye held out her arms and took Mike into a tight embrace. 'Happy birthday. Shit, I feel dreadful. Did I know?'

Mike shrugged. 'You've had a lot on your mind.'

Alistair turned to Sally. 'We should have remembered; it's the same day we . . . ' He waved his index finger back and forth in the space between them. 'Did you know?' Sally nodded, and Alistair regarded her for a second, perhaps deciding whether or not to pursue the line of enquiry to a conclusion. 'Of course you did,' he said. 'Of course.'

'I should probably . . . ' Mike indicated the door.

Alistair looked at Sally. A silent question passed between them and Sally nodded. 'We're going to supper,' Al said. 'There's an Italian . . . I'm sure they could fit another couple of chairs — '

'Thank you,' Mike said. 'But I'm going to dial a pizza, watch a movie and drink a couple of glasses of whiskey.'

'You sure?'

Mike nodded. 'I'm positive.'

Alistair turned to Faye. 'You like Italian?'

Faye shook her head. 'I do, but I won't. Thank you. I need a bath, a bar of chocolate and a long sleep. Maybe Mike could have a whiskey for me?'

Mike raised an invisible glass. 'Mike can manage that.'

The four laughed, a gentle sound of relief and fatigue and maybe reconciliation.

'Next week,' Faye said. 'Thursday. It's my last night. Last night in the ... you know, play. Maybe you could come. We could have drinks after — if you want, unless you're busy?'

Mike, Alistair and Sally exchanged glances: *Shall we?*

And they all decided that they should.

★   ★   ★

Mike had the cigarette in his lips as he stepped out through the automatic doors. But patting his pockets, he found his Zippo missing and was forced to borrow a light from an old man in a hospital gown, his left arm hooked up to a mobile IV stand.

'Bum one of those?'

Mike turned to find Al at his heels.

'Hey. Since when did you start smoking again?'

'Since one minute ago. Don't tell Sal, she'll ... you know Sal.'

Mike fished out a cigarette, lit it off his own and passed it to Alistair.

The two friends stood shoulder to shoulder, staring through the darkness to the street lights and passing traffic beyond the car park.

Al took a cautious drag of his cigarette, didn't choke or die and took another. 'Remember when you used to bum mine?'

'A bad habit compounded.'

Al laughed. 'What was it you called them?'

'OPs.'

'That's right. Other People's.' Al took a longer

pull this time, exhaling a thin stream of smoke into the frigid air. 'Sally and Faye are talking to the nurse,' he said. 'Some paperwork.'

'Okay.'

'Do you think Faye will . . . ?' He turned to Mike and let his eyes finish the question.

'She's scared. Knocked about. But I don't think she wants to have a . . . you know. An abortion.'

'I hope not. For a while, I hoped she would.' He looked at Mike, gauging his reaction. 'What does that make me?'

'Human, I guess.'

'That's too easy. What the fuck, Mike? How did this happen?'

'I don't know, we were . . . I don't know, Al. It happened.'

'Be honest with me. I'm going to ask you something . . . and I want you to be honest with me.'

Mike drew on his cigarette.

'You love her?' No need to qualify who.

Mike lowered his eyes, looking down and off to one side. He could admit he had, once; he could reject the question; he could lie. But Alistair knew the answer — why else ask the question? Mike lifted his chin and found Al's eyes.

'Yes.'

Alistair acknowledged Mike's honesty with a small nod, then turned again to face the passing traffic. He took a final drag on his cigarette before dropping it to the ground and grinding it out. 'Then let her be happy.'

Alistair patted Mike on the shoulder then walked back through the sliding doors.

The doors closed and Mike nodded.

'Yes,' he said. He ground out his own cigarette and set off in the direction of the road. It was a long walk home.

37

They sat three abreast in the theatre. Sally in the middle, with Alistair on her right and Mike to her left. Faye had reserved tickets for them; three rows from the stage, just left of centre — 'Best seats in the house.'

Mike had kissed Sally's cheek when they met in the lobby, and Sally had pulled him into a tight hug, pressing her face sideways into his, sending a message that only he could receive or understand. He had regarded Alistair over Sally's shoulder, and Al had smiled. When Mike released Sally, he felt the same tug and loss that he experienced saying goodbye to Jojo, and always would. Sally felt it too; he saw it in the miniscule movements of her lips and brow and eyes. Alistair embraced him, and all that needed to be said between the two friends was conveyed in that unhurried clutch amid the flow of oblivious theatre-goers. Something had settled; there was no awkwardness now, only their friendship, although it was different to how it had once been. More restrained perhaps, but made of denser stuff.

They sat three abreast and the lights went down.

And in that dark and quiet theatre, Faye had caught each of their eyes. Early in the performance, pondering her teacher's self-serving philosophy, she had looked out across the audience and found them. She had smiled without professional restraint, communicating something different to each of them: *accord, agreement, apology.* Or perhaps they simply saw in that uniform smile the thing they each hoped to see.

Walking to the theatre — and in truth, several times in the handful of days since making love to Sally for the last time — Mike had anticipated the point in the play where Faye's character, Rose, invites her teacher to draw her. In Brighton, they had shared a moment and a memory; Sally nudging Mike with her elbow, him mouthing the word *Cliché*, Sally pressing a thumb to her lips to contain her laughter. The way she had twenty years ago in their life-drawing class, just hours before they'd made love for the very first time.

At the same point in this final performance, Mike waited for the elbow in his side, but it didn't come.

Faye found them again, during the final bow. She looked at each of the three in turn, blowing three small kisses across the space between them: *One, two, three.*

The director came on stage with flowers, he said a few words and the crowd rose to their feet, clapping. Faye took a final bow and there were tears in her eyes as she turned and left the stage.

They had all, in fact, been moved to tears. And they would come to wonder if, in that moment, they had already understood what they had not yet recognised.

38

They were halfway through their second round of drinks when the idea slowly found its form: *Faye isn't coming.*

But no one said it yet.

She had sent them ahead while she said her farewells to the rest of the cast, specifying a bar north of the river — a good taxi ride from the Brixton Playhouse, but only a short walk from Faye's flat. She should have been with them by now.

All three of them had their phones on the table, and Mike picked up his now to call her. There were any number of rational reasons why Faye might have been late, but no one was surprised when her phone went straight to voicemail. Their faces said this, but no one spoke it out loud.

At a few minutes past the hour, their glasses stood empty for the second time. They fiddled with their straws and watched the remnants of their ice cubes melt, but no one suggested a third round.

Alistair chewed the pulp from a lime wedge.

Sally checked her watch.

Finally, Mike pushed his glass into the centre of the table. 'She's not coming, is she?'

Sally shook her head.

Alistair said, 'Nope,' and the plosive 'p' hung in the air like a full stop.

The three of them stood as one and pulled on their coats.

39

Faye's key was under the mat, and they could smell or feel the absence of her as they walked through the door, the sounds of their voices echoing the way they will in an uninhabited space.

No clothes in the wardrobe, no books on the shelves, no toiletries in the bathroom. The floorboards and surfaces clean, the dishes stacked, the cushions plumped up and anticipant. The plants remained and had been watered.

On the coffee table stood a bottle of red wine, a corkscrew and three glasses.

Beside the bottle, a card; beneath it three sealed letters.

Alistair and Mike sat on the sofa. Sally took the armchair, opened the card and read:

"'That bottle of wine cost thirty quid, so make sure you damn well drink it.''

Alistair laughed, reached for the bottle and the corkscrew.

"'There's ice-cream in the freezer, too. Rocky road!'' Sally looked up. 'There's an exclamation mark,' she said, tracing the shape of one in the air.

Mike and Al nodded, acknowledging the reference.

Sally continued: "'Before I go on, I should tell you that I'm safe. And happy, in a wonky sort of way. The baby is safe too — I can't wait to find out whether it's a boy or a girl. I feel like it's a she, but time will tell.''

Sally paused and brushed at a tear on her cheek.

Alistair asked, 'You okay?'

Sally nodded and continued:

''There's a letter for each of you. Please don't share them. Don't offer and don't ask. What I've written is for your eyes only, as a certain spy might say. Sorry, I'm being frivolous, but only because this is so fucking hard. I'll miss you all, but we'll meet again. Faye.

''P.S. If I misjudged this and the person reading this card is a cleaner or an estate agent, do enjoy the wine. But please throw the letters in the bin.

''P.P.S. I'm keeping the money. F.''

Sally placed the card back on the table. 'There are three 'x's at the end. Three kisses.'

She accepted a glass of wine from Alistair, took a sip.

Mike took up his own glass. 'At least you hadn't given her the whole — '

Alistair cleared his throat. 'We . . . we got to the theatre a little early. Had a coffee with Faye before the show. And . . . ' He shrugged.

'All of it?'

'Half of it,' Sally said, pressing a thumb to her lips.

Mike raised his glass. 'This had better be a bloody good glass of wine.'

They laughed then; an act of release more than amusement, although there was that too. And a good measure of admiration for Faye.

They knew, after all, that this was right and fair — not the ending they had planned or imagined, but the right ending, nevertheless.

The laughter faded, they picked up their letters, sat back and read.

Dear Sally

Dear Alistair

Dear Mike

They read in silence, looking up occasionally and meeting another's eye. They stopped at certain words and phrases, rereading and rereading, and bringing the words in.

Friend . . . lover . . . father . . . child . . . family . . . love . . . together . . . alone . . .

Some words hurt and others soothed, and every one was honest. They smiled and reflected. And on occasion, they held the sheets of paper more tightly to their chests.

They each finished in their own time, sipping their wine and waiting. Folding their letters away, then taking them once more from the envelopes to read again a particular line, paragraph or word.

Blame . . . mistake . . . deliberate . . . accident . . . respect . . . timing . . . trust . . . life . . .

But eventually they finished, all the letters ending the same way:

We only regret the things we didn't do.

Faye x

40

They washed the glasses and replumped the cushions. Rinsed out the empty wine bottle and dropped it into the recycling. Making small talk as they did so, too tired, heads too full of words for the bigger conversations that lay ahead.

Mike pulled on his jacket and Sally did the same. She noticed Alistair had made no move to put on his own coat. As she turned to him, Al pulled the cotton bracelet from his wrist and placed it inside his pocket. When he smiled, it was shaped by sadness and resolve.

'You not coming?'

Alistair kicked off his shoes. 'Thought I might stay here tonight.'

Sally went to him, put her arms around his neck and kissed him. She kissed his neck, his cheek and his mouth and Alistair pulled her to him, one arm around her shoulders, one around her waist as he pressed his face into her neck.

Mike watched from the kitchen doorway as Sally kissed Alistair one last time. She took a half-step away from him. 'You'll be all right?'

'Sure. Got a whole tub of Rocky road in the freezer.'

'I'm serious.'

Al nodded her towards the door, towards Mike. 'I'm fine. I'll . . . I'll be fine.' He looked at Mike now and smiled. 'I'll be fine.'

On the steps outside Faye's flat, Mike pulled his cigarettes from his pocket, removed a smoke and placed it between his lips. He put his hand to his pocket and stopped.

'No lighter.'

He put the cigarette back in the box, the box in his pocket.

Sally threaded her right arm through his. 'You should quit anyway.'

They set off walking, turning either left or right without thinking because it didn't matter. They would simply walk; maybe they would walk all night.

'Probably,' Mike said.

Sally slipped her left hand into her pocket and closed it around the cold weight of Mike's brass Zippo. 'Definitely.'

'That the doctor speaking?'

'Did I tell you about Mr Johara?'

'Mr who?'

'Patient of mine — Nadeem Johara. He's . . .' Sally paused, not wanting to cry. She'd done enough of that. 'Fifty-four,' she said. 'Wife, two girls, pancreatic cancer.'

'That's the bad one, right?'

'It's not a good one. If he makes it to next Christmas, next summer even, I'll be surprised.'

'How old are the girls?'

'Five and seven.'

'Fuck.'

'I don't think I've met a happier man. I went to see him at home, met his wife and these two

312

beautiful, *beautiful* girls. And I thought: maybe that's the secret, you know. Family.'

Mike said nothing, just pulled Sally closer to his side.

'But I think I was wrong. I mean . . . family, I'd love a family . . . but really, it's love, isn't it? Maybe it comes from a family, or maybe it comes from just one person. But . . . love. You know?'

'Yeah. I know.'

Up ahead a fox darted out from a hedge, stopping in the street to face these two humans leaning against each other.

Sally recalled Faye telling her how she'd seen a fox in Brighton, followed it around a corner and seen what she'd seen. How it had set the whole thing in motion. How it had led to her and Mike walking this street, watching this fox watching them.

She laughed, the sound clear and resonant in the empty street. The animal turned tail and vanished into the night.

'What's funny?'

Sally turned and kissed him. 'I'll tell you another time.'

'When?'

'When we're old,' Sally said, and she continued walking.

Mike watched her go for half a dozen steps, then followed after, walking quickly to be by her side.

Epilogue

It will be time soon.

Christmas is a long-ago memory; all the Easter chocolate has gone. London is half a year behind her, the clocks have moved forward and the mornings are light when she wakes. Even when she wakes at six, like she did this morning. Stomach full of baby, bladder full of water, head full of story.

Writing it all down has helped. At first as an idle exercise, then as therapy, and then shaping the narrative into the five acts of a play: The night in Brighton; The Aftermath; The Pregnancy; The Arrangement; The Heroine Absconds. Some details she has changed, some motivations she has had to imagine. A process of adapting.

Four acts are written now, the fifth close to complete. She could finish it today, this morning, but as she nears 'The End' she has become prone to distraction, doubt and procrastination. Sitting at a desk is uncomfortable now, too. Her hands are swollen, the keyboard moves further away every day as the baby inside her grows and kicks and rotates into position. No morning sickness, though. No infections, no haemorrhoids and minimal stretch marks. An easy pregnancy, her mother has said.

And Mother, you don't know the half of it.

Faye is unsure how the play ends — just as she is unsure what happened to the real-life

314

protagonists after she exited the back door of the theatre and the driver loaded her cases into the boot.

'Going anywhere nice?'

'Home,' she told him.

In the first few weeks after her vanishing act, she waited for the others to track her down. But they didn't come. Haven't yet.

She has sent emails to Alistair alone, updating him with his child's progress, telling him she is well. That he will see the baby when the time is right. She asks him, every time, to not reply. She doesn't want to know what happened to him and Sally and Mike, not yet. She needs to maintain the distance she has created. Al has respected her request. Almost. He sends the same reply every time, just two words and a polite kiss: *Stay well x*

After the first two months, she stopped anticipating the arrival of an unfamiliar car in the driveway. But now, as the day approaches, she has begun again to wonder if they, or one of them, will come knocking at the door. They will know the time is close, but Faye trusts them to wait.

Faye hears the floorboards creak upstairs and glances at the clock on her computer screen: 7:03. She hopes her mother will go back to bed for an hour — give her the time she needs to finish the story.

And then they will talk again of names. Her mother has a list of old relatives scribbled on the back of — yes — an envelope. Jack and Bob and Arthur, Julia, Mary and Agnes — uncles, fathers, aunts, mothers. If it's a boy, Faye will name the baby for her own father, for the grandfather the child will never know. If it's a girl . . . she likes the name Sally. Always has. But then again, maybe not.

Upstairs her mother turns on the shower and Faye looks again at the script on her computer. The line where she left off last night:

Naomi takes her final bow, meets the eyes of Liam, Lois and Phil. She blows three kisses towards them, turns and exits stage left.

She could end it here, she thinks, but won't the audience want to know what became of the four — the actress, the ad man and the should-have-been sweethearts?

Surely these last two are together now. Faye likes to think they are.

Her agent has read the first three acts and says it's good. She joked: 'People will ask if this is you, sweetie.' And Faye had laughed her most convincing laugh.

She laughs again now, but this time the sound is genuine.

She reaches forward to continue typing, but as her fingers touch the keys, Faye is gripped by a strong contraction. Not one of the trivial twinges and tightenings she has grown accustomed to. This is painful — a fist clenching inside her, the violence of it radiating from her womb to her muscles and bone and skin. She feels it in her toes and her teeth and she cries out.

Her fingers have mashed indiscriminate keys typing out a long capitalised line of incoherent vowels and syllables and bad punctuation. Typing out a scream.

'Mum!' she shouts, but Faye's mother doesn't answer. The only sound from upstairs the thrashing water of the shower.

It's frightening and exciting at the same time. Faye takes a deep breath and then another. The contraction subsides, fades but doesn't fully relax. This is it. A certainty formed in her body rather than her mind. Before this day is done she will hold her baby, she will be a mother. She continues to breathe and the contraction continues to ease.

Faye saves her document, saves the typed scream at the bottom of the page. The ending will have to wait.

She fills her lungs with air and shouts again. 'Mum! Mum! It's starting.'

Acknowledgements

Thanks to: Lily Cooper, Emma Herdman, Joanna Kaliszewska, Rachel Khoo, Sara Kinsella, Sara Marafini, Thorne Ryan, Lydia Seleska, Louise Swannell, Peter Ford, Andy James, Kate Proctor.

To Stan at the North Literary Agency for selling this novel. And to Kate Howard for buying it.

To Dorothy Jones for honest notes, unflagging support and for being my mum.

And to Sarah Jones, my wise and patient wife. For helping me make this book better and for buying me a replacement lucky writing top when the elbows wore through on the last one.

We do hope that you have enjoyed reading this large print book.

Did you know that all of our titles are available for purchase?

We publish a wide range of high quality large print books including:
Romances, Mysteries, Classics
General Fiction
Non Fiction and Westerns

Special interest titles available in large print are:
The Little Oxford Dictionary
Music Book
Song Book
Hymn Book
Service Book

Also available from us courtesy of Oxford University Press:
Young Readers' Dictionary
(large print edition)
Young Readers' Thesaurus
(large print edition)

For further information or a free brochure, please contact us at:
Ulverscroft Large Print Books Ltd.,
The Green, Bradgate Road, Anstey,
Leicester, LE7 7FU, England.
Tel: (00 44) 0116 236 4325
Fax: (00 44) 0116 234 0205

THE TWO OF US

Andy Jones

Fisher is fizzing with the euphoria of new love — laughing too loud, kissing more enthusiastically than is polite in public. How he met Ivy is academic; you don't ask how the rain began, you simply appreciate the rainbow. The two of them have been an item for less than three weeks — and they just know they are meant to be together. The fact that they know little else about each other is a minor detail . . . But over the coming months, in which their lives will change forever, Fisher and Ivy discover that falling in love is one thing, while staying there is an entirely different story . . .

THE SINGLE MUM'S WISH LIST

Charlene Allcott

Martha Ross dreams of being a singer, but she's been working in a call centre far too long. She's separating from her husband, the father of her son. And she's moving back in with her parents, toddler in tow. Life has thrown her a few lemons, but Martha intends to make a gin and tonic. It's time to become the woman she's always wanted to be. At least her mum's on hand to provide childcare — and ample motherly judgement. Soon Martha realises that in order to find lasting love and fulfilment, she needs to find herself first. But her attempts at reinvention — from writing a definitive wish list of everything she wants in a new man, to half-marathons, business plans and meditation retreats — tend to go awry in the most surprising of ways . . .

THE DROWNED VILLAGE

Kathleen McGurl

It's the summer of 1935, and eleven-year-old Stella Walker is preparing to leave her home forever. Forced to evacuate to make way for a new reservoir, the village of Brackendale Green will soon be lost. But before the water has even reached them, a dreadful event threatens to tear Stella's family apart . . . In the present day, Stella is living with her granddaughter Laura, who helps to care for her as she attempts to leave double heartache behind. A fierce summer has dried up the lake and revealed the remnants of the deserted village, and Stella is sure the place still holds answers for her. With only days until the rain returns, she begs Laura to make the journey for her — and to finally solve the mysteries of the almost forgotten past.